THE MISTS OF GLEN STRAE
BOOK TWO OF THE HIGHLAND BALLAD SERIES

KRISTIN GLEESON

Published by An Tig Beag Press

Cover designed by JD Smith Design

ISBN:978-0-9956281-0-6

❀ Created with Vellum

OTHER WORKS BY KRISTIN GLEESON
In Praise of the Bees
CELTIC KNOT SERIES
Selkie Dreams
Along the Far Shores
Raven Brought the Light
A Treasure Beyond Worth (novella)
RENAISSANCE SOJOURNER SERIES
A Trick of Fate (novella)
The Imp of Eye
The Sea of Travail
HIGHLAND BALLAD SERIES
The Hostage of Glenorchy
The Mists of Glen Strae
The Braes of Huntly
Highland Lioness
NON FICTION
Anahareo, A Wilderness Spirit
LISTEN TO THE MUSIC CONNECTED TO THE BOOKS
Go to www.kristingleeson.com/music
Receive a FREE novellette prequel, *A Treasure Beyond Worth,* and
Along the Far Shores
When you sign up for my mailing list: www.kristingleeson.com

The trees were dark and closing in on Abby. She swayed on her horse, conscious that the weight of her body seemed more than she could manage. The murmur of a soft but drenching rain filled the air as it fell against the leaves. Any protection the trees might have provided had long since disappeared under the rain's determined and persistent fall. Though it was early summer, Abby was drenched and chilled to the bone. Her dress hung in heavy damp folds, and her hair, a mass of soaked clumps, fell loose about her neck, the glorious golden red colour now a dark rust. It was only her back that was dry, protected by the lute slung across it in its leather bag.

The light had faded almost completely, and all she could see now through the drips that gathered on her lashes were long shadows of branches and shrubs. Ahead, the ground sloped upwards and the trees opening up to sky and the rough terrain that signalled bogland. As she drew nearer, the light improved only a little. It was clear that dusk had descended and night would soon be upon her. Should she leave the dubious shelter of the trees or venture forth into the unknown and potentially dangerous ground?

She edged her horse into the uneven terrain to survey more closely what lay ahead of her. She narrowed her eyes, straining to see through the dim light. Was that a small cottage in the distance, perched against the hillside? She saw some movement and made out a few cattle grazing casually on the pitiful bits of grass available.

Someone seized her arm and pulled her off the horse. She fell, jarring her shoulder against a hidden rock when she hit the ground. The rest of her was cushioned by the spongey bog grass. Automatically she reached behind her to check the lute. It was safe.

"Who're ye?" A voice demanded.

She looked up and brushed the wet hair out of her eyes. Several faces peered at her, clad in an assortment of wet straggly hair, beards, plaids, boots and bare feet.

She made an effort to mask her fear. Did these men belong to the laird at Glenorchy? She didn't recognise them, but that meant nothing. He could have easily have sent these men looking for her. It had only been days since she'd escaped their clutches. They certainly couldn't belong to the Comte de Damville. The men before her bore no resemblance to them.

"Weel?" said the voice, the tone impatient.

The voice belonged to one of the clean-shaven men, a blue wool bonnet pulled down over his head. From what Abby could see of him, he didn't look old enough to have a beard. Yet he seemed to be in charge.

Abby sat up and rubbed her sore arm. "I could ask the same thing," she said.

"But this is no your land." The Scots accent was thick and heavy.

Abby regarded the youth carefully. She could just about make out the fine features, the clear blue eyes and something else that reminded her of someone.

"This land belongs to you?" Abby asked, doubt clear in her tone.

"Aye. It belongs tae the clan."

Hope began to blossom inside her as she realised who it was this youth reminded her of. Had she finally found the MacGregor clan? It was only now that she acknowledged she'd been lost and was only hoping she'd been heading in the right direction.

"What clan is that? Is it MacGregor?"

The youth frowned. "Aye. It's MacGregor.

"Oh, thank goodness. I've been searching for days. Can you take me to the laird?" She put a reassuring smile on her face. "Please."

"The laird is it?" The youth swept a glance over her and gave a disdainful look. "And just who is it that wants tae call on the laird?"

Abby rose to her feet and tried to arrange her clothes in some semblance of decency. Her hem was torn, her ill-fitting kirtle had slipped to reveal a little too much of her breasts and one of her sturdy leather shoes had slipped off her foot. The lute hung awkwardly at her back. She pushed it back into place, hoping that they wouldn't notice it, and even more importantly, that it had fared no mishap.

"I'm Abby Gordon." She searched around for something that would convince them she was someone of note. "I know the laird's son. I was lately in his company."

The youth gave her a hard glance. "MacGregor's son? Well now we ken ye're lying. MacGregor has sons. Two of them. One is safely tucked up in bed and too young to be in company such as yours. And it would be impossible for ye to ken the other. He is held hostage by those foul Campbells at Kilchurn Castle."

Abby's heart sank. She had known it was impossible that Iain had gone to Glen Strae. It would have been too risky for him. But still, deep in her heart she had hoped to find him there.

"It was Iain. I met him at Kilchurn, but he's no longer there. He's gone."

"Gone?" The youth's tone was sharp. "Gone where? When? How?"

"He escaped. Several days ago."

The youth snorted. "Och. It took him long enough. And where did he go?"

"I don't know."

The youth gave her a considering look. "And why does someone who was at Kilchurn Castle, the home of the sworn enemies of the MacGregors, want to see Himself?"

"Iain told me to go to Glen Strae."

"And why would we believe ye?"

Abby held out her hand, where on her first finger was the ring Iain had pressed on her for safe passage through Glen Strae.

"He gave me this."

The youth grabbed at her hand and studied the ring. "Where did you get this?" His voice was high pitched and full of surprise.

Abby hid a smile with effort. Clearly the age of this youth was less than she'd thought and his voice was still struggling with the transformation from boyhood. "As I said. Iain gave it to me."

"Iain gave it to ye? I say ye lie. Iain would never give away that ring." The youth glanced over Abby's shoulder. "What have you got in the bag?"

Abby put a protective hand behind her back. "Nothing. Just my lute."

"Your lute?" The youth swept a glance over her bedraggled figure and scoffed. "Give us a wee look at yon lute, then."

Abby carefully slipped the cord over her head and brought the leather bag around to the front. She loosened the string that held it shut and pulled the instrument out just enough so that its neck was visible.

The youth looked at the lute and then her, his eyes narrowed.

He turned to the large dark-bearded man at his side. "I say she's a spy. Take her to MacGregor. See what she has to say for herself when she comes face to face with him."

THE TREK WAS LONGER than Abby thought it would be. With Dark Beard, which is what she'd taken to calling in her mind the man leading her horse, they crossed a small river, the mist hanging all around them as they skirted the rise in the land and headed towards a valley. For a moment, when the mist cleared, she could see in the distance the faint outline of two mountains rising high and disappearing into cloud.

It was much later, after the sun had risen in the sky and the mist had burnt away, that Abby could see a castle in the distance, though it was more of a glorified keep than a castle. This must be Iain's home. Soon she would come face to face with Iain's father, the laird.

She scanned the fields and clusters of houses around it, hoping for some clue as to what she might expect. The cottages were made of clay, stone and turf and though small, were in good repair. In the fields nearby a number of cattle grazed. Stolen from the Campbells? Or stolen back from the Campbells? At this point it might be difficult to tell who owned the cattle, mused Abby.

"Is that the laird's home?" she asked Dark Beard.

She glanced around and noticed that the youth who had confronted her had disappeared and it was only the surly silent men who were left now.

"Aye," Dark Beard managed to grunt.

A bark rang out and Abby turned back around to look for the source of the sound. Bounding awkwardly across the field beside her came a dog, one leg tucked up.

"Cú!" shouted Abby.

The men around her exchanged uneasy glances, but said nothing. Abby slipped off her horse and went up to the shepherd's hound she had befriended at Kilchurn Castle after she had stumbled upon him injured in the woods. She'd no idea then he belonged to Iain when she helped and protected him from the Campbell's vicious hounds. She knelt down and greeted the dog with joy, stroking his head and fondling his ears. It was reassuring to find someone familiar who was happy to see her.

One of the men grunted something and she looked up. He urged his nimble Highland pony forward and the others followed, except for Dark Beard who still held the reins for her horse. He frowned and gestured for her to remount. She gave the dog one last pat, sighed and rose, brushing away a wet lock of hair that had fallen in her eyes. Silently, she mounted the horse and Dark Beard moved his pony forward, giving her barely enough time to find her seat properly.

It was a short distance to the castle now. The morning was well upon them and people were busy at their work in the fields, in the cottages and in the small sheds beside them. Bare legged men were clad in long shirts of saffron or brown and topped with plaids of mud brown or the occasional blue colour, draped and belted, some threadbare but still serviceable. Over their kirtles, women had plaid draped over their shoulders or wore short woollen jackets with open sleeves.

The men who accompanied Abby were dressed similarly to those she saw here, their legs and feet bare for the most part, but large mud brown woollen mantles topped their shoulders and were folded around their bodies. All of the clothes were a good camouflage in this landscape.

The group made their way through the gatehouse archway and into the small yard. Unlike Kilchurn, there were no large stables, smithworks or other signs of prosperity to fill the yard with people busy at tasks. There was a lone shed, large enough for several Highland ponies, but nothing more. Turf was piled up beside the shed and a cart stood on the other side. A few dogs milled around hunting for scraps. They looked up and gave some half-hearted barks.

Dark Beard helped Abby from her Highland pony, careful this time of the lute that was still slung across her back. He took her arm and led her inside. The sudden darkness made her blink and she could hardly see as he shuffled her along a small corridor. A strong odour of roasting meat wafted out from behind a door to her right. Dark Beard's insistent grip, and the henchmen that followed, made it impossible to linger and imagine the meat filling her belly.

Dark Beard led her through another door and this time light filtered in from two large windows to reveal a sizeable hall, panelled on three sides in a dark wood, where claymores, targes and other war implements hung. In the middle was a vast hearth, bare of any fire. A large trestle table of rough-hewn oak stood at one end. Near it, on the wall, was a large tapestry woven with the incomprehensible motto in Gaelic, *Rioghal mo dhréam*, emblazoned on it.

Abby stood there while Dark Beard barked orders in Gaelic and two of the men disappeared back through the door. Silence fell and Abby strained to hear something that might tell her what was happening. There were no shouts, no murmured whispers, nothing. The room was proof against anything that went on beyond it.

The door opened and a large, dark-haired man filled its frame. A livid scar crossed his right cheek and disappeared into his beard. The Laird MacGregor, Iain's father. Despite the hair colour, there was nothing about him that suggested anything of Iain.

Clutching a stick, MacGregor began a laboured progress across the flagstone to a large chair at the end of the trestle table.

Though incapacitated, the plaid, of muted browns and blues, swayed about him with a grace that added to his imposing demeanour. It was then that Abby realised that there might be some resemblance that went beyond the physical. Until he turned his eyes on her that were so deep a blue and so much like Iain's she caught her breath.

The men gave MacGregor a short bow. "Well?" he said, his tone sharp. His voice was deep and gravelly, from years of shouting across a battlefield, Abby had no doubt.

"MacGregor," said Dark Beard. "We found this woman wandering on clan lands and it was thought best we take her tae ye." He added a few more phrases in Gaelic.

The laird looked over at her again and examined her carefully. Once more she was conscious of her bedraggled appearance and resisted the urge to straighten her bodice and skirt. The strap of the lute case crossed between her breasts, and she was certain in the journey from horse to this hall the pitiful stomacher had shifted to an indecent show of breast.

"Why would I want tae question a lass of that sort, Fergus? Except that she might try tae cast a spell on me?"

Fergus stroked his dark beard in embarrassment while the men behind him sniggered.

"Och, I can see why ye might be thinking that. She's no much tae look at," he muttered. He grabbed her hand, pulling her closer to the laird and displayed the ring. "She asked tae see ye, laird. And she says Iain gave her this ring."

The laird glanced at the ring for a moment and gave her a direct look. Abby stiffened under his scrutiny, flustered by eyes that so resembled Iain's and were now filled with anger and something else. Hope.

"How is it you've seen my son?" he growled. "He's at Kilchurn Castle."

"Not any more laird," said Fergus. "He's escaped."

MacGregor held up a hand. "Wheeest a moment, Fergus. Let her answer. What's your name?" he asked Abby sharply.

"Abby Gordon, my laird."

He frowned a moment. "Your mother wasna a Campbell was she?"

Abby shook her head. It might be best at this moment not to mention her mother's name.

"Och, a Gordon's no sae bad," he muttered. "I can live with a Gordon." He eyed Abby. "Your father's no a relation tae the Earl of Huntly, is he?"

"What?" Abby asked, startled. "N-no."

The laird looked thoughtful for a moment. "And where is Iain, then? Will he be coming home, soon? I'll no be having him avoiding custom and tradition nae matter what he might think suits him. He kens that. Forbye, he wouldna scoff at that."

Abby gave him a puzzled look. "I'm afraid I don't know where Iain is. I came because Iain said I could come here if I needed help and—"

MacGregor waved his hand. "Of course ye maun come here, lass. It has tae be done formally."

"Formally?" said Abby, completely bewildered.

"The betrothal."

"Betrothal?" said Abby.

"Intended bride. Don't they say 'betrothed' in the Lowlands?"

"I-I don't know, my laird. I have lately been in France," she said feebly.

Her mind reeled. Should she correct him? She could hear the men behind her stirring restlessly and a few mutterings in Gaelic. The clink of a sword against another. She'd no doubt that the men would strike her down without hesitation if they thought she threatened the laird in any way.

"Och," said MacGregor. "That'll explain the strange lilt in your speech. And are your parents still there?"

"Yes," she said. It seemed best to keep her replies as brief as possible while she gathered her wits and cobbled an explanation that wouldn't anger the laird and bring worse down up on her from the men behind.

"At court, are they?" asked MacGregor.

"Yes. My father is part of the Queen's household."

The laird eyed her speculatively. "A soldier, then?"

"Not exactly."

"Nae matter. There's time enough for all that. For now we must get ye set up. Ye look fair drooked in your wet things." He looked over at Fergus. "Take Mistress Gordon tae Mistress MacNab and tell her we have an honoured guest who is soon to be part of this family."

CHAPTER 2

*A*bby tugged at the gown that she had hastily donned, trying to make smaller what was clearly too big for her. The gown obviously belonged to a woman larger than she, and no amount of adjustment could conceal the fact it was borrowed. It was a fine gown, beautifully made and one that wouldn't be out of place at the Scottish court, Abby suspected, where more soberly clad figures were the norm in the face of the growing number of Protestants who foreswore elaborate colours and dress. It was far too fine, it seemed to her, for an ordinary meal with the family.

No mention had been made of its owner when Mistress MacNab, a glowering florid-faced woman, handed her the garment and told her she'd should think twice if she thought someone would be back to dress her hair. Abby had struggled into the gown with some bemusement and wondered what manner of attendance Mistress MacNab thought she was used to. She'd always dressed her hair herself in the simplest manner possible, except for the brief time she'd been Henri's wife, living at his home.

At the thought of Henri, Abby blinked in surprise. She'd not thought of him in days, perhaps weeks, and now when his name came to her mind it was without the familiar stab of pain. She still felt the sorrow that someone could die so young and suddenly, only hours after their wedding, but there was nothing of the dispiriting pain that had gripped her when it first had happened, late last year. Her descent into widowhood had evoked no compassion from Henri's family; only blame and retribution that she'd carried the illness with her from court.

Abby glanced around the room, distracting herself from the morose and angry thoughts. That it was a chamber fit for a guest was clear, from the sizeable, if not new tapestry of quality that hung along the wall in addition to the large, curtained bed. A brazier stood in the corner and the heat from the red hot coals took the edge off the chill. The window was small, but surprisingly contained window panes, and rather than overlooking the courtyard, as she supposed it would, showed a breathtaking view of the mountains.

It was when she turned away from the view and cast her gaze once again into the room that her attention was caught by the portrait hanging on the wall by the door, above a small writing table. She'd noticed it earlier. Now she drew nearer to examine it and saw that it showed three children and a woman. The woman was tall and fair-haired with full lips. Considered on their own, the lips might be thought as sensual, until they were taken with loving, open expression in the grey eyes that gazed down at the children surrounding her.

The oldest child, tall and dark unlike his mother and wearing a solemn expression, could have been no more than ten. He was dressed in doublet and hose with a large swathe of plaid draped across his chest and over his shoulder. The middle child, a girl, was also dark, but unlike her brother, wore a rebellious expression, her chin thrust out. The youngest, chubby-faced and fair, sat on his mother's lap and could be no more than four years of age. She looked at the oldest boy again and saw the eyes weren't grey like his mother's, but blue. The blue that had caught her breath the first time she saw them looking at her at Kilchurn Castle. Iain.

She gazed at the woman again with more care, knowing that it was Iain's mother that faced her now. There was no doubting the beauty, the fine features that she'd passed on to her son in many subtle ways, but there also was a depth of feeling present in her eyes and the smile that spread across her face. The painter had been skilled, and for a moment Abby wondered how it was that an artist of such experience would come here, to this remote place. But the whole chamber spoke of good taste, refinement, culture. She reminded herself that Iain had been to the Scottish court, could play the lute and that the very cultured mistress and lady of Loch Awe and Kilchurn Castle was cousin to his mother. The lady in this portrait bore some resemblance to Lady Arbella, she could see that now. And like Lady Arbella, there was an unmistakable sign of illness around the eyes and at the corners of the mouth.

It was on this close examination that Abby noticed the gown Iain's mother wore. There was no mistaking that either. It was a rich blue silk with matching foresleeves and seed pearls embroidered along the neckline. Fur trimmed cuffs were folded back to reveal wide sleeves of fine embroidered linen. Her hair was caught back in a French hood with a stiff circlet that matched her gown. Around her neck was a large gold and ruby necklace. Except for the headdress and the necklace, Abby was clothed identically.

Again, she wondered why, of all the gowns that might have been given to her, this one was chosen. She thrust aside the kernel of suspicion and looked at the image of the young Iain. The child seemed so serious. Was it because he knew his mother was ill? She could see the firm jaw, the cheekbones and the hint of the man to come. There was no arrogance there, no confident tilt of the head that she remembered, or the humour that glinted in his eye when he was set on teasing.

She sighed, turned away from the painting, and patted her hair. There was nothing that could be done to improve it. She had run her fingers through its tangled locks and already it was drying into large curls. Without hair pins or combs she had little choice in her hairstyle and decided the laird and his family would just have to cope with the result.

The laird was already seated at the table when she arrived a short while later. On his right side was a fair-haired youth that Abby couldn't mistake for anyone but the young child in the portrait, Iain's brother. There were three other places laid, one beside the youth and the two others at the laird's left. The youth and the laird rose from the table, though it was an effort for the older man. He was dressed much as before, draped in plaid and shirt, his legs bare except for the boots that encased his feet and calves. The only addition was a large bearskin draped across his shoulders.

"I bid ye welcome tae our table and our home, Abigail Gordon," said the laird. "Ye maun forgive my attire. I'm afraid I left off court dress after Margaret died." He resumed his seat and indicated the youth who remained standing. "This is my other son, Alisdair."

Alisdair gave her a careful bow. "I am pleased tae make your acquaintance, Mistress Gordon."

Unlike his father, Alisdair, slim and fine-boned, had chosen to wear a brightly coloured brocade doublet, though the skirt was unfashionably long, nearly reaching his knees. Underneath it he wore dark coloured hose. Like his father and brother his eyes were blue, but they were a lighter blue, the kind that would turn grey on a bright day.

Abby chose not to correct the laird over her name, murmured

her greetings and after the laird indicated, took the seat on his left. A moment later a young man dressed in a long black cloak, plain doublet and hose rushed in and bowed to the laird.

"I apologise, my laird, for my late arrival," he said. "I lost track of the time."

The laird gave a long mmmphh. "Reading that reformist muck again?"

The man reddened. "I like to keep fully conversant of all ideas that are abroad, whatever they might espouse." He moved over to the vacant place beside Abby and sat down.

"So long as you don't have my son blethering that tripe, I dinna care what ye read. Better that he had a proper tutor, one that can show him the ways of soldier, like I had."

"I assure ye, Father, I have my own mind," said Alisdair. "Master Gower may teach me, but he doesna tell me what tae think."

"It's what he might teach ye, that worries me," said MacGregor.

The door by the stairs opened and Mistress MacNab entered carrying a large plate of fowl, followed by a young servant boy bearing a steaming pot of what might be pease porridge. A flagon of ale was already on the table in addition to simple plates, bowls and cups of pewter and horn spoons. Mistress MacNab and the boy placed the food at the table's centre, stood back and waited for the laird's signal.

It was difficult for Abby not to compare the fare she saw here to the sumptuous dishes she'd seen served at the elaborately set table of Kilchurn Castle. Then she had been merely an observer, posing as a household musician, just another young man who worked for the laird. Her guise had enabled her to play her much loved lute and learn from her father's old music teacher, and it had kept her safe from those who might want her killed at the French court, safe for a time, at least.

"Where's Morag? She kens she should be in the hall for dinner."

Alisdair shrugged. "I dinna know." His accent came in thick and the tone tinged with humour. "She is likely tae be out racing the dogs in thon fields as in the barn, mucking out the coos."

"Weel, field or no, we willna wait any longer."

He nodded to Mistress MacNab and she began the process of doling out the pease porridge while the boy poured the ale. It was only after the pease porridge was served into the bowls and the fowl which Abby thought might be duck, placed on the plate beside it, that the door opened again and young woman entered, a little breathless. She was dressed in a modest gown of brown velvet and matching foresleeves. The neckline was square cut and untrimmed. Across her shoulders she'd draped a plaid. Her hair was stuffed under a hood and a circlet had clearly been shoved onto her head and pinned without interest. She made her way quickly over to MacGregor, kissed him lightly on the cheek and took the remaining vacant place beside Alisdair.

"And where were ye, that ye couldna see fit to come tae the table on time?"

She smiled and answered her father in Gaelic.

"Speak in Scots. We have guests, Morag. Which ye would know had ye come earlier."

For the first time Morag looked around the table and saw Abby, who gave her a tentative smile. On closer inspection she could see the resemblance to the young girl in the portrait. There was no mistaking the rebellious expression, nor the fact that the real person was glaring at her now.

"What is this woman doing here at our table, and" she added in threatening tone, "wearing Mother's gown?"

The expression on the MacGregor's face darkened. "Where are your manners, Morag? Mistress Gordon is our guest and should be treated as such."

"Guest? Was she nae picked up out of a ditch like some witch or wey faced hoor?"

"Wheest!" said MacGregor. "Ye'll nae speak of Iain's betrothed in such a manner. He is my heir and so she has every right tae the gown."

"Betrothed?" Morag said. "Is that what she told ye? She's nae more betrothed than I am." Morag left off a stream of Gaelic, her voice rising.

MacGregor thumped his fist on the table, causing the dishes to shake with the force. "Did I no tell ye tae hold your girning? What good cause have ye tae think this lass here is a spy? Ye've only just met her this moment."

Morag reddened, but her eyes sparked with anger. "I know what Fergus told me."

"Fergus told ye Mistress Gordon was a spy?" asked Alisdair in a calm voice.

"Nay," Morag, her tone more even. "He told me the circumstances surrounding their meeting and…it's obvious she can only be a spy."

"Surely ye're being hasty, sister. What evidence is there tae support such a conclusion?"

Morag glared once more at Abby and in one astonishing moment Abby realised the identity of this person who accused her so vehemently. She was the youth who led the small band of men who'd encountered her in the forest. Abby paled at the thought.

"Aye, your brother is right. Ye're overwrought. There is nae reason tae suspect Mistress Gordon of spying." MacGregor turned to Abby. "Forgive her. She is a spirited lass, but she is goodhearted for all that."

Morag stiffened. "There isna anything tae apologise on my behalf. I stand by my conviction. Did she tell ye that she was at

Kilchurn Castle, among the Campbells?" Morag spat out the rival clan's name.

"Aye, she did. And that was where she met Iain. Isna that so, Mistress Gordon?"

Abby opened her mouth, but before she could speak Morag interrupted.

"And did she tell ye that Iain escaped?"

MacGregor nodded. "And glad I am. 'Tis time that lad tae saw sense and stopped tarrying among those gowked Campbells."

"Mother's cousin is there, too," said Alisdair in a mild tone.

MacGregor waved a hand at him. "Yes, yes, lad."

"She came from Kilchurn Castle, without Iain, though he's escaped. It is only reason tae call her a spy. She's been sent here tae look for him."

"But she has Iain's ring," said Alisdair.

"She does, and she says that Iain gave it tae her, but I say she stole it, for he wouldna give it up willingly. She probably enticed him tae her bed and took it then."

"That's not true," said Abby, trying to contain her anger. She'd had enough of Morag's insults, though her accusations were closer to the truth than was comfortable. "Iain gave it to me of his own free will."

"There, ye see? She's nae spy, nae matter how much ye may argue." said MacGregor. "She has Iain's ring. And as ye point out, he wouldna hand it over except tae someone he carried verra much about, a woman who would be his bride. She canna be a spy."

"We have only her word that he gave it tae her willingly," said Morag darkly.

"And that's enough for me," said MacGregor. "Forbye there's an end tae the matter." He patted Abby's arm. "I ask again for your pardon of my daughter. She's a wee hot-headed at times."

"I wonder where that may have come from," said Alisdair in a low voice, his voice filled with humour.

MacGregor gave Alisdair a sharp glance. "Nae more your wit, laddie." He turned to Abby and frowned. "Did Iain say when he might be coming?"

"No," said Abby. She took a deep breath. "That is to say, he had no clear plans. His decision to leave Kilchurn was quite sudden, at night. Some matter arose for him, I believe they'd captured a man he knew…" she trailed off, not certain if she should say any more on the matter.

"A man, ye say. One of our clan?" asked MacGregor.

"I know of nae MacGregor captured by the Campbells," said Morag. "Unless ye mean Davie Guthrie, but he was kilt."

"I don't know who the man was," said Abby.

It wasn't a lie, especially; she didn't know the man's identity, though she was fairly certain it wasn't Davie Guthrie, for Iain would have said.

"So how is it ye decided tae come here?" asked Morag.

"I—"

"Morag, let the lass be," said MacGregor. "It's obvious she came here hoping tae find Iain."

"That's right," said Abby. "Iain did say to come here, and after he left…."

"You thought it best tae leave since as his betrothed your presence would be unwelcome at Kilchurn," said MacGregor.

"Yes," said Abby. "More or less."

It was actually much less, and at present it didn't seem wise to explain that her departure was as sudden and as secret as Iain's. She only hoped no one from Kilchurn Castle would think to find her here.

"Ye're a Gordon, I understand," said Master Gower to Abby. He gave her an owlish blink and cast a glance at the laird. "Are ye a relation to the Earl of Huntly? Perhaps your father might be able tae intercede on behalf of the laird."

"Yes, yes," said Alisdair, his tone excited. "We could petition him, Father. If the Earl of Huntly is on our side, then surely the Council of Regency and the Dowager Queen would see fit tae give us back our lands."

"I'll no go begging for what is rightfully mine," said MacGregor darkly. "And I'll hear nae more about it."

"I'm sorry, there is no relationship," said Abby. "My father is in the Queen's household in France."

"He is?" asked Morag. She gave Abby a suspicious look. "And were ye raised there, in France? Your accent doesna mark ye for a Scots."

Abby drew herself up. "French is the common language of the court, naturally. Though the Queen speaks Scots quite well." She hadn't actually ever heard the Queen speak Scots, but her father had mentioned it.

"And your mother, is she also at the French court, in the Queen's household?" asked Morag.

"No," Abby said. "She's dead." At least as far as her father was concerned and since she had told Iain this, she decided it was best to maintain the fiction.

"I'm sorry to hear of your loss," muttered Morag.

MacGregor gave Morag a meaningful look. "Aye, it's a sad thing tae lose a mother."

"And sad tae lose a wife," murmured Alisdair. He picked at his food for a moment and then gave up. "Iain was in good health when last ye saw him?"

Abby cast her mind back to her last meeting with Iain, playing the lute and exchanging cryptic messages warning of danger disguised as Italian song lyrics. Was there something more behind those lyrics than just warning and explanation?

"Yes," she said finally. "He was well. And only had time to tell me that he would have to leave soon, not where he was bound."

"We'll find out where he's gone," said MacGregor darkly. "The lad's wanderings have always been a sore trial. This time I'll make certain he puts in an appearance. There will be nae shirking his duty."

"Thank you," said Abby. She put on a bright smile.

"There is nae need tae thank us," said Morag. "It's just as important for us to find Iain. For when Iain's here we'll ken the truth of your claim."

"Dinna mind her, lassie," said MacGregor. "I know ye speak the truth. In the meantime we can write to your father and begin the formal arrangements for the betrothal."

Abby nodded, speechless. There would be much explaining to do when and if Iain showed up.

*a*bby plucked the string again on the lute, listening for the correct sound. She adjusted the peg slightly and plucked again. She smiled. Yes. The lute, after much effort and quiet concentration, had been restored to its original rich tone. The task had calmed her mind and allowed her to focus on something pleasurable for a short while. She'd debated taking the lute out of its leather sack, worrying it might attract attention and bring on more questions and suppositions about how it came she had Iain's lute in her possession. After two days, though, she could no longer bear the boredom of the bedroom. Except for the occasion of the painful main meal where the laird stared fixedly at her while Morag sat sullen and silent, Abby had confined herself to the bedroom while she thought about what to do.

She strummed the lute and immersed herself in the sound that came. Her fingers began plucking out simple tunes, ones that had been with her since her father had taught her on his knee when she could barely hold a lute. The thought of her father brought the worry once again. Had he written yet? Was he still at court playing his lute as always for the Queen and doing nothing more harmful than sleeping with all the ladies who flocked around him?

She shifted her playing away from tunes that she associated so much with her father and just allowed herself to aimlessly pluck out a different piece while she focused on the pure pleasure of the sound. It took her some time before she realised the tune that had emerged. She strummed a deliberate discordant sound. She would not play "Iain Glinn Cuaich". That path only took her to unwanted and impossible reminders, or back to her present situation.

She set the lute aside. There was nothing for it. She must find a way to get back to France without enlisting the direct aid of the laird, unless perhaps she could convince him she needed to speak to her father directly about the betrothal. It seemed an unlikely ruse, but perhaps not impossible. In the meantime, she could try to find out the location of the nearest port from which she could sail to France. It might be possible to take up her disguise once more and get herself across in some manner that way. Alisdair seemed close enough in size to her and might unwittingly play a part in securing her disguise and giving her information about a route.

Abby stood up, glad to be able to take action. She made her way to the door and headed along the short corridor to the stairs. The kitchen seemed the best place to ask where Alisdair might be found. Mistress MacNab might have a low opinion of her but she surely couldn't refuse a direct answer for such a simple question.

She made her way down the stairs, taking care with her skirts on the stone steps. There was no denying the castle's sturdiness, but it was old and the stone steps were worn in places. She was thankful again she'd asked for the clothes she'd come in and wasn't reduced to wearing the ill-fitting dress belonging to Iain's mother. The gown was simple enough and though not her own, fitted her better than the fancier one. Morag had certainly noted her change of clothes at the meal yesterday, if no one else had.

She rounded the door to the kitchen and entered. It was a smaller room than the kitchen at Kilchurn, but there was something comforting about it. A big fireplace dominated the room, containing spits that hung over the fire that burned there. A large pot sat on three legs at its side and a few smaller pots hung on the crane over the fire, simmering away. Abby sniffed the air. Stewed beef, she thought.

Mistress MacNab was bent over the pots and rose when she saw Abby enter. She gave Abby a speculative look.

"I'm sorry to disturb you Mistress MacNab, but I was wondering if you could tell me where Alisdair is."

Mistress MacNab gave her a puzzled look. "Alisdair? Why I suppose he's where he always is. With his tutor."

"And where would his tutor be, Mistress MacNab?" Abby said patiently.

"In thon solar," she said.

"And the solar is …upstairs?"

"Aye. Ye canna miss it."

"Thank you, Mistress MacNab."

For some reason she'd found the exchange amusing rather than frustrating, and with a smile, she took herself off up the stairs again. The solar was as Mistress MacNab had said, "unmissable."

SHE ENTERED THE SOLAR, expecting to find Master Gower and Alisdair seated at a table, bent over a text. Instead she found Alisdair seated by himself, quill in his hand and paper before him, writing intently. The light from the window poured on his fair hair, giving it a red cast. She stood there for a moment, unnoticed, until she cleared her throat. Alisdair looked up and gave a guilty start.

"Oh, Mistress Gordon, I thought ye might be someone else." He put the quill down and gave her an easy smile.

"I'm sorry to interrupt, but I wondered if you might have some time to answer a few questions. No one else seems to be about and I hate to disturb your father."

"Nae bother at all, ye're no interrupting." He looked down at the letter and sighed. "It will most likely come tae nothing anyway."

She glanced at the paper, wondering about the nicely formed letters that crowded the page. Clearly it was a formal piece of correspondence.

"Is it important? Perhaps I can help. I know something of court ways."

A small gleam of boyish hope lit his eyes and made him look younger than he had up to now with his calm manner.

"Aye. Perhaps ye might help. I'm trying tae compose a letter of petition. Should I address it to the Chancellor, the Justiciar, or the Dowager Queen, Mary of Guise?"

Abby's eyes widened. This was indeed a formal piece of correspondence. She thought how best to advise him. "What is the nature of the petition?"

"It's tae ask that they restore our lands. The lands that Campbell now holds. I ken that my father doesna approve, but I will try and send it in secret."

"And on what grounds do you ask?"

"The grounds that they belonged to us. It belongs to the Gregorach and has done since the time of McAlpin of the Picts himself. Gregorach blood runs through the people who live there. It was only through some deft bit of trickery that the Campbells took the lands over the years. More and more they took, when once we had half of Scotland."

Abby blinked at the force of the words. It was evident this statement had been said more than one time and with great emphasis. The pride behind it was undoubted and strong.

"It's a powerful heritage and I can understand why you would want to fight for it."

"Aye. My father is the MacGregor, the head of the clan, whereas Glenorchy, is nae the clan chief, the MacCailean Mhor, though he might like to think so."

Abby took in his words. "So your father is chief of all MacGregors and the laird of Glenorchy is only chief of the Campbells at Glenorchy?"

"And some other lands. The Earl of Argyll is the clan chief for the Campbells."

"Can you not appeal to him?"

Alisdair shook his head. "Argyll is Lord High Justiciar, tis true, but he is nae friend of the MacGregors. He'll support his kin and the writs that give Glenorchy legitimacy." He frowned. "We havena any written charters or deeds that show we own the land. Glenorchy, and his father, obtained documents declaring their ownership, disregarding tradition."

Abby sighed, seeing the situation more clearly. "With Queen Mary in France and still under age, her mother might be the one to appeal to. The Regency is now in her hands since Arran was forced out."

Alisdair brightened. "Could ye write tae the Queen mother and say that ye're engaged to the MacGregor heir and on the strength of your connection to her daughter, would she help?"

She smiled faintly. "I'm afraid my acquaintance with the Queen is too slight to presume to write such a letter."

Alisdair's face fell. "Aye, I knew it was too much even as I spoke."

An idea began to form in her mind. "Perhaps it's not as far-fetched as I thought. I could try in person. With your father's help, I could return to the French court and speak to my father. He has the Queen's ear and she's close with her mother. I'm sure she would speak words in your favour if my father was to ask."

Alisdair shook his head and gave her a rueful look. "Father wouldna permit anything like that. He thinks it begging for what is rightly ours, and that he willna do."

"But would we need to tell him? Perhaps we could say that I have to return to my father to make the arrangements for my dowry and my belongings." She held out her hands. "I have only what I stand up in."

He gave her a curious look, a twinkle in his eye. "Ye had a hasty departure."

She flushed. "Yes. The situation became uncomfortable rather suddenly."

"Ye mean after Iain saw fit tae leave. Suddenly, in the dead of night, nae doubt."

She wasn't certain if he meant Iain or herself. Alisdair was a canny lad for all his youth. But his wry humour gave her no doubt as to his relationship with Iain.

"Yes, Iain left in the night. He hadn't planned to, but the situation changed after a man that he knew was captured."

"Aye. So ye said." Alisdair gave her a thoughtful look. "I know Iain tae be a loyal friend and companion, as ever any Highlander would be. Especially tae his kin, though my father might say different."

"He and your father don't see eye to eye, do they?" Abby said it as a statement of fact.

"Aye, weel, they can both be pig-headed. Father wants Iain tae take up some of the clan responsibilities, tae be known among the clan, tae fight the battles that he feels should be fought."

"Which battles are they?" She could hear the tone of affection for both his father and his brother and realised how difficult it must be for Alisdair not to be caught in the middle.

"Against the Campbells and any other clan that might challenge our rights. There are rents, and tolls for the drovers when they bring the cattle through the passages to sell at the autumn trysts. By ancient custom we are owed one cow in fifty."

He went on to explain the intricacies and it was clear to Abby how much Alisdair knew of the law. But it was of Iain she wanted to know more, not the legal rights and obligations of the MacGregors.

"And Iain doesn't feel it necessary to take up these responsibilities?"

"Father thinks Iain cares only for spending his time womanising, drinking tae excess and wasting his time enjoying other pursuits that have no place in Glen Strae."

"I would have thought those practices would have constituted Highland pursuits," Abby muttered softly. Certainly her experience at Glenorchy led her to believe that.

Alisdair nodded grimly. "Aye, ye see it too. The hypocrisy. My father thinks Iain acts in this manner just tae annoy him."

"Well you could be right in that," said Abby. She remembered how Iain dressed at Kilchurn castle in a worn plaid and a mangy skin that she knew was aimed at annoying the laird. Or Glenorchy, as she now thought of him.

Alisdair flushed. "Aye, well, I ken Iain does act in that way sometimes with Father. But he feels goaded. Iain isna as Father says. He is kind, compassionate. And he doesna drink any more than anyone else." He leaned over and squeezed her hand. "And I'm certain he wouldna betray ye with another woman."

She gave him a weak smile. "Thank you. I'm certain you're right." She suppressed the almost hysterical urge to laugh.

ALISDAIR'S WORDS still rang in her ears as she opened the door to her room. A figure stood beside the bed and turned as she entered. It was Morag, her headpiece straight and perfectly adjusted, the grey wool gown smooth and darker grey velvet sleeves attached. She gave Abby a dark look and pointed to the lute that still lay on the bed.

"This is my brother's lute. Why is it ye have it?"

"He gave it to me when I was in Kilchurn. But I brought it here to return it to him."

Morag eyed her up and down disdainfully. "You play the lute?"

"Yes, since I was very young. My father taught me."

"Your father? And ye say he is a Highlander?"

"He is Scots. Not a Highlander. He was at the Scottish court before he went to the court in France."

That was as much as she knew. Her father had told her little of his early life and if she pressed him about it he had fobbed her off, or changed the subject.

"Ye say he is a Gordon? The Gordons are a Highland clan."

Abby blinked. She knew so little about Scotland and the various clans she wouldn't know a Highland clan from a Lowland one. How would she explain herself?

She decided to try for honesty. "My father spoke little about his background. I grew up at the French court, for the most part, and there was little enough said from others."

Morag nodded and seemed to accept her statement. "So ye came tae bring back Iain's lute. Ye left in a hurry yet ye still brought Iain's lute. And why is that I wonder?"

Abby sighed inwardly. How would she make Morag accept her? "I brought the lute because I knew how much it meant to Iain. I had little time to take anything else and to be truthful, nothing else seemed as important as the lute."

"Not even a change of clothes? A lady who comes from the French court?"

Abby could picture the kind of lady Morag had painted her, but nearly laughed at the image. She was as about as far from that simpering lady as anyone could possibly be.

"I assure you, I'm not attached to my gowns as you may think."

"What exactly caused ye to leave with such haste?"

It was only fair, Abby supposed, that both brother and sister should ask her this question. She knew Morag wouldn't be satisfied with the vague answer she'd given MacGregor and Alisdair. She chose a different tack.

"One reason is already known. The situation became awkward."

"And the other reasons?"

Abby gave a slight smile. "I think we all have things we would rather not share. At least at present."

"Ye are a spy. As I first said." Morag gave a smile of satisfaction.

"As I said to you from the first time we met in the glen, I am not a spy."

Morag flushed and narrowed her eyes. "What do ye mean?"

"I think you understand. I imagine your father doesn't know you are riding around dressed as a man. But I'm prepared to keep your secret if you will stop making unwarranted accusations about me."

Morag started to speak but stopped herself, studying Abby for a while. "I will hold my tongue," she said finally. "But if I do find any cause that shows ye other than what ye say ye are, I will break this promise."

"There is nothing that will give you cause to do so," said Abby.

She hoped that would prove true. At least until Iain got here, if he ever did. In the meantime she would try to convince

MacGregor that the best course in pursuit of her marriage to Iain was to send her to France.

The sound of horses approaching came from outside. Morag went to the window and looked out.

"Armed men are coming and they're no MacGregors."

Abby joined Morag and looked out. She could see the mounted men wearing swords. Several ghillies ran alongside, also armed, but dressed in the plaid she remembered from Glenorchy. It wasn't until they drew closer that she recognised the man at their head. The Comte de Damville. The man who sought her capture, not because she'd posed as a man when she was a household musician at Kilchurn; that he knew and cared little about. No, he was convinced she was a spy, just as Morag was. But his connections were more deadly and his questioning more insistent. She should have known when she'd escaped his clutches days ago that he would come looking for her here. She'd only hoped that he wouldn't dare. But he had. Of course he had.

Below, the approaching men halted in the face of the other men emerging from the keep. MacGregor was at their head, unarmed, as the hospitality code dictated, but from his demeanour, clearly wary.

Abby couldn't hear their conversation, but a few bows were sketched, gestures made towards the house, followed by nods. The whole group processed through the gate house and disappeared into the courtyard. Abby's heart sunk. It would only be a matter of time before Damville told them everything. Would MacGregor hand her over? She must try to persuade him not to.

CHAPTER 4

The knock came just as she anticipated. Morag had left in a rush as soon as the men had disappeared from view. Presumably she would be called upon to arrange the hospitality, but Abby also knew Morag wouldn't be able to suppress her curiosity. With Morag present for any discussion involving Damville, it was only a matter of time before she demanded that Abby come and account for herself at the very least. She might even convince MacGregor to hand her over with only Damville's story as justification.

With those fears in mind Abby descended the stairs, following the young lad who'd been sent to fetch her. She took a deep breath, straightened before she entered the hall and clutched her hands tightly in front of her to keep them still.

MacGregor sat, his frame filling his large chair. Seated beside him was the Comte de Damville, his doublet, bonnet and cloak still elegant despite its travel stained appearance. On the table in front of him was a plate of honey oat cakes and a cup of whisky. Morag stood beside her father, hand on hip, her face speculative. Abby could read nothing in MacGregor's expression as he eyed Damville and toyed with a cup of whisky.

MacGregor's and Damville's men lined the room. The swords had been collected beforehand and stored in the gatehouse. There would be no easy route to violence at least, thought Abby, though she wouldn't put it past Damville to use his eating knife to some deadly end.

Damville looked over at Abby. "Ah. Here she is. The escaped captive."

So he hadn't minced his words. Her status as prisoner was already known. The question was, had he described her as his prisoner, or Glenorchy's?

"Monsieur le Comte," Abby said. "I didn't expect to see you here."

"I am sure not, mademoiselle. You often underestimate too much, if I may be so bold to point out."

"No, Seigneur, I must disagree on that point." Their tone with each other had been civil and Abby's voice was calm, though her heart was racing.

"I have just been explaining to Lord MacGregor the situation that has brought me here."

"I see. And just what exactly is that situation?"

"Why of course, you know yourself. That you have escaped from Kilchurn while under the laird's custody and then when I managed to capture you, you escaped again by foul and under-handed means."

Abby forced a playful smile. "I seemed not to have caused permanent damage, for I see you are able to mount a horse and sit at table. Or is the whisky you drink potent enough to dull the pain?"

Damville's expression darkened. "You will bide your tongue. I am here to take you back into lawful custody, not to hear flippant chatter."

"And under whose law and into whose custody am I to be taken?"

"Why the law of Scotland and the Laird of Glenorchy, Justiciar of Argyll."

Abby paled at his words. She knew that Argyll was Justiciar for the whole of Scotland, but Alisdair hadn't mentioned that Glenorchy was Justiciar for this region.

"And ye think that gives ye the right tae come here and take anyone as ye please?" said MacGregor. His tone was low enough but there was an edge to his voice.

"Father, can ye no see she's a spy? Why else would they want her?"

"Wheest, daughter. I'll have nae clacking."

Damville turned to MacGregor. "I beg your pardon, Lord Glen Strae. I meant no offence. I merely am here to retrieve a person that should be of little note or interest to you. I will be on my way in the time only that it takes to collect my sword."

MacGregor frowned. The incorrect manner of address had clearly annoyed him and Abby felt a little surge of hope.

His accent became broader, his eyes sparking. "I dinna care whose law ye say ye have on your side. Ye willna take anyone frae under ma roof wi'out ma say."

"I honour you for your manners and hospitality, but you mustn't feel you need to extend it to this woman who has transgressed the law."

"Has she? And in what way?" asked MacGregor.

Abby opened her mouth to speak but Damville interrupted. "Why, she entered the household of Kilchurn under false pretences, disguised as a musician. A young man."

Morag gave a harsh laugh. MacGregor looked over at Abby and raised his brow, a sceptical look on his face.

"Can ye no see, Father? Someone who is deceitful in that manner is no tae be trusted," said Morag before Damville could say more.

"As you know yourself, there can be good cause for pursuing a course that may at first seem to be deceitful," Abby said.

"But such action in the laird's household in such troublous times can only point to ill intentions," said Damville. "And given your background I think it's reasonable to assert that you could be, as this lady has said, a spy. And there is also a matter of witchcraft," said Damville.

"Witchcraft?" said Abby. "This is the first I've heard of this."

MacGregor looked at her with renewed interest. "Are ye saying she's a witch?"

Damville waved his hand. "Not I, monsieur, *non*. But Mister Johnstone, the priest, he has some reason to suspect and wants her questioned."

Abby stared at him. She shouldn't be surprised that the priggish minister who'd hated women with such force would have come up with the preposterous charge. But she knew better than to scoff at it. Many women were burned for witchcraft with little enough cause.

"Mister Johnstone, the priest?" said MacGregor. "Or do ye mean Mister Johnstone the Protestant squawker?" The disdain was evident.

"Ah, Lord MacGregor, you must excuse me. I am not clear on these matters here. As a Catholic I am only familiar with the terms of my faith."

MacGregor nodded. "So, I being asked tae gi' this woman tae ye, because ye say that she ha' dressed up as a man and Glenorchy's toady thinks she's a witch?"

Damville smiled thinly. "I would not put it quite like that. I am here on behalf of the Laird of Glenorchy to request that you return this escaped captive so she might face her accusers and answer for her offences." He thought a moment. "In accordance with the law," he added.

MacGregor nodded. "I see. " He paused. "I ken well that

Glenorchy likes his bits of law writ doun on paper, but here, at Glen Strae we see things in a different manner. We hold tae the ancient ways."

The door opened and one of MacGregor's men entered. He slipped in beside one of the clansmen that lined the hall. Bearded and clad in plaid like the others, it took Abby a few moments to recognise him. It was Angus, the man who had brought her from Paris, across the sea to Kilchurn Castle. When she was dressed as a young man called Gabriel. What was he doing here among the MacGregors?

With a sinking heart she returned her attention to the discussion. Damville was frowning.

"But surely," he said, "You wouldn't harbour a criminal in your midst."

"Ye say she's a criminal, but ye have nae proof of it."

Damville drew himself up straight. "You have my word, Seigneur, as a nobleman and a Frenchman."

"Aye. Your word. And I suppose Glenorchy's word," said MacGregor. "But the truth of the matter is that the woman ye seek tae place in your custody is my future daughter. And I canna have ye takkin her anywhere, ye ken."

Damville looked over at Abby with disdain. "Is that the lie she told you? Well I beg to differ. She is no more his affianced than I am. What proof does she offer?"

"I have the ring belonging to Iain MacGregor," said Abby. It was time she said something if only to draw the matter to a close, since it seemed that MacGregor would stand by her. She held out her hand. "A ring that he wouldn't have given up willingly to anyone, save his kin."

Damville gave her a scornful look and turned to MacGregor. "If indeed she got that ring by his consent, how does that mean they are to be wed?"

"It has nae other meaning in ma family," said MacGregor

darkly. "And let that be an end to it. Tell Glenorchy I canna comply with his wishes. As a Highland gentleman he should understand my position."

Damville rose and gave a stiff bow. "In that case, Seigneur, I will take my leave."

MacGregor gave a nod. Behind him, Morag frowned and started to speak, but thought better of it. She glared over at Abby. Damville made his way out, his men following him. The few Campbells who made up the rear, threw sneering glances towards the MacGregors they passed. Angus spat at a Campbell after the man had muttered something and the spit landed on the man's cheek. The man drew back his fist to give Angus a punch until MacGregor's voice rang across the hall.

"Angus! Campbell! Hold still."

Angus lowered his fist and the man did likewise. With a glare the man departed after his fellows.

"Angus," said MacGregor. "We've nae seen ye in these parts for a good while. What brings ye here? Have ye news of Iain?"

Angus moved forward and bowed to MacGregor. He glanced over at Abby and gave her a puzzled look. "Aye, of a sort, my laird."

"Good," said MacGregor. "First get yourself something tae eat in the kitchen. And then when ye're refreshed, we'll have a talk."

"As ye say, MacGregor," said Angus. He looked over at Abby. "I have one or two questions of my own."

He left the hall and the other clansmen filed after him, leaving Abby alone with Morag and MacGregor.

"Sit down, lass," said MacGregor. "We'll await the news together and pass the time in a little conversation. I'm most curious about the things I've just heard."

SHE RAN her hand over the leather sack that lay on the bed, her mind racing furiously.

"Hurry it up, lass," said Fergus, growling through his dark beard. "Himself doesna like tae be kept waiting."

She raised her eyes from the bed and gave him a polite smile. His earthy smell filled her nostrils. He stood before her, arms crossed, his plaid and furskins wrapped around his large belly carelessly and held together with a leather belt. For a moment she wondered exactly how many live creatures lived beneath the skins and plaid. The thought distracted her for only a moment before her mind returned to what she faced below stairs in the hall where Himself, MacGregor, awaited her and presumably a well fed Angus. Unable to bear the tense silence, she'd asked MacGregor if she might fetch something from her room that would support her case. With a wary look he'd given her permission, but not before ordering Fergus to accompany her.

Now she picked up the leather sack and straightening, nodded to Fergus. "I'm ready."

She clutched the leather sack to her chest, as if it might protect her from what was to come, and followed Fergus back to the hall. As she descended the stairs she could hear voices through the door that led to the hall. She opened the door she realised it was laughter. She entered. All eyes turned to her and the laughter ceased. She could feel a draft at the back of her neck. The fire crackled.

"Is it true?" said MacGregor in a dark voice, his eyes narrowed.

She clutched the leather bag tighter to her. "Is what true, my lord?"

He frowned at her, clearly not appreciating the form of address she gave him. She cursed herself for the slip. MacGregor. She must remember to call him that.

"Wee Angus says that when he collected ye in Paris tae bring ye tae Kilchurn Castle ye were a laddie, but now it seems ye're a lassie, sae either ye witched yourself or someone else did it tae ye, but however it was done they should be paid handsomely, for ye're a much bonnier lassie than ye were a laddie."

Abby flushed and looked at Angus. There was humour in his eyes, but something else. Calculation?

She moved forward and stood before MacGregor, who was still seated in his great chair. Morag had taken the seat Damville had occupied and Angus stood to the laird's left.

Abby took a deep breath and gave MacGregor a direct look. "Is it the witchcraft you want me to clarify? Or that I was dressed as a boy."

MacGregor gave a grim smile. "Weel, in view of the accusations of the froggie lord, I would prefer it if ye explained everything."

She tightened her hold on the leather bag and nodded. "Of course. Well, to the accusation that I am a witch, or that I employed the services of a witch, I deny it. I employed no witchcraft and to my knowledge no one has employed it on my behalf."

"But ye were dressed as a boy?"

Abby held her head firmly and nodded again. "I did. It was to cause no one any harm that I took on that disguise, merely to provide me the opportunity to earn my keep playing the lute." She opened the sack and removed the lute from it. Iain's lute. Would MacGregor recognise it? "If I might play something to help explain my reasoning?"

"Och, Father, why are ye listening to her blether?" said Morag, her voice filled with scorn. "She'll say whatever comes tae her heid."

"Give her a chance," said Alisdair from the doorway. No one had noticed him enter during the exchange between MacGregor and Abby. "She should be able tae state her case."

Morag laughed. "Ah wee Alisdair. Ye're aye fond of the legal terms."

"And sae we will, laddie. We'll gi' her a chance tae explain herself."

MacGregor turned and nodded to Abby. Abby laid the leather sack on the table and asked for a stool. When one had been fetched, she settled herself upon it and took up the lute. She fiddled with the tuning for a few moments and then ran her fingers along the string to play an arpeggio, revelling once more in the rich tone. She plucked the opening bars of one of the pieces she'd played at Kilchurn, one that Master Kerr had taught her. It was not particularly complex, but it was short and would allow her to warm up her fingers so that she might show her skill in the next piece, a complex branle that she'd learned from her father.

It wasn't until she was half way through the branle that she allowed herself to glance across at MacGregor. He studied her hands carefully, a thoughtful look on his face. On his right Morag frowned. Alisdair, taking the seat to MacGregor's right, looked at her in wonder, his face shining with appreciation. She took heart in that, but when she brought the piece to an end, she tried a different approach. She plucked a few strings, giving space to the change in mood and to fix the notes in her head. Then she took a deep breath and began to sing "Iain Glinn Cuaich."

She managed only the first two verses, her confidence in her memory and pronunciation of the Gaelic uncertain, but when she finished the hall was silent. Not one foot shuffled or throat was cleared. She lifted her eyes from the lute and looked at MacGregor. Grief flashed across his face, but only for a moment, to be replaced by polite interest. Morag scowled at her darkly, though Alisdair smiled warmly, nodding.

"*Go álainn,*" Alisdair murmured. "Beautiful."

"Where did ye learn that tune?" asked MacGregor.

"From Iain. At Kilchurn. The Lady Arbella asked Iain to teach it to me."

MacGregor frowned. "Aye. Weel, there's no denying that ye play fine enough, as much as I ken these things, but how does that explain your actions?"

"I hoped it might show you that I am worthy to earn my living playing the lute, but as a woman, I wouldn't be permitted to do so in any household. In light of that, I had no choice but to take on the disguise."

"And they didna notice ye were a lassie?" asked MacGregor. He surveyed her thoroughly. "I find that a wee bit difficult tae believe."

Abby looked at Angus. "Ask him. He was with me for an extended period of time."

"Ye didna notice she was a lass? Not even on board ship?" MacGregor looked at Angus who flushed darkly.

"Och, now there was little time tae take notice for all that I had tae do. The lad—the lassie was sick, and I left her tae that. And weel, on the road, it was different. We kept our distance, ye ken, and I had my mind on other things."

Abby suppressed a smile as she recalled the times on the ship he'd rubbed her back and hovered over her in concern while she emptied all the contents of her stomach.

"Mmmph," said MacGregor in that indecipherable way the Scottish had. He turned to Abby. "And what about Iain? When did he see through the disguise? I'm assuming he did, since ye say ye became engaged."

She bit back the retort that would remind him that he was the first to make the assumption that she and Iain were engaged, she'd made no claim. At least not at first.

"Iain saw through the disguise, as did Lady Arbella," she said. "But few others. At least not until after Iain had left. And when they discovered it the…the minister, a Mister Johnstone, made accusations of a varying nature and convinced Glenorchy to treat me severely. They locked me up and I was able to escape."

"Are ye telling me that Glenorchy is dabbling wi' Reformists?"

Abby nodded, glad for the distraction from her own story. "Yes. Well in that he has given Mister Johnstone the hospitality of his castle. And he allowed the man to preach on Sunday." She thought back for a moment to Johnstone's thunderous railings against women in a sermon during which Iain, seated next to her, had managed to fall asleep.

"Was there nae priest in evidence?"

"None that I saw," said Abby. She knew by now that the Highland form of religious affiliation was loose, but Catholic nonetheless, though the Reformers were making sharp inroads into the Lowlands.

"And just how did ye escape the clutches of Glenorchy? Kilchurn is a stronghold. Did ye beguile the guard at your door? Put a glamour on him?" There was a trace of humour in MacGregor's voice.

Abby relaxed a little under the more benign tone. "Ah, no. I have no skill in that direction, MacGregor." She stroked the neck of the lute. "It was Glenorchy's youngest daughter. She helped Iain escape, and as a favour to him, she did the same for me."

"Glenorchy's youngest daughter?" asked MacGregor. "What was Iain doing charming Glenorchy's youngest daughter?" The trace of good humour had disappeared. "I thought it was ye Iain was engaged tae."

Abby bit her lip. "I should explain about that."

"What are ye saying? I hope Iain isna engaged tae Glenorchy's lassie. God gi' me strength, that lad will never do what is required of him."

The door opened once again, this time more loudly and with some flourish. "Did I hear my name mentioned?"

Abby turned to see Iain, clothed in a dark doublet somewhat the worse for wear, dark hose that was partially covered by scuffed boots that looked far too small for his large frame and in a sizeable faded plaid folded and wrapped around his middle and across his shoulder. His face was drawn, a dark stubble contributing the appearance of an outlaw rather than a dashing courtier.

"Iain. Aye, and about time ye saw fit to appear," said MacGregor. "There is much here tae answer for."

Iain bowed and made his way slowly across the room, his eyes flicking briefly on Abby, but he made no remark. Abby's mind froze. What would he make of her presence? There was no doubt now that the truth would come to light. It was only a question of time.

"Aye, before I ask ye any more, I'll have ye greet your future lady wife." MacGregor nodded to Abby.

Iain turned and regarded her, his expression unreadable. "My future wife. And I thank ye for that. I would like nothing better than tae greet my betrothed."

Morag spoke to her brother in Gaelic, her tone sharp and disdainful.

"Aye, sister, I can vouch for her," said Iain.

Morag gave him a dark look but said nothing more. Iain made his way to Abby and leaned down to kiss her cheek.

"I'm glad tae see ye safe and well, quean," said Iain. He smiled at her.

The endearment, pronounced 'quine' took Abby aback for a moment, because she'd only heard her father say it once, to her mother, one of the few vague memories she had of the two of them together.

Abby returned his smile tentatively. "And I you, Iain."

Iain took her hand and looked at his father. "If it's all the same tae ye, I would prefer tae go tae my bed. I've covered many miles today and I'm sore tired. Tomorrow I'll happily answer anything ye might want tae know, Father."

MacGregor regarded Iain carefully before giving his assent. "Tomorrow then."

Iain smiled, satisfied. "And if ye don't mind I'll have my betrothed accompany tae my chamber, though ye have my word nothing untoward will happen between us."

"If only it would Iain. Then maybe I'd ken that ye were more than a scallywag wi' nae backbone," muttered MacGregor with a snort.

Abby rose and placed the lute in its sack, wondering what Iain wanted with her. He slipped his arm across her shoulder and pulled her into his side, by all appearances intimate and loving. She was only too glad to help the charade and slipped her arm under his plaid and along his back. It was then she felt the damp patch there. It wasn't sweat. No there was something sticky about it. It was a moment later that she realised it was blood. And quite a lot of it.

CHAPTER 5

$\mathcal{I}$ain lay back on the bed and sighed. Now, with the light from the window on him, she could see the beads of sweat forming on his forehead, underneath the riot of dark curls. His face had taken on a grey tinge and his eyes were glassy.

"Iain, you're badly injured. What happened?" asked Abby.

His face became more pallid, alarming her further. Without further ado she began the process of removing his clothes, taking care for the possibility of an open wound. It took some doing but she managed to remove his ill-fitting boots without much protest from him and tossed them on the floor. That task done, she leaned him forward from the bed against her and he groaned slightly. His eyes were closed now, so she uttered some reassuring words and told him what she intended to do. She surveyed the plaid that was wound around him and began the process of untangling it. With the plaid removed she could see the large rent in his doublet. He'd obviously used the plaid to conceal the bleeding which had now soaked nearly all the doublet's expanse.

Abby gave a grim smile and unbuttoned the doublet with a briskness she knew was necessary in light of all the blood now visible and, by all appearances, still flowing. He needed the wound staunched somehow, and soon, before any more blood was lost.

It was when she began to peel the doublet from his shoulders and slipped it from his arms that she saw the other wound on his left shoulder that soaked the once white linen shirt with its blood. It was nearly as severe as the wound as his side and Abby winced at the sight of it. She eyed the bedcovers and after a moment grabbed up the plaid and laid it across the bed. She eased Iain carefully onto it.

"Iain," she said.

His eyes fluttered opened and attempted to focus. *"Francach?"*

She smiled at his use of the more familiar term he'd used with her in private, back at Kilchurn Castle. "Iain, I must go and get some water to wash your wounds. I'll need a needle and thread, too."

Iain looked at Abby, his eyes clearer for a moment. He grabbed her arm with his right hand. "Be careful. Tell no one that I'm wounded, except Angus. He'll help you."

She nodded and he released her arm, closing his eyes once more. She gave a worried frown and made her way to the door. She slipped out of the room quietly, with only a quick glance at the figure on the bed and saw the grey colour had returned.

She made her way down the narrow stairs, wondering if the stables or the kitchen was the best place to find Angus. She opted for the kitchen with the thought that she could find water there and perhaps obtain a needle and thread on some pretext from Mistress MacNab.

In the kitchen she found Mistress MacNab busy banking the fire for the next day, her face more red than usual from the effort. Spying Abby, she rose with a questioning look.

"I was wondering if I might have some water to take to my

room and perhaps a needle and thread? I'm afraid that I tore my nightshift."

"Is there nae water in your room?" asked Mistress McNab. She frowned. "I thought I told the lad tae take it up tae your room."

"He did. I'm afraid I, er, used it."

Mistress McNab gave her a dubious look and muttered something about fancy French manners and chills. She went over to the large bucket and ladled some water into a pewter jug from the table before handing it to Abby.

"There's nae need tae go mending your own garb," said Mistress MacNab. "I'll see tae it in the morning."

"I don't mind doing the mending myself, Mistress MacNab."

"Nonsense," said Mistress MacNab. Her tone held a slight edge. "I'll see tae it in the morning."

"I would prefer to do it myself, tonight," said Abby, trying to keep her tone reasonable. "You see it is in a rather delicate place and I would like to repair it before I retire."

Mistress MacNab sniffed and nodded. "Very well. It's no for me tae say what ye should and shouldna do. I've told ye I would and I canna do more than that."

She disappeared into a room next to the kitchen and a while later returned carrying a small packet.

"There's needles and some thread in there. See that ye return it on the morrow, mind. My mending basket is never empty. Morag has little desire or talent for it and Peigi, the wee slip of a girl who comes up tae help, is as likely tae sew her finger tae the cloth as mend it."

"Thank you, Mistress MacNab," said Abby.

She gave a faint smile and took the packet, picked up the jug from the table and made her way back up the stairs, relieved. It seemed she'd managed thus far to keep Iain's state secret, but it was clear she would have to make a tear in her nightshift in a 'delicate place' and mend it. She was certain Mistress MacNab's eagle eyes would notice if there was no mended garment when next she washed the household linen.

She found Iain lying on the bed as she left him, half undressed, blood seeping from both wounds, though not as much as before. Perhaps lying still had helped staunch the flow. She could only hope so.

She set the jug on the small table beside the bed where a stump of a candle was wedged into a pewter holder. The room was chilly, she now realised. The window kept out the worst of the wind, but the light was muted, especially now dusk was descending. She looked around. The room was smaller than hers and spare, just a bed with a kist containing clothes at the end of it, the small table, and another table and chair by the window. On that table lay an inkwell and some old quills beside a pile of books. The hearth was bare.

She blinked a moment and made her decision. Quickly, she left the room and retreated back down the short corridor to the stairs and descended one flight to the level that held her room. It was outside her door that she met MacGregor.

"Are ye off tae your own rest now, lass?"

"Yes, thank you. I bid you goodnight," said Abby.

"Aye, sleep well," he said. He raised a brow. "Ye dinna suffer from sleepwalking?"

She flushed and shook her head. "I sleep soundly."

He nodded and went off to the far door, and disappeared inside. Abby let out her breath and entered the chamber. There was no sign of it being disturbed and the fire she had hoped for was lit against the late spring chill. It would be well into summer soon, but as she'd been warned, the warm sunny days she knew in France would be few and far between here. She glanced out of the window and saw the mist forming around the mountains. A chill night. It was important she knew, to keep

Iain warm. And pray that no fever would come from his wounds.

She brushed those thoughts aside, went for the tinder and collected some kindling and wood to lay a fire. With those items in tow she carefully opened the door and with the way clear, returned to Iain's room, praying that Morag or Alisdair wouldn't be entering their own rooms at that moment. She was in luck and found Iain, his eyes open, attempting to rise.

"Don't move," she said firmly. "You'll only make the wound worse."

He lay back on the bed with a grunt. "Tae be honest wi' ye, *Francach*, I dinna think I can go anywhere. My side aches like a hoor's quim."

Abby suppressed a smile at his remark and took comfort in the fact that he felt well enough to joke. "Stay there without moving while I light a fire. This room is fit only for making butter."

"And just what do ye know about making butter?" said Iain.

"Hush now." Abby smiled and turned to the job before her. She laid the fire in a very makeshift fashion, for she'd little enough experience. It took her all of three times to light it, but finally, she had a feeble flame going. She rose and made her way back to Iain, who lay with his eyes closed, a bit of colour in his cheeks.

"I need to remove your shirt. It's stuck to your wound in places, so it may hurt," she told him.

"Do what ye must, *Francach*."

She looked at the shirt and without hesitation ripped a piece from the bottom. She dipped the cloth into the jug of water and patted the wound at his side gently. Iain winced.

"I'm sorry," said Abby. "I'm trying to loosen the fabric."

Gently, and with painstaking care, Abby eased the ragged ends of the cloth away from the skin and eventually loosed the shirt first from his side and then his shoulder. What little colour that had returned to his face was gone by the time she'd slipped the shirt over his head.

She made a quick intake of breath. His wounds were as bad as she'd feared. The cut in his side was long and deep. She hoped it hadn't struck any vital organs. The slice on his arm was nearly as severe, but seemed to have missed the muscle.

"I have to stitch your wounds, I'm afraid."

"Aye." He gave a grimace.

She glanced at him. "It's going to hurt."

He nodded. "Just get on wi' it," he said, his tone grim.

She said nothing but went to work cleaning the wounds with the cloth. It wasn't long before the water in the jug was as red as the blood stains on the shirt lying on the floor and the cloth piece dyed pink. Eventually, the wound was as clean as she could make it and Abby reached for the packet Mistress MacNab had given to her. She removed the thread and a needle and went over to the fire. It was a sturdy darning needle, not much for fine mending, but it would have to do. Iain probably cared little if he had a scar. Didn't all men revel in them?

She reached for a small stick from the fire and used it to light the candle stub by the bed and replaced it when she was done. Everything was set, she'd only to complete the task. With the candlestick in hand, she took up the chair from the table and set it on Iain's left side. She placed the candlestick on the chair and studied the wound. The light wasn't the best, but it would have to do. She knelt beside Iain, her eyes level with his side.

"Brace yourself, now," said Abby, lifting the needle to Iain's side.

He grabbed her hand. "Before ye go poking more holes in me, would ye do me the courtesy of giving me a bit o' stick to bite on? I wouldna want tae ruin your pretty lugs or wake the house wi' my screeches, for that matter."

"Of course. I'm sorry I didn't think of it."

She rose from the bed and fetched a stick from the small pile that lay in wait beside the fire and handed it to Iain. He placed it between his teeth and gave her a nod. She resumed her kneeling position and began her work.

She placed each stitch with care, making an effort to keep her fingers steady. She'd done this only once before, when her father had fought a duel over some slut at court. At least that's what he'd said. The woman's name she'd never learned, nor who had sliced his arm in the fight. But he'd told her calmly how to proceed, mixing his instructions with reassurances, so by the end, when his arm was safely bandaged, she could even take a bit of pride in her work.

Now, beads of sweat gathered at her lip, and she kept wiping the moisture from her hands while she stitched. Luckily, the bleeding had all but ceased. It was more a matter of Iain's reaction; his constant effort to keep the pain under control upset her and made her nervous.

When she'd finished his side she straightened a moment, easing her back. She drew her hand across her brow, the top of her cap now as damp as the tendrils of hair that poked out of it.

She took a deep breath. "Now for the shoulder. I don't think it's as bad as your side, though I'm concerned about the muscle."

Iain eyed her curiously. "Where did ye learn sae much about healing?"

She gave a grimace. "My father. He's been in a scrape or two."

He raised a brow. "Has he? Aye. Weel, the French court I expect is full of hazards."

She gave a weak smile and took up the needle and pulled a fresh thread through it. Iain replaced the stick in his mouth and gave her a grim nod. She leaned over him and began the process of stitching up the shoulder.

It didn't take her as long as the first wound, in part because she was more confident, and also because it wasn't as severe as she'd first thought. Iain had only stiffened once or twice and this time there was no muffled groan as there had been when she'd worked on the wound at his side.

With both wounds stitched, Abby ripped up the cleanest parts of his shirt to make bandages. It wasn't easy, but she managed to wrap and bind the best of the fragments to his arm. It was his side that made her resort to her own petticoat because there wasn't a fragment big enough to circle his body. Iain had given her a dubious look and a bawdy comment when she'd lifted her dress and untied her petticoat. She'd only glared and continued her work.

When she was finished with the binding she scooped up the ruined shirt and stuffed it in the leather sack that held the lute. She would see to it later. She reached for her petticoat.

"Thank you, *Francach*," said Iain. "I owe ye much for that."

"It was the least I could do to repay my debt to you," said Abby.

"For what?"

"Well, for a start, you didn't betray me to your father."

"Aye, weel, we can talk about that later," said Iain. "Go now, and get some rest."

"I'll stay here with you," said Abby. "In case there's a fever."

"Just fetch Angus. Tell him tae bring a drop of whisky. That will fend off any fever, I nae doubt."

She gave him a sceptical look and he smiled back at her. He took her hand, lifted it to his lips and kissed it. He held it there for a moment. His eyes slid from her to the door. The next thing she knew she was on top of him, his arm gripping her tightly and his lips on her mouth.

"Be still," he whispered.

The door opened and Abby broke away and turned her head. Alisdair stood in the doorway, a flagon and two cups in his hand.

"Alisdair, did ye no think a man of my age requires a knock before a person enters his chamber?"

Abby reddened and leaned her head back on his shoulder, conscious of the bandage that covered it. She felt him stiffen and hoped she hadn't caused it to bleed again.

"I'm sorry, Iain, I didna think," said Alisdair with a grin. "I just wanted tae welcome ye home. And since ye did plead tiredness, I had nae notion ye might be…er… occupied in something other than sleep."

"Och, we're just getting reacquainted. Nothing more than that."

Alisdair eyed the floor and raised his brows. "I see ye've already reacquainted yourself with her lips and her petticoat and are on your way tae acquainting yourself tae the rest of her."

"Can I no embrace my betrothed?"

Alisdair shrugged and smiled. "The lady doesna object, so I'll leave ye tae your acquainting." He held up the flagon and cups. "It's obvious ye have nae need of whisky, sae I'll tak these off wi' me. I can see now why Father said just now that ye are tae be handfasted as soon as possible." He bid Abby a warm goodbye and shut the door.

The moment the door shut behind him, Iain groaned. "*Francach*, if ye dinna mind I would appreciate it if ye could take your head from my shoulder. Your head's a fair weight."

Abby lifted her head and body from Iain's and slipped off the bed to stand. She stared at him, wondering if she had heard Alisdair correctly. She was to be handfasted. She had no idea what it was, but she suspected it was something neither she nor Iain had bargained for.

CHAPTER 6

The fierce sound of a cataract of water woke Abby. She opened her eyes and lifted her head, groggy with sleep. A large muscled back and thick dark curls on a tousled head blocked the light from the window. Iain was sitting on the bed, his legs swung over on the floor. She was seated on the other side, slumped over the bed. She blinked and saw the bandages that wrapped the torso and the arm and recalled the events of the night before.

Startled, Iain turned and noticed her. He snatched the blood-caked plaid and drew it quickly over the top of his bare lap. "I didna thought tae wake ye, lass."

"You made enough noise to wake a bear," said Abby with humour.

Iain snorted and rose. With some wincing he drew the plaid around his waist and tucked it in.

"Ye were sound asleep," he said firmly. "And now that ye are awake I would be grateful for some help. I seems I canna manage my clothes wi' my arm and such."

"You should be in bed still," Abby said tartly. She studied him carefully, looking for signs of fever, but could see none. At least not yet.

Iain frowned. "I've nae time for bed. There's much I have tae do."

"And what would that be? More gallivanting around hills and fighting? Just how did you get those wounds?" She'd meant to make her voice light and joking, but it sounded more combative than anything.

"It is nae concern of yours, *Francach*. Now I would appreciate it if ye would stop your havering and help me dress."

Abby pursed her mouth, but held her tongue. She looked on the bed and saw that he'd lain out fresh clothes beside him, presumably taken from the kist at the end of the bed. On the floor were the breeches and hose that he must have peeled off with difficulty at some point. He'd still been clothed in them the night before when she'd sat beside him watching for signs of fever, afraid that her crude attempt at sewing his wounds wouldn't be enough. She must have fallen asleep in the early hours of the morning, her head resting on the bed. Now she felt stiff and dishevelled; her mouth a cesspit.

While she collected her wits, Iain took up the fresh linen shirt and struggled to put his head through the opening. Abby moved forward to help him, taking care for his injured shoulder and side.

"Never mind the hose and breeches," he told her. "I'll wear the plaid."

She gave the plaid he wore a sceptical look. It looked worse, not better in the light of day. She shook her head.

"Not this one," said Iain.

He nodded to the bed. Beside a leather jerkin and short jacket with open sleeves was a neatly folded plaid. She took it up and held it out to him dubiously.

"I don't know how to manage it."

He gave her a mock frown. "Ye call yourself Scottish?"

He shook his head and grabbed the plaid from her hands. With one swift motion he unfolded the bloodied plaid and it dropped to the floor. Abby felt herself blushing. Though his thick linen shirt with its full sleeves showed no more than a small area above his knees, it seemed that he was naked before her. She forced herself to keep her eyes on him, fascinated and somehow drawn to him.

Deftly he created folds with the plaid, and with her help, wrapped it around his waist, leaving a long length that hung down behind him. At his instruction she took his belt and buckled it around him. With the plaid held firmly in place, he reached for the leather jerkin and looked for her to help him once again.. She fastened the ties, checking first that the bandage around his chest and arm were still in place. All the while her eyes were focused only on her task, hoping her fingers wouldn't tremble under his gaze.

"All seems well with your wounds," said Abby, her tone full of purpose. "But try and keep from using that arm as much as you can. You don't want to break open the stitches."

Iain looked at her, his expression unreadable. He took up the jacket from the bed and slipped it on over the jerkin, with Abby's assistance. That done, he caught up the trailing length of tartan from the back and pulled it up over his shoulder, tucking the tail inside his belt.

"I ask your help wi' the boots, lass, if ye don't mind."

Abby nodded. He sat on the chair. She scooped up the boots where they lay on the floor, and with less effort than the night before, she helped him put them on. Fully dressed, he rose, stamped the boots in place and stood before her, one side his mouth turned up in a smile. His stance, his height, his dark curls wild about his face made him an imposing sight. A sight she would tuck in her memory, in her private most thoughts that even she wouldn't dare label with anything more than "treasured."

"Now," said Iain in a firm voice. "There are a few things we need tae discuss before ye go anywhere."

He indicated the chair and she took it without a word, gathering her thoughts. She supposed he was going to ask her how it was she came to be here, and why his father believed they were betrothed. In the hours while she watched him last night she had tried to come up with the best explanation possible. Now, in the cold light of day, she knew all the words that had crowded her mind were feeble and of no use. She took a deep breath.

"Yes," said Abby. "You're right. I suppose you want to know why I'm here." Hadn't her father told her to take the offensive if caught out, so there would be a chance to put your opponent off guard?

"Nae, lass. I ken that wi' little trouble. They discovered ye were nae laddie and ye did as I told ye and came here."

She blinked at him. Her father hadn't told her how to deal with a response that takes all the wind out of the explanation. "Yes, that is, they did discover me, but…it was Mister Johnstone, in Glenorchy's presence. But then Damville thought I was a spy, so they locked me up."

Her explanation had come out in the most cobbled ungainly manner and she felt flustered and annoyed.

"They locked ye up?" said Iain, his tone helpful.

She frowned at him. "Yes. After they beat me to try and get me to confess. To being a spy, I mean." She sighed. "With some help, I escaped when they were all distracted with Margaret's death."

"Margaret died?" Iain was alert now. "How?"

She bit her lip. She had pushed those events aside, trying not to remember Margaret's pitiful life as fiancé to the Glenorchy heir. A woman who had looked to her for comfort and help and, in the end, Abby had been too concerned about her own situation to bother with.

"A fall down the stairs. They say it was an accident, but I'm not so sure."

"And what do ye think?"

She shrugged, unable to give voice to her thoughts. "She was in an unenviable position and there are one or two who won't be unhappy that she's out of the way."

Iain's face remained expressionless. "Perhaps. But accidents do happen."

"Perhaps." She shrugged. She wouldn't speak about it any further since it was clear he wasn't going to believe her view.

"And so ye escaped, ye said, wi' some help. Who was it that helped ye?"

She eyed him a moment, but she could read nothing from his face. It mattered little, she supposed, if she told him, since it had been Glenna's express wish that he should know.

"Glenna," she said. "And she gave me the lute to bring with me, as well. Unfortunately, on my way here Damville managed to capture me. But I escaped him, too."

She smiled again at the memory of the great whack she gave him that left him doubled over. She hoped she'd given him enough damage so that it would be some while before he had pleasure of any kind from women.

"Ye're a braw hand at escaping," said Iain, shaking his head. "There's nae doubt ye have courage, lass. But it would be better if ye had half as much sense as courage."

She bristled at his words. "I have more sense than many a man at the French court."

"Aye, that maybe so," Iain said reasonably. "And do they go posing as women when they can only clomp around like they've just got off a horse?"

Abby stiffened, remembering how he'd told her she was too

feminine in her walk. "Of course they don't, but they make fools of themselves in more ways than you can imagine. Besides, I had a bloody good reason for going to Kilchurn posing as a boy," she said hotly.

"Och, ye were tae be companion to Lady Arbella, but instead ye decided tae play the lute. A very good reason tae risk life and limb."

"It wasn't that at all. I was hiding, and I thought it best to pose as someone entirely different. A boy." The words tumbled out of her mouth before she could stop them. Why had she done that? Hot tears clouded her eyes as all the events and fears of the months past crowded in on her. She lowered her head and studied her hands. A finger slid under her chin and lifted it. She fought for control as she looked at him.

"Why were ye hiding, lass?" he said. His eyes searched her. "What happened?"

She tried to look away but his hand held her chin firmly.

"Ye can tell me," he said.

She frowned, wondering if she dared confide in him. But something about his look, his firm warm touch on her chin made her want to trust him.

She sighed. "I overheard a plot to poison the Queen," she said softly.

"Our Queen? Queen Mary?" His voice was calm, reassuring.

She nodded and then the whole story tumbled out, finishing with her father making light of it, but insisting it was time she go to Scotland to acquaint herself with the land of her birth.

"Your father was right tae send ye tae Scotland, whatever the reason. Ye should know where it is ye come from."

She gave him a dubious look but said nothing. "I've heard nothing from my father since I've arrived. I'm not certain he really cares where I am."

"Nay, that isna so, I'm sure."

She shook the self-pitying thoughts away, no matter that it made for a more reassuring explanation of her father's silence.

"No, you're right," she said. "That's why I came here. To find help to get to France. I'm worried about my father."

He dropped his hand and turned away. "Ye're sure ye've heard nothing since ye arrived? There hasna been even a message tae Master Kerr tae inquire about your safe arrival?"

"No, nothing," she said.

He moved over to the window and stared out. "I'm certain all is well, lass. But in the meantime, we'll see about making arrangements for ye tae go there."

She felt warmth spread through her at his words. Though she knew nothing had changed. There was still no word from her father, but the fact that Iain was helping her and that she might soon be on her way to France, made all the difference.

A thought occurred to her. "The handfast, Iain. I-I'm sorry. Your father just assumed. Since I was wearing your ring." She looked down at the ring on her first finger and began to take it off.

He waved his hand at her. "Leave it for now, lass. And dinna concern yourself about the handfast. I'll think of something. My father has long been trying all means tae get me wed and heirs bred. And I'm well practised in outwitting him. So ye have nae need tae worry that ye'll be bound tae me."

Abby nodded and spoke words of relief, but they rang hollow in her ears. She eased the ring back in place and rose to leave.

IT WAS LATER, in her room, that all the events seemed to catch up with her. She stared out of the window, watching the rising sun cast long shadows across the rough field below her and the mists that hung around the rugged mountains. In the short time she'd been here, Abby had learned what she could about the area, if only to think how she might contrive a way to the coast and take ship for France. Unlike the countryside of her former in-laws, there was nothing gentle about the scenery here. Glen Strae was a long and twisting valley that rose high to the tufted bog and moorlands then suddenly change character with the force of the burn that thundered down from Fionn Lairig, The White Pass, as waterfalls and cataracts from the melting snow and spring rains. These Highland glens and pastures didn't support much more than basic breeding stock, so they sold off the cattle at the autumn trysts and markets to fill the bellies of the Lowlanders. The Highlands were no place for a woman who didn't know the terrain and with that certainty Abby was glad that Iain had said he would help her.

With a sigh, she pulled off her cap and shook out her hair. She reached for the small wooden comb that lay on the table. She'd been reluctant to use it before, knowing that Iain's mother had pulled it through her own hair. She examined the comb now, looking for traces of hair, but could see nothing. She was disappointed, but refused to acknowledge it stemmed from a wish to touch and feel a strand of the fair hair that would be a part of Iain's own mother. With a show of purpose she dragged the comb through her hair, unsnarling the knots that had built up over the past few days. Before, she'd not minded that her hair hung in bedraggled clumps. The cap had covered most of the mess, in any case. Now, though, she wished for pins to arrange it in a becoming manner and wished also for a gown that fitted well and was of finer cloth. She wouldn't acknowledge the reasons behind those wishes either.

She took up her cap and pulled it over her hair firmly. There was no need for anything different, she told herself. It would serve for what she must do.

CHAPTER 7

*A*bby inhaled the fragrant aroma of the fresh baked oatcakes and felt her stomach rumble. Dare she ask Mistress MacNab for some? She assembled a pleasant smile on her face and entered the kitchen. Mistress MacNab was bent over the fire, stirring something in a pot, her face flushed from the heat, sweat clinging to the simple linen kirtle and jacket she wore. The flaps of her once crisp linen cap drooped. Behind her, a young girl, whose clusters of frizzed curls and rounded cheeks marked her as a relative of Mistress MacNab's as anything else might, was carefully stacking the oatcakes on a wooden platter on the table. A boy, not much older than the girl, was placing a bucket of water beside Mistress MacNab.

"Don't crowd me in so, Willie," Mistress MacNab snapped. She lifted her arm against her brow. "It's as hot as the de'l himself."

"Sorry, mam," said Willie. He backed away with the bucket, slopping some of the water in his haste and splashing Mistress MacNab's skirt. She gave a loud "tsk."

The girl looked up at Abby. "Mam," she said softly.

"What is it noo, Ailish?" said Mistress MacNab. She turned to face Abby.

Abby forced herself to smile wider. "I'm sorry to trouble you, Mistress MacNab, but would you mind if I had a bite to eat? Perhaps one of the oatcakes?"

Mistress MacNab's face darkened. "Are ye no a guest of the laird? Ye maun help yourself of course. I would honour the laird's generous hospitality even tae one such as ye, though it is hardly time yet tae be breaking the fast and me still tae see tae the parritch, the meat and all the rest that will be served at the proper time." She stopped abruptly and pursed her lips.

Abby gave her a little nod and moved forward. Though her appetite had disappeared she was damned if she would back down. She picked up an oatcake, murmured her thanks and left the kitchen, closing the door. Through the wood she could hear the muttering, but chose not to listen and made her way out to the yard instead.

A loud bark greeted her and Cú came bounding towards her. She bent down and stroked his head, murmuring words of praise and assurance. At least someone was glad to see her. Despite his warm welcome, she was careful to keep his muddy paws away from her gown. She'd managed in the last few days to brush it down and to get Mistress MacNab to give her a clean cap and a linen necklet to go over the bodice. Her hair was arranged now so that a few puffs of hair appeared on either side of her forehead as was the fashion at the court.

The effort she'd made was to reassure her that she would be returning to court soon, she told herself. But she still had no idea when that might happen since she hadn't seen Iain since the morning when she'd helped him to dress after treating his wound. And that had been two days ago. There had been no sign of him at meals and when she'd asked, MacGregor had only grunted and told her that Iain was out on the land.

"I'll no object tae that, lassie," he'd said. "Though I know ye must be fierce wanting tae see him. He needs tae see the state of things, ye ken."

She'd tried to take his words in her stride and refrain from impatience, but it wasn't easy. Morag hadn't helped either with her restless eyes and the constant prowling around the halls of the castle. It was Morag's Highland pony that had woken Abby from a restless sleep this morning as she'd rode away, presumably in an effort to find an outlet for her increasing agitation.

Abby continued to stroke Cú, marvelling once more at his recovery from the wounded dog she'd first discovered. She hadn't seen him around the yard lately and found that she'd missed his friendly presence. He gave a little bark and bounded off again, this time towards the stables. She followed him on a whim, wondering if he had something to show her. He stopped just outside the stables, wagging his tail impatiently.

She drew closer and it was then she heard the voices. She recognised them at once. They were loud enough to hear, but after a few moments she realised they were speaking in Gaelic. Though she didn't understand what they were saying she could tell that Iain's tone was both familiar and urgent as he explained something to Angus. So they knew each other. But why had Iain never said? Abby searched her memory and concluded that perhaps there had never been a reason. Angus would certainly not want the Campbells to know he was a MacGregor when he'd first brought her to Kilchurn Castle.

Angus strode out of the stables, interrupting Abby's thoughts. She greeted him, damning the flush she knew that spread across her face, but he hardly took notice, nodding only at her words. He made his way to the kitchen and disappeared inside.

"Ye're up wi' the birds, *Francach*," said Iain.

Abby turned and saw him framed in the stable entrance, unkempt in his belted plaid, rumpled shirt and stained jerkin and his hair a mass of tousled curls. Her courtier's eye could only imagine what the nobles of Paris would make of him.

"The weather was so fine, I felt I had to get out, before the mists came in."

Iain gave her a lopsided smile. "Ye have the weather right enough. The mists will soon be descending down the valley and with it the rain."

"Fine soft weather," she said, giving her own turn at her father's expression.

Iain gave a little laugh. "Aye."

"So, you're back again," she said, for wont of anything better.

"I wasna aware I was away."

"Your father said you were out on the land."

"Aye, I was. On the land, as ye say, but I wasna 'away', so how could I be back?"

She gave him a puzzled look.

He gave her a shadow of a smile. "The land is MacGregor land wi' all its glens and mountains, that I've lived and breathed since I was a wean. It's all home tae me, lass."

She blinked, taken by surprise at this small insight into him. "Yes," she said. "I see. You are home."

They regarded each other for a moment and Abby savoured the silence between them. There seemed no need for words for that brief time. It was a moment she would recall later and savour it for what it was.

Hoofbeats broke the silence. Fast and urgent, they clattered into the yard and Abby turned away from Iain reluctantly. It was Morag. She drew up beside Iain.

"Tell Father to gather the men, Iain. We must go quick. The Campbells have struck us up at the shielings and have killed several of the men and women."

"The shielings? The cattle are up there already? But it's only just summer."

Morag snorted. "How would ye ken when is best and not? Ye've not been here this while. Will ye tell Father, or must I?"

"How do ye know? It might not be true," said Iain.

"Have ye gone weak in the head as well as the knees?" said Morag, her voice rising. "I tell ye I know it tae be truth because I just spoke tae young Tadhg, Roro's son. He'd been sent for help."

"When did it happen?" asked Iain.

"Yesterday, at dusk. They were all settling in for the night. The lad has been on the go since then. I left him at Old Peigi's."

Iain moved went over and reached to help Morag down from the Highland pony. She reined it away.

"There's nae time. I'm already saddled. I'll go tae Roro and let him know, too."

"You'll do nae such thing," said Iain sharply. "You'll come wi' me and tell Father exactly what Tadhg said."

He grabbed the reins with one hand and dragged his sister off the Highland pony with the other. Abby could see him wince with the effort and she thought of his injured side and arm. Morag squirmed against his hold but he maintained an iron clad grip on her and escorted her towards the castle entrance. Morag protested loudly as Abby followed closely behind, worried more for Iain's pain than Morag's.

"I'LL KILL every last one of the Campbells," said MacGregor, his voice filled with fury.

The hall was silent, though men lined the walls. Frowns and furrowed brows creased faces bearded and clean shaven. They all seemed to speak one thing. Vengeance. Abby could feel the surging energy in the arms and hands, itching for broadswords and dirks. These were the household men, the men from the neighbouring farms, all summoned to hear of the perfidy committed by Glenorchy and his men.

Morag stood by her father, her hand on his shoulder, her eyes glittering. Master Gower and Alisdair sat at the table near MacGregor. Iain stood apart from them, arms crossed, his expression unreadable since he'd entered the hall and Morag had relayed her story to her father who'd just come down from his room. MacGregor's roar of anger had fetched in Mistress MacNab, her children, Alisdair and Master Gower, as well as numerous men from the yard.

It was hours later now, and dusk was beginning to gather. The story had been told again and again as new men joined the ranks, but with everyone within a day's walk of here gathered, their arms at the ready in the stable, the laird was ready to make his judgement.

"Ye canna, Father. Ye ken that. The Council of Regency will have us outlawed. Glenorchy will see tae that."

"Glenorchy will be dead," said MacGregor. "And nae Campbell tae tell the tale."

"If Glenorchy is dead, there is more certainty that Argyll will have us outlawed."

"MacCailean Mhor? He wouldna dare take us on," said MacGregor.

"Father, you maun see reason," said Alisdair, his voice containing a note of pleading. "Glenorchy is Justiciar for all of Argyll. He has influence. We will be outlawed."

"Alisdair is right, my laird," said Master Gower. "It is entirely possible that the Campbells could have the clan outlawed. And that would mean the lands would be forfeit most likely to the Campbells and the Campbells would have the right to take up arms against the MacGregors."

"Och, there's nae law that thon southroners can pass that will keep here amongst the Highlands," said MacGregor. He patted his son's hand. "Dinna worry your head, laddie."

"Will we attack tonight?" asked Morag. "We could be there before dawn and take them by surprise."

"Ye're not going anywhere, Morag," said Iain evenly. "And Father kens that an attack on the castle is foolhardy. Any response we make must be well planned and in consideration of all the consequences."

MacGregor frowned. "Aye, well. Your brother is right, Morag. We canna rush off in a stamash wi' nae plan tae see us through. We'll think this through properly."

"Are ye all cowards then?" said Morag her voice rising. She scanned the room. "All of ye ken that the Campbells have been coming after us for years and we've done little enough in reply. They've taken our lands, our cattle. Is it no right that we make a stand now?"

"Morag!" said MacGregor roared. "Ye'll sit yourself down now and hold your tongue. It's nae for ye tae say what we maun and maun not do."

Morag took an empty chair, her posture rigid and her eyes flashing. Abby could almost feel pity for the frustration she saw in every inch of Morag's body.

"Kilchurn Castle isna a place to assault lightly," said Iain. "We might do better tae send a delegation. Talk to Glenorchy and see what he has tae say."

"Do ye think I dinna ken what Kilchurn Castle is like?" said MacGregor. "Was it no a castle on lands that are ours by right?" He frowned. "And just what do ye think Glenorchy would have tae say? 'I'm sorry for your loss'? or maybe 'will ye have your land back in return for all the trouble I've caused ye'?"

Iain gave his father a direct look. "I'm sure Glenorchy willna have much tae offer us in the way of restitution. But he might be open tae hearing the consequences of any more trouble."

"Aye, and what consequences do ye propose to threaten him with?" said MacGregor.

"Argyll isna a real friend of his and he's the one with influence on the Council, not Glenorchy. We could say we have our own influential connections at court and if he doesna stop we'll petition that Campbell be outlawed."

MacGregor gave a snort of laughter. "As if he would believe such *stite.*"

Iain shrugged. "It's a gamble. And when we send the delegation that might just step beyond its reach, it might do nae harm tae ensure nae letters are sent anywhere afterwards."

MacGregor ran his fingers through his dark beard. "Aye. This might have promise." He eyed Iain. "It's a pity I canna appoint ye as head of these men ye'd have me send. But there's nae doubt that Campbell would seize ye in an instant, for now he has a reason tae have ye kilt on the spot. His vanity and the law would have ye for breaking your word as a hostage."

Iain stiffened imperceptibly. "Aye, well. It canna be helped."

"Nae, laddie. I dinna hold it against ye for leaving, ye ken that. I only wished ye hadn't left it sae long. I'd sooner the Campbell bastard had nae truck wi' my family for any space of time."

"I'll go, Father," said Alisdair. He drew himself up, his narrow chest expanding. "I'll present the case in the best possible manner."

MacGregor gave his son a fond smile. "I appreciate the offer, laddie. But I canna risk ye being taken hostage either. No, I'll send Fergus and some of the others. They'll go at first light."

"Shall I write a letter outlining the different points?" asked Alisdair.

"There'll be nae letter writing," said MacGregor. "The tongue can carry lies and truths and nae others the wiser. I'll nae commit anything tae paper that can be waved in my face at a later time."

"Father, dinna waste your time wi' this talk," said Morag in obvious frustration. "It willna go anywhere and Glenorchy will think us fools. He will think tae take all of our lands if we dinna show him he canna kill our people and not pay the price. A real price. One that is measured in blood."

"Calm yourself, quean," said MacGregor. He laid a hand on her arm. "I ken that ye're hurting, that our kin have lost their mothers and fathers, but Iain's right. It's best that nae more blood is spilt just for foolishly rushing into danger."

Morag pulled her arm away from his grasp and frowned. Her eyes remained stormy, but she said nothing more. MacGregor nodded and turned to Iain.

"Ye'll see tae the arms for those that have none here wi' them?" said MacGregor. "I'll no have them going to Kilchurn Castle only tae be slaughtered on the way. They'll be watching out for us."

Iain nodded and started to move towards the door when his father spoke. "Have Fergus see tae the men, will ye?"

Iain gave his assent and disappeared from the hall. Abby watched him go, wishing she could follow him.

THE NIGHT HAD FALLEN like a shroud, the mists providing such cover against any stars that might have lit Abby's way as she made her way across the stables. It was here she hoped to find Iain talking with the men, calming them, assuring them, or at least providing clear instructions for sensible behaviour when they went to Kilchurn. As much as she might dislike Glenorchy and his sons, she had no wish for ill to befall Glenna. She only hoped that Lady Arbella was still away with her daughter Elspeth.

She peered inside the stable, scanning the stalls where men were scattered, sitting and standing, talking among themselves, the Highland ponies moving restlessly among them. The tension was obvious, underneath joking tones and snorts, never mind that the tongue they used was Gaelic. She saw no sign of Iain, but Angus was there. Spotting her, he left the man he was talking with and came to her side.

"Mistress, did ye want something?"

His face showed only mild curiosity, but Abby could only wonder what he must think of her. She'd noted he studiously had avoided her name, just as he'd avoided her presence in the days since his appearance.

"I-I was looking for Iain." She blushed which annoyed her, making her tone sharper than she'd intended. "I thought he might be here in the stables."

"He's gone off tae bed. He intends tae come wi' us tomorrow."

"But I thought he wasn't to go to Kilchurn."

"Nay. He'll come away just before we get there."

"But is it safe?"

Angus cocked an eyebrow. "Iain kens what he's about."

She thought of Mistress Brigson's small farm just outside of Kilchurn Castle. The woman had MacGregor blood running through her and had proven her loyalty to Iain a few times already.

"Yes, yes of course." She forced a smile. "Thank you Angus."

She turned and made her way back across the yard, conscious of Angus's stare. Let him wonder what she was about. He wasn't the only one who could keep their share of mysteries.

CHAPTER 8

The last time she'd been here it was at Iain's invitation. Now, she was hesitant as she knocked on the door. She wasn't certain of her reception but reminded herself she had good cause.

She heard him grant permission for her to enter, pushed the door open and saw Iain at the small table folding a sheet of paper. A letter? He looked at her in surprise.

"I was expecting Angus. Is there something ye require?" asked Iain.

"I thought I would take the opportunity to check your bandages. I haven't done so since I first tended the wounds."

"There's nae need, the bandages are still in place," said Iain. "Though I appreciate your concern."

"I do think it's necessary. It won't take a moment. Your bandages might have shifted and I would feel better if I knew there was no sign of inflammation or putrefaction."

He considered her a moment and then gave a nod. "If ye insist."

He rose and began loosening the ties that held his jerkin closed. Abby moved to give him assistance. He started to wave her away but she cut him off.

"It will be quicker and less chance of damage if I help you. Though after the effort you made to take your sister down off the horse, I wouldn't be surprised if there was already damage done."

Iain gave her a wry look. "Aye, well, it was either that or have her rushing off tae whip up anger where it will do more harm than good."

"I could see that, and though it might have done your wound little good, I don't see that you had any other choice."

She eased the leather jerkin off him, first his good arm and then taking greater care on the other, injured arm. She was glad to see there was no sign of blood on his shirt. It was his side that she was most concerned about. Still, what lay under the bandage was the most important indicator.

Iain pulled his shirt from his belted plaid and began to pull it over his head with one hand. Abby helped him, though her eyes sought the colour of the bandages beneath. There were bruises on his chest that spread out under the bandages, but no sign of blood. She gave a nod of satisfaction.

Taking the shirt from him, she placed it on the bed beside the jerkin. She leaned over the bandage at his side, checking it for seepage. Though the bandage itself was grubby with sweat, there was nothing to suggest it was putrefying.

"It's a little loose here. I'll just unwind it, check the wound to be certain that all is healing well and put the bandage in place once more."

Abby kept her tone brisk. It helped her to avoid any distraction that his naked chest and close proximity might cause. Iain seemed to respond to her cue and just nodded, leaving anything that might have been said in objection unspoken.

She continued with her work, unwinding the bandage and checking the wound. She was relieved to see that her carefully sewn stitches were still in place and only at one edge was it a little puckered and red. She touched it lightly with her finger and felt Iain stiffen under her probing. Well it was to be expected, she thought, and decided not to apologise for causing pain. It most probably wouldn't be appreciated anyway. In her experience of her father, men didn't like to be reminded of any weakness. At the thought of her father her insides tightened. Was all well with him? She gave a sniff.

"Och, *Francach*, I ken that I am nae sweet smelling flower the noo, so there's nae use sniffing tae tell me so."

She gave a small laugh, grateful for the diversion. What he'd said was true, though. There was nothing sweet-smelling about Iain at the moment.

"I'm sure there's a mare somewhere who would find your odour irresistible," she said and tried for a bright smile.

The bandage back in place, Abby turned to the arm. That dressing came off more quickly, but though the cut was smaller, she could see that the wound was red and angry and one of the stitches had come loose. She prodded it carefully, provoking a sharp intake of breath from Iain. She was relieved to see no pus emit, but she wasn't happy with its state. She bit her lip.

"Iain, is there any salve about I could put on this?" she asked. "Perhaps Mistress MacNab could make up a poultice?"

Iain looked at her. "We'll keep this from Mistress MacNab if ye dinna mind. She would feel obliged tae tell my father and I canna have that."

Abby narrowed her eyes. "And just what is it that put you in this state that you can't let anyone know? After your words in the hall earlier, it's clear that you don't support senseless killing."

"I dinna support killing where it's obvious what clan is attacking and witnesses can swear evidence. The consequences tae the clan are too large." said Iain. He sighed and nodded to his wounds "This encounter wasna of my choosing and it was in the dark."

"Do you know who the man was?"

"Men. There were three of them. And nay, I didna see who they were."

She gave him a speculative look. There wasn't a doubt in her mind that he could fend off three men, she decided. He had no reason to try and impress her either; his reluctance to tell her was evident in his posture. And she also had no doubt that there was much more to this tale.

She eyed the angry wound and frowned. "Well I'll just have to make up my own story for Mistress MacNab to get some salve from her. She has little liking for me anyway, so it will come as no surprise that I'm clumsy enough to cut myself badly."

Iain gave a laugh and his eyes twinkled at her. Her breath caught at the unexpected sight of the humour that transformed his face and gave him a beauty any balladeer would praise. She lowered her head to conceal her thoughts and took up the bandage.

"I'll put this back for now, but as soon as I can get the salve, I'll want to tend this again."

She gave the bandage a dubious look. It was even grubbier than the other bandage, but it would have to do. She wound it around his arm, making an effort to appear efficient, conscious that his eyes were on her.

"Och, lass," he said softly. "I'm grateful for your help. That's twice now. Or more accurately, three times."

She looked up at him. "Three times?"

"Aye. Back at Kilchurn. Do ye no remember? Ye came tae me in the night and told me about thon Charlie's capture."

She nodded. There was no fear that she'd forgotten that night. He'd greeted her at his chamber door, sleepy and clad only in his shirt. Though she'd been dressed as a lad, he'd known her for a girl.

"You knew the man well, then?" At the time she hadn't been

sure. She'd only seen the two of them conversing on the road when he'd told her the man was a poacher.

"Aye, I did."

"Was he a MacGregor? Do you know what happened to him?"

"He was a MacGregor. And I say 'was' as there's nae doubt he's dead."

"He wasn't a poacher."

Iain gave her a ghost of a smile. "Nay, *Francach*, he wasna a poacher. He was a cousin and a friend. And a good one at that. "

"I'm sorry to hear he's dead. The MacGregors have suffered much of late, it seems."

"Aye. And thanks for your condolences."

"Was he the reason you left Kilchurn?"

Iain cocked his head. "Ye have many questions and it grows late." He looked down at her fingers that were just tying the final knot to the bandages. "If ye're finished here, I think I'll take some rest while I may."

Abby nodded. The dismissal couldn't have been any plainer. She knew she'd been stretching his patience with her questions. Her only surprise was that he'd given her the answers to all but the final one.

IT WAS NO USE. She couldn't sleep. Not with the recent encounter with Iain still playing across her mind. Coupled with that were the thoughts of her father. Should she write to him? MacGregor had hinted that he would write. Wouldn't it be best if she were to write first? If he was there to receive it. If he was still at the French court, playing his lute and dallying with the women. She never thought she would wish for the reassuring evidence of his flirtations as she was at this moment.

With a sigh, she rose from the bed and went to the window.

The mist had descended again, obscuring any view that might be had in the darkness. She turned, took the large plaid that she'd tossed across the kist at the end of the bed and wrapped it around herself, then picked up the sack that still held Iain's lute and withdrew the instrument from it. Idly, she plucked out a few notes, twiddling and turning the pegs to tune it. Though the light was poor, her fingers found the strings with ease from years of practice. She hummed the piece softly while she played, hoping it would soothe her anxious thoughts.

If she hadn't paused in her humming she might not have noticed the muffled voices outside. The mist that made sight so difficult carried sound. The voices were distinct enough and accompanied by the sound of the slow progress of horses. Abby set her lute aside and made her way to the window. She moved slowly, reluctant to see what was going on below.

She cast her eyes down and blinked against the dark. Several figures and several Highland ponies were making their way down the track away from the castle. Abby caught her breath. There was no mistaking one of the figures. Her memory of the encounter those many nights ago was fresh enough. Morag in her disguise. Abby cursed under her breath. Where was Morag heading with the men? Most definitely not for an evening's innocent canter across the bog. It couldn't possibly be that she was defying her father and intent on avenging the deaths of her kinsmen.

Even as she denied the possibility Abby was out the door and making her way up the stairs to Iain's room. She knocked on the door lightly but there was no answer. She knocked again, this time a little harder, but still no response. She tried it and it opened, creaking with age and damp. Inside, she peered at the bed. Even without effort she could see that it was empty, the bedclothes hardly touched. She scanned the room but could see nothing out of place. In fact there was nothing there to indicate Iain's recent presence in any way. No cast aside plaid, no hose, shoes or any other item of clothing scattered around the room. The paper and quill that she'd seen him with earlier was gone.

Abby turned with a frustrated snort and left the room, closing the door quietly behind her. Without any further thought she rushed back to her room and was shoving her kirtle on top of her nightshift and thrusting her feet into the oversized leather shoes that she'd worn when she'd first arrived. She spared only a moment to lament that the boy's clothes were still at Kilchurn.

Inside the stable she noticed that Iain's Highland pony was gone. Had he seen his sister go? Somehow it seemed doubtful since she hadn't observed his distinctive figure among the men that were making their way down the track earlier. She saddled her horse, struggling in the dim light, and swung up onto it. She spared a moment to wish that it was one of the nimble Highland ponies underneath her so that she might negotiate the tufts and rocky paths that much better and quicker. She could only hope that they were on the track still and what her horse lacked in nimbleness he would make up in speed before the bogland was reached.

HER EYES WERE weary from straining against the mist and poor light, trying to see the figures ahead. She had no plan and the foolishness of her journey had become abundantly clear almost as she'd set out. What possessed her to think she could attempt to overtake a group of people who knew this land like the backs of their hands? And who were mounted on the ponies that under- stood instinctively how to pick their way through the most diffi- cult terrain with little effort. Her own horse had slowed to a walk and she dared not urge him faster for fear he might break a leg.

The fact that she had little idea where she was heading she dared not voice in her head.

She was about to turn her horse around and hope that he would know the way back to the castle when a voice emerged from the darkness and a hand grabbed her reins.

"Just where do ye think ye're going, *Francach*?"

She had no need to see his face to know it was Iain. That familiar, derogatory term for her was music to her ears at that moment. She sighed in relief.

"Iain, I'm so glad to see you."

Iain was beside her mounted on his pony. "It's fortunate for ye that it was me. I could ha' been anyone, and wi' murder and worse for ye as a result. Could ye nae do anything more foolish?"

She knew he was right, but still she stiffened. "You need not trouble yourself on my account. I'm perfectly fine."

Iain gave an exasperated snort. "Ye know that for the lie it is so I'll say nae more on the subject. But ye will tell me why ye're sae foolish tae take a journey in the middle of the night in a place ye ken nothing about?"

With some effort she suppressed the remark that rose in her mind and the pride that prompted it. Iain was right and there were more important things to address than her pride.

"It's your sister. I think she's gone out with some men to avenge the deaths at the shielings."

"What?" Iain said sharply.

Briefly, Abby told him what she knew of Morag's activities. Iain cursed roundly when she'd finished and let off a long string of Gaelic expletives for good measure.

"You didn't hear where they were headed, though I can guess."

Abby nodded. "To the Campbell shielings?"

"Aye. Though she's a fool tae think they won't have extra men there. She'll be cut down and all the men with her."

"Oh," said Abby. "Can we stop them?"

Iain gave her a direct look. "*We* will do nothing. Ye will return and I'll see if I can stop them."

Abby only now took in the broadsword that hung from its belt strung across his chest, the dirk in its scabbard on his belted kilt and the sack that hung from his pony. Though Iain's ignorance of his sister's actions had made it clear to her that the fact he was here had nothing to do with Morag, she hadn't realised until this moment the reason for his presence this time of night. He'd been intending to leave the castle. Go away without any word to anyone, presumably not even his father.

"I will not return to the castle," she said sharply. "For if I do, how can I be certain you will go after your sister and not continue on your coward's journey, escaping in the dead of night? If you wanted release from any obligation to me you only needed to say so. I will gladly tell your father we aren't suited after all and there's an end to it. I will find help to get to France elsewhere."

Iain grasped her arm tightly. "Will ye just hold your tongue, lass? It isna what ye're thinking at all."

"I can fathom no other explanation, I'm afraid," said Abby stiffly. "But that matters not at this moment. Finding Morag is what's important."

Iain frowned. "Aye. We'll talk about this later." He grabbed her reins. "I suppose ye'll have tae come wi' me, since I dinna think it wise for ye tae go back on your own."

They made their way forward in silence, the pony setting a fast clip and the horse following him with a bit more confidence. The time passed and all the reassurance Abby felt when they first set out slowly evaporated as they saw no sign of Morag and the men.

❧

IT WAS ONLY a faint noise when she first heard it, but Iain had already pulled up. She stopped just behind him. He turned to her and put his finger to his lips. Quietly he dismounted and moved forward. The noise came closer. Shouts and the neigh of a pony. Iain turned and came back to her.

"I want ye tae take the twa beasts tae yon craigs," he said, nodding to a cluster of rocks a short distance from where they were. "Stay there with them and dinna move until I come tae collect ye."

She nodded and allowed him to help her down from her horse. He handed her the reins and she made her way to the rock outcrop, turning briefly to watch Iain disappear from view, into the mists. She felt helpless and frustrated that she could do nothing more than mind the ponies, but she knew better than to think she might be helping Iain if she accompanied him up ahead. The noise of fighting was clear. Her heart sank as she thought of Iain's wounds. Two figures appeared, one gripping the other tightly and dragging the unwilling companion to an area near Abby. A bonnet fell to the ground from the struggling figure and dark hair tumbled out. Morag.

Abby instinctively rose from her place behind the rocks and rushed over to Morag's crouching figure. As she approached she could see the rage across Morag's face as she struggled against her captor. Abby cast around for something she could use to hit the assailant and found a hand-sized rock. She scooped it up and headed toward the looming figure, the rock in two hands, ready to hit the assailant with all her might until she saw who it was. She lowered her hands.

"Fergus!" she hissed. "What are you doing?"

Startled, Fergus turned to look at her and Morag took the opportunity to wrest herself free. She stood up, but before she could make her escape, Fergus gripped her again and pulled her back on the ground.

"I had nae choice. Iain said tae take ye away and that's what I'm doing."

"But this is my fight too," Morag hissed.

"Nay, lass. It's the clan's fight and wi' Iain leading it, as it should be."

"Iain has nae stomach for this, do ye no see? I'm the one who will stand and fight."

"Is it the Campbells you're fighting?" Abby asked. "Are there many of them?"

Morag turned to look at Abby, her eyes filled with disdain. "And just what concern is it of yours?"

"I'm concerned because your brother is out there fighting God knows how many men because you had some hare-brained notion to go against your father's wishes and carry out your own personal plan for vengeance against the Campbells." The words came out in a great heated tirade as all of Abby's fears and frustration rose up. "Fergus, I'll look after Morag so you can go back."

Fergus gave her a doubtful look. "Will ye give me your word that ye'll stay here, if I let ye go?" he asked Morag. "Otherwise I'll be forced tae tie ye."

She frowned but gave a quick nod. Fergus released his grip, mumbled an apology and took off.

"I was waiting over there behind the rocks where the ponies and my horse are," said Abby. "That's where Iain told me to bide."

She started to make her way back to the ponies and her horse, safe in the knowledge that Morag wouldn't betray a promise to Fergus. As she'd thought, Morag's steps sounded behind her. When they arrived at the outcropping, Morag found a seat on the rocks and turned her head away from Abby. Such an action didn't worry Abby for she had no wish to explain her own reason for being here. The less said to Morag about that, the better.

The shouts became louder. She could hear swords clashing. A moment later, figures emerged from the mist, clad in plaids.

Arms swung wildly, targes were thrust in defensive action. Then there was a shout, followed by a scream of agony. Abby shot up from the rock, searching the figures that emerged once more from the mist. Another cry came and then another. A figure fell to the ground and there were more shouts. Steel clashed hard and angrily, its sound ringing into the night. More shouts sounded again and cries. Someone was thrown on the back of a pony, men mounted and disappeared into the thick mist.

Abby closed her eyes, hoping what she'd seen and heard hadn't happened. Was it only her imagination or was the figure that fell tall, beardless and dark-haired? She looked over at Morag. Her face was white with shock.

Abby turned back to see the figures coming towards her. Leading them was Iain, his leather jerkin slashed and drenched in blood. Close behind him came a grim-faced Fergus, leading two ponies. The other men straggled behind, about eight in number, each with their head down, pony in tow.

Abby went quickly to Iain, Morag following close behind. "Are you badly hurt? Your wound? Has it opened?"

Iain blinked at her. "What? Nay, this isna my blood."

"Ye killed one, did ye Iain?" said Morag, her voice triumphant. "That will teach the Campbells."

Iain turned to look at her. "Aye, I killed one of them, though I dinna seek tae do so. And such killing will teach them nothing that will benefit us, sister." His tone was hard and full of suppressed fury. "Glenorchy willna allow this tae go unmarked, ye can be sure. And all because ye thought tae take it into your own hands. Can ye no see ye've put us on the path tae ruin?"

"I've done nothing more than show Glenorchy that the MacGregor's willna have their people slaughtered wi'out retribution."

"Nay. What you've done is give Glenorchy a reason tae petition the Council of Regency for us tae be put tae the horn."

"The Council willna banish us, surely?" said Morag. "We're descended from MacAlpin. We're royal."

Iain snorted. "Glenorchy has their ear and their favour. That's all that matters." He gestured to the men to mount. "We'll waste nae more time here. It's best that we get back and let Father know what happened."

Morag paled and all the certainty and triumph that had been there a moment before vanished under the press of Iain's words.

CHAPTER 9

The ponies snorted restlessly as they made their way up to the gatehouse, sensing the tension and unease that hung in the air. No word had been spoken since everyone remounted and headed back to Glen Strae. Questions still hovered in the air and with those questions, dread. How had the fight come to be? Had the Campbells attacked the small MacGregor band, or was it as Abby feared, that Morag and her men had found what they searched for, a group of Campbells guarding their lands, their cattle and their rights? Who was killed and who was injured of the Campbell band, Abby wondered. She prayed that it was no one of importance, even though the thought of Glenorchy's younger son dead would, in a different situation, have given her a certain satisfaction.

It was only after the ponies had been stabled and Iain had dismissed all the men but Fergus that an explanation started to unfold.

Iain gave his sister a piercing look. "Well?"

Morag shifted uncomfortably and glanced at Fergus. "Well what?" she said with a small note of defiance.

Iain's face became severe. "This is nae game, sister. And ye are nae child tae give petulant answers as if ye were caught pulling a dog's tail. Tell me exactly what happened so that I might find a way tae repair at least some portion of the damage."

"Ye saw it," said Morag, her chin set stubbornly. "There was a fight."

"Were ye defending yourselves or did ye attack them? Ye were on Campbell land."

"We were on MacGregor land!" said Morag hotly.

"They attacked us, Iain," said Fergus with a sigh. "But it might be they were provoked."

Iain looked at Fergus and nodded. "And might it be that the provocation came from my sister?"

Fergus frowned and nodded.

"I was only telling them tae go back from whence they came," said Morag. "That they were trespassing."

Iain sighed and levelled a gaze at Morag. "Ye ken very well that the land is Campbell, now, and nothing you can do will change that."

"That's only because nae one has the courage tae fight them for it," said Morag angrily.

Iain gripped his sister's arm. "Will ye no ken that there is nae use in fighting the Campbells when each time ye attack they will only have cause tae have us punished?" His voice was cold.

Morag gave him a disdainful look. "Not while I have any MacGregor blood left in me."

"It may be well tae put your life on it, but ye also put the rest of the clan at risk, as well," said Iain. "What will Roro's tenants and the other glens do when they are turned out of their homes and left tae wander the hills?"

"It willna come tae that, will it?" Morag said in a whisper.

"It might." He released her arm. "I want ye tae promise me that ye willna go raiding again."

She pressed her lips together and nodded. "But Iain, they ken it was ye who killed the Campbell man."

"Aye, leave that worry tae me," said Iain. He stroked her hair. "I want ye tae go tae your chamber, quean."

The last words he spoke in a caressing tone. Morag leaned against him and whispered, "I'm sorry."

He kissed her head and pushed her away. "I know. Off wi' ye. It's getting light.

Morag made her way out of the stable and across the yard. Iain turned to Angus and sighed. "Fergus, man. What were ye thinking, allowing her tae lead the men amuck?"

Fergus shifted uncomfortably and refused to meet his eye. "I'm sorry, Iain. But ye ken what she's like, when she gets a notion in tae her head. I thought if I go wi' her she mightna come tae harm and I could keep her from her worst notions."

Iain snorted. "Aye, well. It's done, and let's hope we can manage tae minimise the harm. But I expect in future there willna be any more night time riding."

"No, Iain. I promise ye I will do my best."

"Best isna good enough, Fergus. I expect ye tae tell MacGregor if she even thinks about something as daft as this. Ye ken?" Iain spoke firmly, with a hint of warning in his tone.

Fergus nodded and Iain dismissed him. The rest of the men had melted away to their beds. Iain looked at Abby. His face was drawn and pale, and the fatigue in his eyes was telling.

Abby moved over to him. "Have your wounds opened?" she asked quietly. She touched his arm lightly and saw him wince. "Come, let me have a look."

Iain shook his head. "Nay. There's nae time for that. I maun go tae my father and tell him what's happened. We need tae be prepared for what is tae come."

"And what is that?"

He gave her a grim look. "Banishment. Unless we can persuade the Campbells otherwise. But I'm no hopeful of that."

"Can't you plead directly to the Council of Regents? Or the Dowager Queen herself?"

"I wish I could, lass. But there is nae person who would hear me over Campbell. And the Dowager Queen is a *Francach* and has nae connection or reason tae love a Highlander, let alone a MacGregor. Glenorchy has influence, as I've said."

Abby gave him a silent nod. His reasoning was sound, she just wished it wasn't so dismal. She followed him silently out of the stable, wondering how MacGregor would take the news.

MacGregor was waiting for them when Iain and Abby arrived in the hall, his face set in a dour expression. He wore trews, his plaid draped around him and pinned at his shoulder with a huge brooch. He indicated the chairs at the table and the three sat.

"What's this I hear about a raid?" he asked. "And after ye were telling *me* tae keep calm."

Iain gave him a wry smile. "I did do that, didn't I?"

"Dinna play the fool wi' me, mannie," said MacGregor sternly.

Iain's face took a solemn expression. "Ye're right. It's a serious matter, there's nae doubt."

"Suppose ye tell me exactly what happened and then we'll see how serious it is."

"It wasna planned, I can assure you. I was out wi' the men to ensure there wasna any trouble and we came upon the Campbells. There was some taunting and then the fighting broke out."

"And ye dinna stop it?" asked MacGregor.

"Well, ye know yourself, that isna possible."

MacGregor gave a long "hrrmmph". He turned to Abby and his eyes narrowed.

"And ye had nothing tae do wi' this mess?"

Abby shook her head, hoping no one had seen her leave the keep earlier. "I heard the men ride out and waited in the stables for their return."

"What's happened?"

The three of them turned to see Alisdair enter the room, tousled-haired, his shirt still untucked, his hose and pantaloons hanging carelessly on his young frame. "I heard the horses. Did the men go out in the night?" His voice held disbelief. "They wouldna, not after Iain's words, would they?"

Iain gave him a rueful look. "Aye, they did. We did. Just tae try and keep the peace, but it wasna possible."

Iain filled Alisdair in on the rest of the events just as the door opened again and Morag entered. She wore a plain dark gown and her hair spilled out from her French hood that did nothing to help the pale, drawn face underneath it. Smells from the kitchen followed her in.

"Did I hear aright from Mistress MacNab? The Campbells attacked some of our men last night?"

Iain frowned at her. "I wouldna quite put it like that, dear sister. A fight broke out between ourselves and the Campbells and one of their men was killed."

"But not any of ours?" asked Morag, her face a show of concern. She took a seat next to Iain and put a hand on his arm.

"Nay. Only a few injuries."

"How fortunate," said Morag.

"I wouldna count ourselves fortunate," said Iain.

"But it is something tae be thankful for," said MacGregor. "And that there's one less Campbell tae trouble us."

"Father, ye canna mean that," said Alisdair. He began to pace a little. "As much as ye may be glad, it willna be the end of it."

"Do ye think I dinna ken that, laddie?" said MacGregor.

"We must send a message, Father," said Alisdair. "Explain what happened. Try and make them see reason."

Iain rose and went to Alisdair. He put a hand on Alisdair's shoulder. "I fear it may be too late for that."

Alisdair gave him a pleading look. "Surely not, Iain."

Outside, shouts rang out. Everyone made their way to the window. Below them in the courtyard a mounted rider came in through the gatehouse, another man leading the horse. Abby recognised the man as one of Glenorchy's soldiers. He was shouting at the MacGregor man who held the reins.

"Iain," said MacGregor. "Go see what the *stamash* is."

Iain nodded and left without a word. He reached the court-yard below a few moments later and approached the growing group of men surrounding the mounted horseman. Abby watched him exchange a few words, his manner calm, and then reach up for something that the man proffered him. With a nod to the Campbell man, and a few words to the surly looking men milling around him, Iain departed to return to the hall. It wasn't long before he appeared, made his way to MacGregor and handed over a letter, folded and sealed.

"From Glenorchy?" MacGregor said.

Iain nodded. "I dinna think it's good news."

MacGregor grunted. He broke the seal, unfolded the letter and began scanning its contents. He read it through twice walked to the table and threw it down.

"What am I tae do wi' that?" MacGregor bellowed.

Iain looked at him calmly. "May I read it?"

"Ye had better, considering it was ye who prompted it!" MacGregor said sharply.

Iain went over and picked up the letter, scanning its contents quickly.

"What does it say?" asked Morag, a tremble in her voice.

"It says, my dear sister, that Glenorchy intends tae petition the

Council of Regency tae have our lands forfeit and our clan disbanded. In short, he wants us put tae the horn."

A small gasp escaped Abby. Though Iain had predicted this might happen, it hadn't felt real until this moment.

"Surely there's something we can do," said Abby.

Morag turned fearful eyes to Iain. "There is, isn't there?"

"Aye," said MacGregor darkly. "We can fight them. Let them try and disband the MacGregors. Let them try tae find us in our misty glens. They couldna win."

"And we'll we be holed up for all the years tae come, waiting, watching for the next attack?" asked Iain. "Would ye ask that of your clan?"

"I wouldna have tae ask," said MacGregor. "Any MacGregor would offer tae do that, rather than give up their name."

"He canna have us put tae the horn without rightful cause," said Alisdair. "I'll check with Master Gower. I'm certain we can find something tae counter it with."

Iain looked at Alisdair. "Aye, ye do that laddie."

Alisdair approached his father who was standing by the table his arms crossed, his face thunderous. "We could write our own letter," said Alisdair, "explain how it wasna intended. Explain about the deaths at the shielings. They'll will see it isna our fault."

With some effort MacGregor smiled grimly. "I know ye're trying tae help, but I dinna hold out much hope for any words on a piece of paper tae a Council of Regency that wouldna ken one end of a glen from another."

"I'll take the letter myself," said Alisdair. "I'll explain what happened. And with Master Gower's help, I could make them see the right of it."

"Ye havena any influence," said MacGregor. He frowned. "Our only connection is through your mother's family. And that may count against us since Glenorchy is married tae Arbella."

"Lady Arbella might speak on the MacGregor behalf," said

Abby. She glanced at Iain, remembering the strong bond he had with his mother's cousin. "What do you think, Iain?"

Iain gave a dubious look. "Aye, she might."

MacGregor studied Abby. "There might be other connections, come tae think on it. Lass, ye said your father is at the French court with the Queen. Have ye been tae the French court?"

"Yes," Abby said slowly, dreading where this might be heading. "I was raised there."

MacGregor brightened. "Could ye no convey a daughter's greetings tae her mother at Stirling, or wherever it is the Dowager Queen holds her court, now?"

Abby opened her mouth to speak, but no words came out. "I'm not certain it would have much effect. I-I don't really know the Queen more than to exchange a few words."

"Wheeest, that matters little. Ye can still say much about her health and her interests tae a woman who is starving for news of her daughter so far away in France."

"I imagine her brothers serve her quite faithfully in that manner. As does the Queen herself."

MacGregor gave an impatient snort. "Aye, nae doubt. But there are always the questions that canna be asked in a letter."

"I suppose so," said Abby doubtfully. "If you would like me to try I will do what I can. Shall I write the Dowager Queen and ask if I might visit?" She looked at Iain but could read nothing from his expression. What of her plans to go to France? She sighed.

"When ye write, ye can mention that ye are tae wed tae MacGregor's heir, and while we wait for the reply, we'll make it so," said MacGregor. "Your connection will give us the best chance of persuading the Dowager Queen to our cause, I think. And she can counter anything that is put before the Council of Regency."

Abby looked at MacGregor in alarm. "Marriage?"

"Handfasting. In two days' time. That should give Mistress MacNab enough time tae prepare something."

"Does that suit Iain?" asked Abby.

It was the best question she could come up with and one that had plagued her before. She looked over at him, reluctant to see the expression she would find there. He gave her a faint smile and she read the apology in his eyes.

He swept her a small bow. "Milady, I would be honoured."

Abby forced a smile on her lips. "The honour is all mine," she murmured.

It was later, as she was about to ascend the stairs to her chamber to wash off the night's events, that Iain caught her arm. She turned to him and saw the apology again in his eyes. But this time there was something more. Was it gratitude? She didn't want gratitude, she didn't want apologies. What did she want? She had no idea.

"Thank you for doing this, *Francach*," he said.

She nodded. "There's no other course of action," she said.

"Nevertheless, my father is asking much. More than he knows."

She reddened. "Some of that was my own fault. I never contradicted the assumptions he made about our relationship."

"Aye and ye're paying the price and more. And I wouldna have ye do it, if I could find another way." He squeezed her arm. "I do promise ye that it willna be for long."

"The marriage?" she asked. She blinked, refusing to let him see how his words were affecting her. She didn't want them to affect her.

"The handfast," he said. "I promise ye it will only be for as long as we have tae. By rights we can dissolve it when we like, as long as we dinna consummate it. And it doesna mean we have tae be together."

"It doesn't?" she said, her voice thin.

"Nay. As soon as we finish at the Scottish court, I promise ye I'll take ye tae France, tae your father. After that, we can part."

She nodded, not trusting herself to speak for a moment. "Thank you," she finally managed.

She glanced down at his hand which was still clutched around her arm. He released his grasp and she turned and made her way up the stairs, her mind a whirl of emotions.

CHAPTER 10

The knock on the door took Abby by surprise. She cleared her throat and bid the person enter. Abby was even more surprised to see Morag, a brightly coloured gown draped across her arms.

Abby rose. "Morag." All other words flew from her mind. Morag entered briskly her mouth pursed, her eyes clouded.

"I've brought ye a gown tae wear for tomorrow. Ye maun wear something decent if ye're not tae shame us in front of the clan." She thrust the gown in Abby's arms.

Abby looked down at the gown and gave a slight smile. It was clearly one of Morag's and not her mother's. It was a rich blue velvet with a matching brocade underskirt but its smaller size and more fashionable cut confirmed its owner.

"It's lovely," Abby said quietly. "Thank you."

"Aye, well." Morag waved her hand dismissively. "It was made for me when Father took it in his head that I might marry one of the MacDonalds and form an alliance against the Campbells."

"He changed his mind?"

Morag sniffed. "As if I might want tae be shackled tae one of those great louts. I told him he was best tae save his energy for other things. It was better that I stayed home and looked after things."

"And he agreed?" Somehow Abby doubted it had been as straightforward as that.

Morag gave her a dark look and shrugged. "He came around in the end. He nattered on a bit saying I must have a husband someday and not tae fash myself about his wellbeing, because there would be a time one day when Iain would marry and his wife would look after things then." She eyed Abby shrewdly. "But I dinna think this is that time, do ye?"

Abby gave her a direct look but felt herself flushing. "We can never know what the future will bring. For now, it has brought Iain and me together. I'm afraid you'll have to accept that, Morag."

Morag put her hands on her hips and examined Abby. "Maybe. But I know my brother. And I dinna see ye as the type of woman who would hold his attention for long. Nae matter that ye have connections." The last word was spoken with huge disdain.

"My connections aside," said Abby, "I think I have more recent intimate knowledge and understanding of your brother than you do. And if you'll remember, I'm doing this to help your family."

Abby tried to restrain the anger that was rising inside her, but it was difficult and she knew she was failing miserably. She didn't want to alienate Iain's sister; in fact she would have welcomed the opportunity to become her friend. She had few enough of those in her life, especially living at court when there was so much hypocrisy and intrigue.

"I didna say ye weren't intimate, or that he might not enjoy ye secretly that way for a time, I just said that ye wouldna be his wife. This is merely a convenience for him and the family, as ye mentioned. And we are grateful. I only wanted tae tell ye that it's nothing more than that. Ye do give him an eye, now and again."

Abby clenched her hands inside her skirts to keep them from slapping the face that was before her. The girl was young, impulsive and underneath it all, miserable. Abby sighed, releasing some of the tension inside her at the last thought.

"I'm sorry. You're right. This is all being done to help the situation."

Morag nodded, satisfied. She indicated the gown. "If ye put it on now, I'll send Mistress McNab to make the necessary adjustments."

ABBY SMOOTHED the front of her dress and adjusted the sleeves. It was a nervous gesture, she knew, but since no one was here to witness it she gave full rein to her anxiety. What would her father say to all of this? Was she mad? She clutched onto the notion that it was the only way she could manage to get herself safely back to France and reassure herself of her father's welfare.

She tried to inhale deeply, but the stiff, tight bodice restricted her. It was a beautiful gown, she had to admit. The sleeves, when they were brought, were trimmed with fur and hung low along her gown. The colour suited her, she could see that from the mirror, and the small French hood that encased her hair was lined with pearls. Mistress McNab had shaped her headpiece so that small puffs of red-gold hair showed at either side of her head. It had been fashionable at the Paris court when she'd left, and an impulsive desire to be a little bit stylish made her ask Mistress McNab to help her achieve it now. Mistress McNab had only muttered something about French vanity, but had complied nonetheless. The result was better than Abby could have hoped.

The door opened and Morag entered, Mistress McNab right behind her. Morag was dressed in a deep red gown with dark velvet sleeves and seed pearls edging the neckline. She looked Abby over and nodded. Abby suppressed a smile.

"Am I suitable?" Abby asked.

Morag nodded curtly. "Aye. Ye'll do." She thrust out her hand. "Here. Iain said tae give these tae ye for today."

Abby held out her hand and watched as a rope of pearls tumbled into to them. She looked up at Morag in surprise. "Pearls?"

"They were my mother's. Iain says ye maun wear them today. It's only fitting." Morag gave her a direct look. "But just today, mind."

Abby nodded, half amused, half uncertain what she thought about this unexpected gift. She fastened the pearls around her neck and gave a small word of thanks.

"We maun be off now, mistress," said Mistress MacNab. "They're waiting below."

For a moment Abby wondered exactly who Mistress McNab was addressing as 'mistress', and gave a bemused smile. "Of course," she said. She must try and act the part, even if both Mistress McNab and Morag would have it differently.

The hall was filled with clansmen and women. Everyone turned to part a path for her and watch her progress to the small clearing at the top of the room. Heather hued plaids were draped and wrapped around linen shirts and long skirts, blending against one another, each slightly different, but each definitely MacGregor. There were a few guests from other clans as well; those that were able to come at short notice, including Colquhouns, McNabs and MacLarens. An excuse to celebrate in summertime wasn't easily passed up.

Abby took all this in as she made her way over to Iain, MacGregor and what she thought must be the priest. Though there was no sign of priestly clothes, she could think of no other reason for the man's presence. She gave it no more thought and took her place by Iain. He stood, bigger than life, dressed in an elaborate lace edged shirt, a deep blue velvet jerkin and a plaid draped and folded around him and along his chest and left shoulder where a large jewelled brooch was fastened. On his feet were long, dark boots polished to a shine and his dark hair was combed into a semblance of order. It was his eyes that caused Abby to catch her breath. They were twinkling and full of light and, together with the wide open smile on his face, they created an image that she knew she would never forget.

She glanced at MacGregor for a moment and saw the nod of appreciation that was echoed in his eyes. She couldn't help but feel a warm glow at the approval. Iain took her hand and she faced the man beside MacGregor, assuming him to be the priest. She was surprised then, when MacGregor began to speak. His tone was formal, but she could tell nothing more than that because he spoke in Gaelic. She looked over at Iain and he gave her hand a reassuring squeeze.

MacGregor intoned some more words, his voice rising and falling. Everyone listened attentively. Occasionally, they emitted murmurs of approval and once, laughter rippled through the group. Abby heard her name mentioned and many other Gordon names following it. Bemused, she watched MacGregor reach out and take Iain's hand and place it on top of hers. MacGregor then took a strip of snowy white linen and carefully wrapped it around their hands. He turned to Abby and spoke some words in Gaelic. She gave him a puzzled look. A frown crossed his face for a moment and he spoke in English.

"I ask ye if ye will promise tae take Iain as your husband."

Abby looked at Iain and he nodded to her in encouragement. "I will," she said.

"*Bheir mi*," said Iain softly.

"*Bheir mi*," she repeated.

MacGregor nodded, satisfied. He turned to Iain and spoke.

Iain answered at length, and though she heard *'bheir mi'* among the words, she had no idea what else he'd said. He looked into her eyes when he'd said it and she saw the hint of mischief and wondered what it meant. She had little idea about the nature of the ceremony, and in the upset of the past few days, she'd not allowed herself to consider what it would mean for her. It was a handfasting that was legally binding, according to Iain, and would become a marriage only if they consummated it. A binding that they could set aside at some future date. She should feel comforted by such reassurance, but if she was honest, she didn't know how she felt. Abby looked at Iain again and tried to discern his own feelings on the matter. All she saw was a wide grin and a glint in his eyes. Mockery? Amusement? Or something more? Her hand felt clammy under his warm dry hand.

After Iain finished speaking, MacGregor added a few more words. The man beside him stepped forward and moved to the small table on his right. He laid out a document, took up the quill beside it and signed it. MacGregor followed suit and gestured to Iain, who took Abby by the arm and led her to the table, where the two of them put their signature below the others. Abby could make out nothing of the words which appeared to be in Gaelic, but it might have been Latin for all it was such a poor hand. With the signing complete, MacGregor gave a shout to the assembled group that was met with a roar of approval.

Iain took Abby's hand and turned her to face the clansmen. She gave a tentative smile as she looked at the generally happy faces that met her. A silver goblet was placed in her hand and in Iain's. Iain raised his goblet, said a few words in Gaelic and then downed the lot. He looked over at Abby and nodded. She looked down at the goblet, the fumes from the amber liquid wafting up to her nose, and then looked at the awaiting group.

She took a deep breath, lifted her cup and said in a loud voice, "To the MacGregors." Before she could give it any thought she drank the whisky quickly. She could feel it burning the back of her throat as it made its way to her stomach. She tried to suppress the cough that rose up, but Iain heard her and gave a light laugh.

"Careful, now, *Francach,* that whisky isna tae be wasted. It's the best quality."

She forced a smile. "I'm fine, I assure you," she said in a tart tone. "What you may judge as the finest quality may not be what the rest of the world holds to be true."

He took her hand again. "Och, now, lass. Enough of the jabs. Let's enjoy the day."

Abby cursed herself inwardly for the remark. It had come out before she could think and there really was no cause for it. But for some reason she was out of sorts and any little remark Iain made pricked at her like a thorn that couldn't be removed.

Beside her, Iain sighed. "Come."

He led her back through the assembled group to the other end of the hall where they had placed the large trestle table. He seated Abby in a chair set near the middle and took the one beside it. MacGregor was already in place beside Abby and on his other side was Alisdair. An older woman, whose features marked her as a family relation, sat beside Alisdair. Morag took the seat on Abby's other side, offering a curt nod before turning to speak to the older man next to her. He was round-faced and wore tartan of a slightly darker hue than MacGregor's.

People began to erect more tables and position benches along them, many gathered from outlying homes in readiness for the day. Though the weather was fine enough at the moment, a change was always possible and nothing could be counted upon. Eventually, they would move outside when the day wore on and the tight formality of the initial hours gave way to more enthusiastic and less inhibited celebration.

Against the din of conversation, the consumption of great

platters of venison, fowl and other roasted meats, and the steady drink of heather ale and clan whisky, Abby sat quietly and picked at her food. With little to say and none to say it to beyond Iain who was throwing comments to all and sundry around the room, she took solace in her goblet. The whisky had long since lost its fire and now gave her a great comforting warm glow that was spreading throughout her body. The feeling was preferable to her earlier discomfiture and irritation and she welcomed it. It was only when she reached for the flagon a third time that Iain put a gentle hand on top of hers.

"Whoa, there, lass. Do ye think ye maybe should have something tae eat before ye pour that down your thrapple?"

She could feel his hand on hers and she fought to suppress the pent-up emotion that welled inside of her. "I'm perfectly fine," she said through gritted teeth.

"Och, we willna quarrel over it, but perhaps a bit of air will do ye nae harm."

He put his hand gently under her arm and lifted her from her seat. She resisted initially, but then her better judgement took over and she allowed him to help her stand. She wasn't prepared to make a scene in front of everyone.

As soon as she was on her feet, Iain slid his arm around her waist. Shouts came from various corners. The words needed no translation for Abby. She flushed. Iain gave the audience a wicked grin and then leaned over and kissed her hard. She could taste the whisky on his mouth. It took her breath for a moment and then the kiss deepened and all the glow from the whisky seemed to pour into her with greater strength. She put her arms around his neck and he pressed deeper, exploring her mouth for just long enough that Abby sighed and wished for more. He pulled away and the moment was gone.

The gathering roared their approval. Iain grinned again and released Abby, taking her hand. She nearly fell backwards with his support momentarily gone and her breath with it, but he moved forward, tugging her behind him. The crowd roared again, shouting phrases and words and offering encouraging gestures urging immediate consummation of the marriage. Iain laughed hard and answered a few as he led her across the hall and through the corridor to the outside door.

It was only when she was outside, in the cool early evening air, that she came to a semblance of herself. Iain stood beside her, his presence still larger than life and the traces of his kiss lingering on her mouth.

"You were most convincing," she said. "I take it they don't know that we have no intention of going through with the marriage."

Iain gave her an amused look. "Nay. Nor my father, forebye he would be sore disappointed. Not only because he wants the use of your connections, but he would have me wed. Tae anyone remotely suitable."

"Even a *Francach*?"

"Ye're Scots, lass, however much ye may think ye're not. A *Gael.* Ye couldna be your father's daughter if ye weren't."

"I wouldn't call my father pure Scots at heart. He has long adopted many French ways. And he married a Frenchwoman after all."

"Maybe, but I think if ye ken your father at all, ye'll see the Scots underneath."

"And just what do you know about my father? You've never met him."

Iain shrugged. "I just ken Scotsmen is all."

A wet nose nudged Abby's fingers. She looked down and saw Cú nuzzling her hand. She knelt to his level. "Cú," she said softly. She stroked his silky coat, glad for an opportunity to be out of range of Iain's keen eyes. She mumbled a few words to him.

"Aye, he's a good loyal dog," said Iain. "And he kens who is good and loyal, too."

She tried to find a fitting reply to what seemed to be a compliment to her, but unwanted tears welled up for a few seconds. She blinked them back. The door thudded behind them and a figure stumbled towards them.

"Angus?" said Iain.

"Aye, it's me."

Angus drew the ballock dagger that was at his side. Iain's hand snapped out and held fast to Angus's arm, stopping his movement.

"Dinna fash yourself, Iain. I've come only tae say a few words on my oath as a MacGregor." With clumsy effort he removed Iain's hand and fell to one knee, the dagger held up at his lips. "I wanted tae be the first tae swear to protect your lady, Iain." His words were slurred slightly, but his tone was earnest.

Iain put a hand on Angus's shoulder. "Och, Angus, there's nae need."

"There is every need," said Angus. "As MacGregor's heir, your bride will someday be the Lady MacGregor. And I want tae be the first tae tell ye what a fine lady ye've chosen and I will do my utmost tae protect her."

Angus turned to Abby, his face and eyes revealing how much he'd enjoyed the day already. "Will ye take my pledge, mistress?" he asked.

Abby gave him a bemused look. "I-I thank you, Angus."

Angus spoke a few words in Gaelic, kissed the hilt of the dagger and sheathed it. He stood awkwardly, and Abby thought he would lose his balance, but after a moment that fostered great doubt, he righted himself.

Iain clapped him on the back. "I thank ye for your pledge and your kind words."

Angus gave an exaggerated nod. "There isna anything kind

about them. They're truth, Iain. Truth." He flashed a smile at Abby. "After all, I shared a few nights wi' the lass. And watched her puke her guts out. If anyone kens her mettle, it's me."

He laughed heartily and gave Iain a shove. "Weel, mannie. I'll leave ye tae her. I'm sure ye'd want tae get on wi' the bedding sooner rather than later."

Angus strode off into the dark, an enthusiastic attempt at whistling the only evidence of his fading presence.

"Where's he going?" Abby asked for wont of anything better to say.

"Tae let out some of that whisky, I expect," said Iain with distinct amusement. "There was certainly enough of it in him."

"Clearly," said Abby. "I'm sure there will be little enough of the day's events remembered when he wakes up."

"Dinna be so certain," said Iain. He sighed. "His pledge was nae idle offering."

The words were spoken quietly and for a moment Abby wasn't sure if she heard him correctly. She had no idea how to reply to his statement and decided to say nothing.

"I suppose we'd better go back in. They will all be wondering where we are."

Iain laughed softly. "Nay, *Francach*, they willna be wondering where we are, they'll be imagining what we're doing."

The words sank in and she stood there quietly, waiting for him to say more. "But we're doing nothing," she said finally.

"That's right, *Francach*, we're doing nothing."

CHAPTER 11

When they arrived back in the hall there was a little of the good hearted teasing, some of it in English for her benefit.

"She looks well-kissed, Iain!"

"Is that kirtle on back tae front, Iain? Do ye nae ken how a gown is put on, laddie?"

"Nay—he only kens how it comes off!"

Abby kept her eyes looking straight ahead. She knew she should toss comments back to them, but she found herself unable to think of what to say. She forced a little laugh and tried to nod to give the impression she appreciated the joke, but failed. Iain saw her to her seat and then disappeared. Miserably, Abby poked at her food and tried to eat a little. Iain had been right. The whisky and nerves had finally taken their toll and her stomach was feeling queasy. She stared at her plate, willing herself to be well.

The sound of plucked lute strings caught her attention. The din that had filled the hall gradually ceased. At the far end of the hall stood Iain, lute in hand, the plucking quill in the other. His velvet jerkin had disappeared, leaving his linen shirt open at the neck and his plaid draped loosely about his legs. Any order that his dark curls had before had long since vanished. The courtier had disappeared and the rogue emerged once again.

A smattering of clapping rang out. Someone brought a stool and placed it in the centre of the hall. Iain bowed, looking directly at Abby and sat down. He strummed the lute, turning the pegs with his free hand to find the right tuning. With the tuning complete, he began the piece. It took only the first few bars for Abby to realise he was playing the first tune she'd performed for his cousin, Lady Arbella, "Lament of the Master of Erskine", a piece composed about Erskine's love for Marie of Guise.

He sang the first verse, nimbly plucking the accompaniment with his quill. All the joy they'd shared in the few times the two of them had played the lute together returned to Abby and she found herself smiling back at him. When he finished the verse he gestured to her and she hesitated only a moment. She could do this. Music was something she was sure of. Her confidence and knowledge was undoubted by her, or by anyone who'd heard her play.

She made her way towards him, her eyes never leaving his, trusting the warmth in his expression. She came alongside him and he plucked a few notes' introduction to the next verse. She took a deep breath and began to sing. After a few lines Iain joined her, his baritone voice offsetting her own alto well. This time, she had no need to worry that she might not sound as she should, a boy who was a member of the household musicians. This time, she could lay free rein to her range and offer harmonies that worked with his notes. He gave her an appreciative smile. The piece came to an end and there was a few shouts of approval and applause. Abby smiled, feeling more in her element.

Iain handed her the lute, leaned across and whispered in her ear. "Show them your talent."

Abby nodded, suddenly lighthearted. With only a moment's

thought she selected "Queen of Scots Galliard", a piece that she'd heard only just before she'd left court. It was a sweet and simple air that someone had said the Queen had composed herself. Abby thought it the perfect choice for now. After only a few bars she could hear feet tapping. She took heart from that and looked up from her fingers to smile at the gathered group. A few nodded their heads to the rhythm as well as tapping their feet, especially after she added a few flourishes.

Iain moved over to his sister and led her round to the centre of the hall and the two began to dance. Abby watched them, fascinated. Iain moved with agility, light on his feet stamping and skipping and clapping his partner's hand, as the dance dictated, his belted plaid moving and swaying with its own grace. Morag matched him with her own skill, her skirts twirling, her feet nimbly making the little jumps and foot movements. It was with reluctance that Abby finished the galliard and the couple came to a halt. Shouts of appreciation came amid the loud applause. Abby rose and gave a little curtsy before handing the lute over to Iain. She returned to her seat, conscious of Iain following her.

MacGregor beamed at the three of them and, once they were all seated, gestured to someone at the side of the hall. A man stepped out, dressed in a faded and once fashionable doublet and breeches, bearing a trumpet. The man lifted the instrument to his lips and sounded an elaborate phrase. The assembled gathering fell silent and MacGregor stood.

The speech wasn't long, and though it was in Gaelic, it was evident from the tones that they included words of praise and thanks. The clerical man stood and bowed and Mistress McNab made a curtsy from the back. With the courtesies completed, MacGregor filled his cup and raised it once more, gesturing to Iain and Abby. Everyone rose, their own cups held and repeated the words MacGregor had spoken. Abby acknowledged the toast and drank from her own cup, glancing across at Iain. He gave her a quick smile and a wink and drank deeply.

The toast completed, the trumpeter was joined by a man holding a rebec. The trumpeter raised his instrument to his lips once more and played a low soft drone. The man on the rebec lifted his bow and began to play the opening bars of a branle. Iain stood and offered his hand to Abby. Startled, she hesitated, then took the offered hand. He led her to the floor. Aware of the eyes on her, she was nervous at first, but the music took hold of her and the joy of the dance rushed in. The two of the leapt from side to side, made the little jumps and twirls. Abby smiled, exhilarated.

Eventually, a few other couples joined Abby and Iain. Abby noticed Morag, still graceful, her steps sure, though her partner this time was less gifted. Tall and burly, he wore a faded belted plaid, his pale bearded face showing the traces of a scar. There was no mistaking the manner in which he regarded Morag, whose own coquettish glances told Abby all she needed to know about the smitten man. Abby caught sight of MacGregor, frowning darkly at his daughter's choice of partner. The man's identity was a question she would save for Iain for later.

When the branle finished, the musicians played another galliard. Iain continued to dance with her and of the few couples that had danced before only two remained, among them Morag and her partner. Abby joined hands with him briefly during the moves and he looked at her and smiled. The smile didn't reach his eyes. It might have been that which made Abby uneasy, but she was glad when her hand was loosed and they moved onto the next figure of the dance.

There were a few more dances, and a few different partners including Iain's brother. The last one was a local dance whose steps Abby tried to learn by watching the many that joined the original dancers. It was full of leaps and stomps which everyone completed with great enthusiasm and it left Abby laughing hard as it ended.

When it had finished Iain took her hand. "Come, we'll slip out now and I'll take ye to your bed. There's none that will take any notice."

Abby glanced around at the crowded room where men and women jostled and shoved each other on the floor, laughing and merry. At the table others were deep in conversation, cups in hand. A few had already moved outside, grabbing a flagon of ale to take with them.

She nodded and followed him as he deftly weaved his way through the group, stopping to talk or toss out a comment. She smiled and nodded behind him in as casual manner as she could muster, until they reached the door and the two slipped through. A moment later, he whisked her up the stone stairs. They met only a few men on the way who were too preoccupied with their own efforts to keep their footing as they descended. They arrived at her room and Iain took her inside.

"There," he said. "Safely bestowed."

She gave him a bemused look. Were they meant to share a chamber tonight? But how did that fit in with the plan not to consummate the marriage?

"Will they visit us here once I am abed?"

Iain smiled, his eyes twinkly. "Nay lass. This is a handfasting, ye ken. Though some may end up abed, by accident or design after the ceremony, ye're safe from that now."

He walked over to the chair and sat down while she perched on the edge of the bed. "I'll bide here a while just tae make certain that no one saw us and will follow us up here."

"But won't everyone notice that we're missing?"

Iain laughed. "I dinna think half of them will notice and the other half won't care, unless there is some mischief in the offing. And I hope I've avoided any chance of that. They will most likely carry on outside with a bit less decorum than inside the hall."

"And your family? Your sister? You don't mind leaving her in the hall as they, as you put it, carry on with less decorum than before?

"My sister can look after herself, I have nae doubt."

Abby gave a faint smile. "I'm sure you're right. Or that man she was dancing with will protect her."

Iain's face darkened. "Aye. Or it could mean trouble."

"Who is he?"

"No one ye need concern yourself with," said Iain. He forced a smile. "Now, I'll leave ye tae your rest." He started to rise.

She blinked at him. Suddenly she realised she wanted him to stay. To prolong the celebration and the heightened joy she'd felt when they'd danced together.

"I didn't realise you could dance so well," she said. It was the first thought that came to her mind.

Iain raised a brow. "Why would ye?"

"Well, you never danced at Kilchurn."

"I was hardly in a position tae dance," he said.

"Maybe not. I'm surprised Glenna didn't mention it. She sang your praises on just about every other subject."

Iain snorted. "Glenna is an unhappy girl full of romantic dreams."

Abby nodded. "She was, poor soul. I hope she finds a husband who is good and kind." She glanced at him. "Did your father never consider a match with her? She seemed to think it possible."

Iain gave a wry smile. "And what do ye think?"

"No, I suppose not." She sighed. "What was it your father said today to everyone at the ceremony? I thought a priest would preside, not your father."

"It's not a wedding, so MacGregor, as head of the clan,

presides over the contract. The promise. He explained tae everyone who you were, your clan and so forth and that as such you were a suitable bride for the heir tae the chief of Clan MacGregor. He also said we only awaited your father's formal consent for the wedding tae take place. He indicated that the lawyer was there tae set it out and see it signed."

One phrase rang alarm bells in her head. "My clan and so forth?"

Iain gave a sheepish smile. "Aye, weel, my father may have stretched the truth a bit."

"Just how much was the truth stretched?"

"He said ye were distant relation tae the Earl of Huntly."

"What? But I'm not."

Iain shrugged. "It doesna matter, *Francach*, since they'll no be a marriage anyway and the handfast ended soon enough. But for now, it's for the best that ye are known tae be well-connected and able to strengthen our case at court. Appearances, ye ken."

"Appearances," she murmured. She searched his face a moment and could see only the calm expression in his face. "Yes, this is all about appearances," she said quietly. She touched his ring that was still in place on her finger, drew it off and handed it to him. "I suppose I must return this to you."

Iain gave her a bemused look. "Nay, that's yours to keep. It's part of the promise, the handfast, ye ken."

She nodded, unable to say anything more, for hadn't it all been said?

He rose from the seat again and made his way to her, lifted her hands to his lips and kissed each one. "I bid ye goodnight, lass. It's been a long day for ye and ye've played your part well."

She stood up. "Where will you be tonight, then?"

He grinned. "Why, entertaining the guests. There will be nae doubt that I dinna bed ye then." He gave her a sweeping bow.

"I suppose with all the celebrations we'll be a few days before we leave for the court at Edinburgh," she said.

"Nay, we'll leave on the morrow. They'll be a few sore heads, but it's only Angus that'll be joining us."

She gave him a stunned look. "But what gowns shall I take? I have nothing suitable."

He cocked his head at her. "Ye look right fine tae me in that gown. Ye'd match any courtier."

She blushed at the compliment, such as it was. Was it the first he'd ever given her about her looks? "But this is your sister's gown. Won't she mind?"

Iain shrugged. "She kens it has tae be done. She's already packed a trunk for ye tae take, with some other gowns and what not."

"Well, if you're certain you won't be suffering too much from the night's celebrations you're intending to continue," she said. "I'll be ready whenever you are."

Iain nodded. "It's best tae get underway as soon as possible. We dinna ken if Glenorchy has sent his own missive yet, and if we can get in there before him, so much the better. Alisdair has already drafted the petition, so there's nae cause to remain a day longer."

Abby nodded. There was nothing more to be said. "I bid you goodnight then, Iain."

"Goodnight, *mo bhilis*," said Iain quietly.

"*Mo bhilis?*"

He gave her a soft smile. "Och, it's no but another word for betrothed," he said.

She smiled weakly. "I see. Well, until tomorrow…*mo bhilis*."

Iain laughed softly and opened the door. Abby watched him disappear and stared at the closed door. What would tomorrow bring, she wondered? After the days she'd had since her arrival, she knew they wouldn't be without event.

CHAPTER 12

She could see her breath, coming in small puffs, in the early morning air. She drew the plaid mantle closer around her and watched as Angus and Iain prepared the ponies. But for them, the yard was silent, as was the castle, everyone abed somewhere sleeping it off or at least trying to. Iain seemed none the worse for wear after last night's revels, but Angus's eyes were pinholes. After Iain had left her, the night had stretched out before her and she'd barely closed her eyes. The day's events and Iain's words had kept circling through her mind.

She felt something nudge her leg and she looked down. Cú. She knelt down beside him. "Sorry, boy. I only wish you could come with us," she murmured into his fur.

The words held more truth than she liked to admit. Cú was the one sure friend she knew she could count on. Not that Iain wouldn't be reliable, nor Angus for that matter, it was just that Cú seemed to embody faithful friendship, loyalty and trust. She wasn't certain what Iain embodied for her. Tumultuous emotions and uncertainty, it seemed, at the worst of times. Bemusement at the best of times.

"The horses are ready," said Iain, coming alongside her. "Time to mount and take our leave." He leaned down and gave Cú a gentle rub on his head. "Watch out for everyone here, eh, Cú?"

The dog gave a small yip and Iain smiled. Abby gave Cú one last pat and went over to mount her horse.

SHE EYED THE COT DUBIOUSLY. It looked clean enough but she wasn't certain it held much comfort. The pallet on top of the wooden boards that comprised the bed itself was thin, the wool inside compressed to almost nothing. A pile of straw in a barn suddenly looked more appealing. She looked over at the small window, where a slight breeze blew in through the open shutters. At least the air would freshen the room. It clearly had been a while since the last female traveller had passed through. These were uncertain times for priories, with some of the lords espousing the new Protestant faith. In their eyes, any religious house harboured nothing but corrupt religious practices.

With a sigh, she removed her mantle and laid it across the bed containing linen and pallet. The other seven beds stood bare, not even a pallet on top of them. Besides the beds there was only a small ewer and bowl on a wooden table. At least she had no other companions in the women's hostel room. Would it be the same for Iain and Angus? She would know soon. The prior had told them the evening meal would be in an hour, after vespers. Abby had declined to join the vespers service, citing fatigue. It wasn't far from the truth after the poor night she'd had. The long day's ride had helped little. Iain had remained silent for the most part, his manner pleasant but distant, leaving Abby alone with her thoughts. And now she was going to have another sleepless night, if the bed was anything to go by. She would rather not be alone with her thoughts, and hoped that the monks here at the priory brewed a strong ale, or even better, wine, that she might drink deeply and gain sleep that way.

The vespers bell sounded. Abby used the time before searching out the refectory to wash her face with the water in the ewer, glad that at least that much was serviceable. With her ablutions completed she left the room, closing the heavy wooden door behind her. She retraced her steps down the stone corridor, pausing at the door to the men's quarters. She tapped lightly on it. Silence. She was just about to tap again when it opened abruptly and Iain stood there, the end of his belted plaid hanging low around his legs, his chest bare. Her eyes automatically went to his chest and was about to avert them until she caught sight of his loosened and grimy bandage with small traces of blood scattered across it.

"Your wound," she said. "I should have asked you last night if I could look at it."

He glanced down at his chest and shrugged. "It's fine."

She frowned. "No, I think it's best that I check it." She glanced at his arm. The bandage was still firmly in place, and though there was no trace of blood, it was just as soiled. "Both wounds." Her voice was firm, brooking no contradiction.

He gave her a wry grin and moved so she could enter. Inside, the room was much the same as hers, except that there were three pallets on three beds and they were, if possible, even thinner than hers.

"I see your quarters are just as luxurious as mine," said Abby.

"Aye. I was thinking that the horses may fare better, tonight. Still, it's better for ye than sleeping out of doors."

"Possibly." She gave him a slight smile and led him over to one of the beds with a pallet. "Stay here a moment and I'll see if I can find some fresh linen to bind you up. They must have an infirmary of sorts here."

He gave her a queer look, but said nothing. She was surprised at his easy acquiescence and quickly made her way out to the corridor before he could change his mind.

The priory was not a large one and it wasn't long before she unearthed a monk fresh from his devotions who pointed her in the right direction. The infirmary was attached to the kitchen and she could smell the aroma of some stewing meat that set her stomach rumbling as she knocked on the infirmary door. She was gratified when the door opened shortly after and a tall, thin monk greeted her. Wrinkles lined his forehead and his jowls hung low, giving him a sorrowful expression, but the deep set eyes looked at her kindly.

"Yes?" he asked her.

She introduced herself. "You must excuse me for disturbing you, I'm a guest here at the priory and I'm here on an errand for my…my husband." Was it better to say husband since she had been treating his wound in such an intimate manner? It was too late now to say anything different. "He has a sword wound to his side and arm and, though it's healing, it needs fresh bandaging. Have you any linen I might use?"

The monk smiled, an action that transformed his face, hinting at the handsome man he once was.

"Please, enter. I'm Brother John." He gestured her through the door.

The small room was filled with herbs, hanging from beams and dried and powdered in carefully labelled earthen jars that were stowed on shelves lining the walls. A bench contained more of the same as well as a mortar and pestle. The scent of lavender filled the air.

"Sword wounds, ye say?" He frowned. "I'm just preparing some balm infused with oil of lavender. It's precious, but it sounds as if ye're need is there." There was something about the soft way he rolled his r's and deep tone of his voice that Abby found reassuring.

"Yes, that would be kind. I thank you."

Brother John indicated the stool that stood by the bench. "Have a seat."

Abby took the proffered stool and looked over at him. "Have you any honey, or anything that I might use to cleanse the wound?"

He regarded her calmly, his hands inserted into his sleeves. "I see you have some knowledge of healing."

Abby shrugged. "Very little, really. It's only what I have gleaned from others."

"Would ye rather bring your husband tae me? I take it he is somewhere here in the priory?"

"Yes, he is." She thought a moment and then shook her head. "It's not that serious, really. I have stitched the wounds and there appears to be no infection. It's just a matter of putting on clean strip of linen to protect them."

"Your husband was in a fight?"

Abby reddened, wondering how much she should disclose to this monk, who for all intents and purposes, was a stranger. "It was an encounter, really. Unexpected. An attack of sorts." She made herself stop talking, already lamenting how much she'd over-explained herself.

"I see," said Brother John, his face expressionless. "Well I'm happy tae give ye what ye might need. From all appearances I would say that your husband is in capable hands."

Abby rose from the stool, suddenly wishing to be gone as quickly as possible. She wasn't certain if it was the way he kept saying "husband" that had her uneasy or the sudden realisation that she'd no idea exactly how Iain had explained their situation to the prior, only that they were MacGregor clansmen passing through.

Brother John gathered some items together and handed them to her. "There's a vial of lavender oil there and a small paste that

I've made up, along with the linen. If he is in the men's quarters there should be water already provided. If not, let me know and I'll have some brought there."

Abby nodded and gave him her thanks. She left without trying to seem too hasty and breathed a sigh of relief when she entered the men's quarters and could shut the door behind her. Iain was still there, staring out of the window. When she appeared he made his way meekly over to the bed and sat down.

He indicated the bundle in her hand "Should I be afraid of what ye have in there, *Francach*?"

She laid the bundle on the bed next to him. "Only if you have the stomach of a wee bairn."

He gave her a strange look. "Nay, I was never a wee bairn."

Abby snorted. "As much as it's easy to believe you came into this world a fully formed adult, I have seen evidence to the contrary in your mother's room."

Iain smiled faintly. "I never said I wasna a wean, I just said I wasna a wee one."

She began to form an 'o' with her mouth, but stopped herself and instead busied herself unwrapping the bandage around his chest, handling the grimy linen with care. When the bandage was fully removed she inspected the wound. It was red and puckered in a few places and some beads of blood had dried on the thread of the stitches, but nothing serious. She fetched the ewer and bowl, thankful that some water remained, and began to clean the wound. Iain remained expressionless, almost stoical during the process, though she knew at times he must be feeling pain.

"Will I do?" he asked, his tone light.

She looked up at him and something about the manner in which the light from the window cast his head and face in a kind of glow made her breath catch. His blue eyes, changeable like the sea, deepened in colour and stared at her. Her mouth, so close to his, opened slightly. He edged forward and his lips brushed hers.

The door opened loudly. Iain lifted his head. "John?"

For a moment Abby thought he was talking about Brother John, and she nearly cursed him for his timing, but then she turned and saw it was a strange man she'd never met.

She rose slowly, suddenly conscious of the picture they presented. It seemed Iain's thoughts reflected her own.

"I'm just having some wounds checked," he said to John, his tone apologetic.

She looked down at Iain and noticed that beneath his seemingly expressionless face, he was flustered.

"I was changing the bandages," she said calmly. "I won't be long if you two would like to converse."

"I apologise for my manners," said Iain, rising. "John MacDonald, may I present tae ye, Gabrielle Gordon."

Abby gave a low curtsy, taking in the light haired Highlander's travel-soiled doublet, mantle and boots that couldn't conceal his air of elegance.

John gave Iain a sweeping look, lingering over his bare chest. "Did ye say Gordon? Gabrielle Gordon? Calum Gordon's Gabrielle?"

"Aye, well. Abby's my... well, we're handfasted ye ken. Just for the wee while to try and help my family."

"I see," said John with all the inference that he didn't see. Not at all.

"You know my father?" asked Abby.

John gave her an enigmatic look and bowed. "I am acquainted with your father, yes."

"From the court here, or in Paris, perhaps. But I haven't met you, so I think not."

"It would be here, Mistress Gordon, or is it tae be Mistress MacGregor?" asked John.

"Leave it be, John," said Iain. "Mistress Gordon will do well enough. And unless ye have urgent business here, I'd appreciate it ye can leave us so she can finish tending my wound."

"I would hate tae interfere with what ye call 'tending your wound', but I came straightaway tae tell ye some news I thought ye'd want tae hear after. I saw Angus with the horses. He told me where tae find ye."

Iain glanced at Abby. "Can the news wait?"

"I think ye might want tae hear this now, as it happens. I just came from Edinburgh. Word of your encounters has reached there. Apparently the Dowager Queen has sent a messenger tae MacCailean Mhor summoning him tae court tae explain himself."

Iain muttered a curse in Gaelic. "Where's the messenger now, do ye ken?"

John shrugged. "Past here, I'll wager. Maybe halfway tae Archinglas."

"What is it? Who is MacCailean Mhor?" asked Abby.

Iain turned to her. "He's the Earl of Argyll. The head of the Campbells. It means the Dowager Queen has found out about the killings and wants tae hear Argyll's account of the events and what he intends tae do about it."

Abby digested the information. "We should leave now, then. Get to the Dowager Queen before Argyll."

Iain smiled weakly. "I think we can have a bite tae eat first." He turned to John. "I thank ye for the information."

John shrugged. "Aye, well. Ye would be a great loss, Iain, which is more than I can say for any Campbells. Ye ken there's nae love lost between the Campbells and the MacDonalds."

ABBY COVERED a yawn with her hand and blinked in the bright morning light. She stepped sleepily out of the door and closed it quietly behind her. There was no sign of Iain or Angus, though the horses were saddled and ready. After remarking on her fatigue, Iain had decided that they could allow enough time for a quick night's sleep as well as something to eat, provided they left at first light. She'd managed to sleep a few hours before the bell for prime sounded and a sharp knock on the door had woken her.

She blinked again and rubbed her eyes. After a moment she made her way over to the stable, thinking that Iain and Angus might be there. When she reached the doorway she hesitated at the sound of voices.

"You're going straight to France after your meeting?" said Iain, his voice low.

"Aye, once I have the message. I'll see ye there," said John MacDonald.

"Let me know if ye find out anything in the meantime."

"Of course." There was a pause. "And ye're saying she doesna know?"

"Nay. And I'd prefer tae keep it that way."

Abby heard footsteps behind her. She turned and saw Angus making his way to the horses. Casually she walked over to him and nodded.

"Ready tae go, mistress?" he said.

"I am. I presume Iain will be along soon."

Angus nodded towards the stable. "Aye, he's just coming. He just wanted tae say farewell tae the MacDonald man."

She nodded. "Is John MacDonald at court much?"

Angus narrowed his eyes. "On and off. His family are prominent, ye ken."

"So he knows Iain well, then. Did he meet Iain at court?"

Angus gave her a wry look. "They're Highlanders. Everyone kens everyone else."

"What about Highlanders?" asked Iain, drawing up beside Abby.

"She was just asking how ye came tae ken John MacDonald."

Iain gave her a shrug. "He's a Highlander."

Abby shook her head. "I see that was a stupid question. I apologise."

"Nay, ye've nae need tae apologise for ignorance of Highland matters," said Iain, humour in his voice.

With confident assurance he put his hands around her waist and hoisted her up on the horse. Behind her he'd strapped a small kist containing her borrowed finery. She still had little notion what was inside. She'd not set eyes on it before it had been secured to her horse the morning before. She could only presume Mistress MacNab had done the honours even before the handfasting. She'd little need for it here at the priory, but its contents would become very important once they reached Edinburgh and the court. She must impress everyone, especially the Dowager Queen.

As they made their way along the track that led from the priory, Abby tried to occupy her mind by composing what she would say to the Dowager Queen and any other members of the court that might influence Iain's case. Anything to keep her from untangling the meaning of the words she'd just overheard in the stable.

CHAPTER 13

Abby sat at the small table and glanced out of the window. Despite the room's limited space, the table was squeezed into the little windowed gable that overlooked the street. The noise of the people and horses below making their way up and down past this small hostelry drifted up through the window. She watched a small boy dodge a wagon and dart inside a building opposite.

"Are ye finished yet?" asked Iain.

He stood behind her, leaning against the wall. She could feel his eyes boring into her. She was supposed to be writing a note to the Dowager Queen's secretary, asking for an interview with the Dowager Queen. The words that had crowded her mind on the journey the past two days since they'd left the priory eluded her now. She was tired, she knew. They had stopped again at another priory on the road, but had barely spent more than a few hours there. They had arrived in Edinburgh only an hour ago and had found a room. Though Iain had apologised that he could ask no court connection to house them at their residence at such short notice, it had been a distracted apology and made with few enough words.

Now, she sat here, quill in hand, paper before her, trying to put together words that would be persuasive as well as urgent, while Iain shifted uneasily behind her. She was well aware that he was uncomfortable with the turn of events and the obligation he'd placed on her. It didn't help her frame of mind, though.

With a frustrated sigh, she scratched the words across the page. It would have to do. When she finished, she blew on the ink and handed it to Iain. He took the note from her and scanned it. After a moment he nodded.

"Good. That's fine."

She breathed a sigh of relief, glad it passed his muster at least. She felt a hand on her shoulder and looked up. Gratitude shone from his face and then was gone.

"Thank you," he said and turned to go.

She nodded. He opened the door and gave the folded note to Angus. It was Angus's duty to take the note to the castle and find a servant to present it to the Dowager Queen's secretary. If possible, he was to wait for a reply. Back here, in this cramped room, she and Iain would suffer their own form of waiting.

THE ATTENDING chamber was crowded with people grouped in various sized clusters, all of them engaged in conversation, so that the noise level had reached a dull roar. The gowns were not of the latest fashion or the richest fabrics, but there was no questioning these people were nobles and their attendants. Abby's own gown of brown velvet with a black kirtle was certainly not out of place, though it was hardly striking.

She took deep breaths to calm her nerves. Beside her, wearing a well cut doublet, breeches and hose, Iain projected all the confidence she wished she felt. Occasionally, he gave nods of recognition to various courtiers, but none came up to speak to him. If her experience in the Paris court was anything to go by, the lack of greetings wasn't a good sign. Had word already spread to the court of the trouble between the Campbells and the MacGregors? If so, then there was no doubt what the general consensus of the outcome was.

"Iain!" A voice rang out.

A fair haired woman, not much older than Abby, made her way to Iain's side, and inserted herself between them, but not before Abby saw the full red lips and the large dark eyes that took in Iain hungrily.

"You are back at court," she said. Her tone and manner of speech was modulated, like the others at court. She slipped her arm through Iain's. "Do say you're here for a while. This place could do with lively company. The Dowager Queen can be so tediously dull in the company she keeps."

Iain gave her an amused glance. "I canna believe any court you grace, Janet, would be dull."

Janet gave him a playful tap on his arm. "You are too much the flatterer. But tell me, you have brought your lute, haven't you? You had such wicked little songs, do you remember?"

"Aye," said Iain. He smiled. "And they werena meant for your ears, as ye well ken."

"Och, you knew I was listening, as did my brother. You were both such devils."

"We were devils, nae mistaking. As any laddie of that age tends tae be."

"You were hardly laddies, with all the women at court vying for your attention."

"Ye're exaggerating, Janet."

"Hardly. But that is no matter, for now I can claim you for myself, before anyone else, for I hear you've only just arrived."

Iain glanced over at Abby for the first time since the conversation had begun. "I have come to court with my betrothed," he said.

"Betrothed?"

Janet turned slightly and studied Abby, who gave her a nod and a slight smile.

"May I present Gabrielle Gordon," said Iain.

"Gabrielle? That is an unusual name for a Scots," said Janet.

"My mother was French," said Abby.

Janet raised her brow and gave a small moue. "I see. The Dowager Queen would find you interesting, I imagine. Forebye, you are a Gordon. Are you one of Huntly's?"

Abby gave an inward sigh. That question yet again. She wondered if her father had suffered it when he'd been at court. "No. I'm not connected to the Earl of Huntly."

Janet looked at her speculatively. "No? Interesting." She turned to Iain. "You're awaiting Her Grace's pleasure?"

He gave a brief nod.

"You will find her in poor humour, I think, today. Châtelherault is proving troublesome again."

Abby's heart sank a little. After years of squandering his position, King James's feckless illegitimate son had been given the title of the Duke of Châtelherault as compensation for handing over the regency of Queen Mary to Marie of Guise, the Dowager Queen. The man was easily led, and usually it was in the wrong direction, by those who sought to exploit his position for their own gain.

"The Dowager Queen still holds authority?" asked Iain.

"Of course," said Janet. She squeezed his arm reassuringly.

A chamberlain came through the door, and after a few words with another man who pointed in Abby and Iain's direction, he made his way towards them.

He bowed to the group. "You are Gabrielle Gordon, lately of Queen Mary's court in Paris?" he asked Abby.

Janet eyed Abby, her face filled with surprise. "Paris?" she whispered.

Abby gave a small nod. "I am." She gave Janet a brief smile, unable to help herself.

"And I am Iain MacGregor, son of MacGregor," said Iain. "Mistress Gordon and I are handfasted."

The chamberlain glanced at Iain and down at the paper in his hand. It was Abby's letter. "Yes, Mistress Gordon mentioned that." He looked back at Abby. "Her Grace is pleased to receive you now."

Abby looked at Iain. His expression gave no indication of his thoughts. "Shall my betrothed accompany me?" she asked.

"No, Her Grace made no mention about it."

She gave Iain an apologetic look and followed the chamberlain back across the room. Behind her she could hear Janet's fierce whispers about Iain's earlier statement. He was leaving no doubt now in anyone's mind at court that she and Iain were to be wed.

ABBY CURTSYED DEEPLY AND ROSE. The Dowager Queen was soberly dressed in black, her hair pulled back under a white stiffened sheer veil. Her eyes were creased with age and lines formed around her mouth, but these marks couldn't disguise the fine features that had marked her beauty.

Around her, the rich appointments that decorated her apartments were faded and from an earlier fashion; the cloth of gold no longer bright, and the once-colourful brocade hangings hung in a listless manner. The small draught that wafted around the room explained the fire that glowed in the hearth next to where the Dowager Queen sat in a high backed chair. She acknowledged Abby's curtsy and gestured to the seat opposite.

"I understand you have news of my daughter, the Queen," said the Dowager Queen once Abby had taken the seat. Her accent was heavy and Abby found it difficult to follow.

"*Bien sûr*. I saw your daughter, the Queen, when last I was at court," said Abby, switching to French. "A month or so ago," she added with a blush. Was that recent enough? Would the Dowager Queen be disappointed, or worse, think she had begged an interview under false pretences?

The Dowager Queen smiled, an action that lit her face and took years away. "She is well? There is no sign that her illness has returned?" she asked in French.

Abby met the smile with more confidence, now. "She was well when last I saw her. In good health."

The Dowager Queen gave a satisfied nod. "You say your father is part of my daughter's household. He is still at court?"

"He is, Your Grace." At least she hoped so.

"Gordon," she said. "Ah, yes. He is some sort of connection to the Earl of Huntly, yes?"

Abby hesitated, not knowing how best to answer it. She knew it would help for the Dowager Queen to think that she was from such noble stock, but one question to Huntly would reveal it for the lie it was.

"And you are part of the my daughter's household? I must confess, I don't remember meeting you when I was there last year."

Abby blinked. "I was away from court at the time, Your Grace. With the family of my intended husband." It seemed like such a long time ago that she'd been Henri's, awaiting her marriage to him at his home.

"You were here in Scotland with the MacGregors?"

"Ah, no, Your Grace. I was in France. Sadly my husband died of the sweating sickness just after we were wed."

"Ah, I see. I am sorry you lost your husband. And now you are —how do they say it—handfasted to the MacGregor heir?"

"Yes, Your Grace."

"And this MacGregor boy, he is a good match? Your father approves?"

Abby nodded, hoping the lie wouldn't betray her. "Yes."

"Yet I hear such things about him. That he killed a man in cold blood. And that the MacGregors are a troublesome, vengeful lot."

"I would imagine you were informed by those who don't hold the MacGregors in high esteem. They would do the MacGregors harm."

The Dowager Queen gave her a small smile. "Perhaps."

"Iain is a good and kind person," said Abby. "He has great integrity and honour, and would kill no one unless he was in danger for his life." Abby felt the truth of her words, which enabled her to give extra conviction in speaking them. "And though I haven't known them for very long, the MacGregors have a similar honour and are good people." With the exception of Morag, Abby thought. Though to be fair, Morag had her own kind of honour as well as courage, although she might be impulsive to the point of foolhardiness in the pursuit of said honour.

"You have a request, I believe. You said as much in your letter. Am I right in guessing it is about the MacGregors?"

"Yes, Your Grace," said Abby. "I would like to plead the case of my husband, Iain and his family, that the clan not be put to the horn, or punished in any way. Once you hear their side of the story I am hoping you will be lenient."

"But this is a matter for Argyll, surely?" said the Dowager Queen. "I have made it clear the earls must be responsible for their tenants' behaviour."

"While it's true that the Earl of Argyll would be responsible for administering justice in that region, he is not truly the

MacGregors' overlord. Not in their eyes. The MacGregors, Your Grace, are of an ancient line that goes back to the original King of Scotland, the MacAlpin. They are proud of that heritage, but also aware that a great responsibility comes with it."

The Dowager Queen gave Abby a speculative look. "Perhaps they are too proud?"

"They are aware of their lineage, Your Grace. Of that there is no doubt. But they are a fair people and wouldn't willingly transgress on another. If you will permit, I can explain the events that led to this situation."

The Dowager Queen gave her assent and Abby briefly recounted what had happened, omitting Morag's part in it. The Dowager Queen listened attentively, her eyes lively with curiosity. When Abby had finished, the Dowager Queen frowned and shook her head.

"This is a familiar story," she said. "Yet you have presented their case in a charming manner, and though I cannot promise anything, I will consider the matter further before I take any action."

Abby curtsyed and thanked her. This was her dismissal. She'd done her best; she'd even called him her husband in the hope that the Dowager Queen would see that Abby was irrevocably linked to the family. It had felt odd to say it and the feelings the term had aroused in her were mixed. To think of Iain as her betrothed was strange enough, but her husband, that conjured up something more. A home, a family, sharing a life together and of course, sharing a bed together. Would that be something she could imagine with Iain? The warmth that suffused her body told her that she could—and only all too well.

She left the Dowager Queen's Chamber and followed the waiting chamberlain back to the receiving room where she'd left Iain with Janet. They were still there, engaged in conversation.

Janet, her ripe figure so evident even in her court dress, leaned forward to speak in Iain's ear. He nodded and looked up, noticing Abby making his way back to him. His face lit up, so full of hope. Abby smiled and tried to convey a positive outcome in her expression. Iain returned the smile.

"She was glad of your news?" he asked when Abby reached his side.

"She was," said Abby.

The chamberlain approached her again and gave a quick bow. "Mistress MacGregor, the Dowager Queen has arranged for you and your husband to stay at the castle tonight. I'll show you to your chamber, now."

Abby gave the chamberlain a careful smile and looked at Iain. He raised a brow and shrugged.

Iain returned the bow. "It would be our pleasure to go with you." He turned and bowed to Janet. "We must leave you now, Lady Janet."

Janet placed her hand on his arm. "But I will see you this evening, at dinner in the hall. You must promise me a dance afterwards. The Queen Dowager keeps a quiet enough court, but we do have music and dancing every night. She does love her music, and as I recall, so do you."

Iain smiled at her and bowed again. "Until tonight, then."

He took Abby's arm and they followed the chamberlain away. Abby made an effort to keep her expression calm, determined not to let Janet see how much her presence bothered Abby. She'd met many of her kind at the French court and they ordinarily evoked no emotion in her, apart from mild disdain. But this woman with her painted lips and fulsome figure had got under her skin and Abby wanted no part of it. She reasoned and reprimanded herself all the way to their chamber.

With the chamberlain gone and word sent to Angus about the change in their situation, Abby suddenly became conscious of the room. A kist, bed and small table were the only items of furniture. One meagre tapestry hung on the wall depicting some long forgotten battle in an unfamiliar place. A small window looked out across the roof top. The castle had few enough chambers for those visiting the court and Abby knew they were fortunate to be given any room at all. Still, looking at the bed, she was suddenly uncomfortably aware how little it was. Two smallish people might fit in well enough, but someone with Iain's height wouldn't find sleep easily. But then sleep wasn't the only thing that happened in beds, as she knew full well from years at court, and even living in her father's apartments there.

Iain gave her a wry grin. "It is a good thing I dinna have much in my baggage. I'd be hanging half of it out of the window."

She returned his smile. "I don't think you'd get it through that window."

He glanced at the bed and then positioned himself against the wall. "So ye're meeting went well with the Dowager Queen?"

"I think so. After I gave her what news I had of her daughter, which seemed to please her, she mentioned the trouble with the Campbells."

"She did?" Iain asked, his brows drawn.

"Yes. She guessed that was the real reason for my request for an audience. At first she seemed to think it should be the concern of the Earl of Argyll's and not hers, but I explained the whole situation and at the end she seemed sympathetic."

Iain raised a brow. "And did she leave it at that?"

"She said she would give it consideration and let us know."

Iain nodded slowly. "Aye, we couldna have hoped for anything better." He smiled at Abby, his eyes filled with gratitude. "Ye did well, *Francach*, and my family and I are deeply indebted tae ye."

He went over to the door. "I'll just go and meet Angus. See to the horses."

Abby looked at him. Was it his embarrassment at their confined situation that made him beat such a hasty retreat?

"Of course," she said, keeping her tone even.

He left before she could utter another word. She stood staring at the closed door for a while, making an effort to push aside where she imagined he might really be going.

CHAPTER 14

*A*bby smoothed her gown one more time and patted her head piece reassuringly. She was wearing the same dress and the pearls she'd worn for their handfasting. It seemed the best choice, given the situation. A formal court appearance at dinner, with all the courtiers, such as they were, demanded the best attire, if only for the sake of Iain's family and their cause. It seemed possible after her discussion with the Dowager Queen today that a decision would be made in favour of the MacGregors. But anything could change that and she wanted to ensure that everything she did helped support them. Was it possible that Iain was favouring Lady Janet for that reason? Abby had no idea how much influence Lady Janet had, but she supposed it couldn't hurt.

This reasoning had formulated in her mind in the hours of Iain's absence. Her kist had arrived and a servant had come to help her dress and arrange her hair. The servant, who was French, had clucked over the unfashionable dress, but had admitted to its quality. The length of Abby's hair gave her more fodder for disapproval, but the servant had worked skilfully and the results were remarkable. Abby hardly recognised the hair that was normally a tangle of curls. After careful brushing, the servant had woven a blue ribbon through her hair and its colour set off her hair and matched her gown so well. The style was unlike any she'd seen at court in Paris or here, but she felt it suited her.

By the time she was ready, Iain had still not reappeared. Would he come here for her? Or was he planning to avoid her altogether tonight? Perhaps she should find her own way down. She made her way reluctantly to the door and opened it. Iain stood there, his hand raised, ready to knock.

He lowered his hand. "Och, I see ye're ready, *Francach*." He looked her up and down, an appreciative expression on his face. "And ye're looking grand."

She couldn't deny the pleasure that suffused her at his compliment. "Thank you," she said. He was wearing the same clothes as before, only this time he had added a matching velvet bonnet trimmed with a few seed pearls.

"Whatever ye've done wi' your hair, it suits ye. Ye'll set the ladies' tongue's clacking, I have nae doubt. I suppose it's the style at the French court now."

"No," said Abby. "It's just what seemed to work with the length of my hair. Since I cut it."

He eyed her hair closely. "Ye cut it? Aye, of course ye did. Ye couldna verra well pretend to be a boy wi' it that way. How long was it?"

She gave him a curious look. There'd been something wistful about his tone that gave her pause. "Down to my waist. At least when it wasn't in tangles. When I was young my father had me keep it braided and pinned so I could manage it better, but it never held and inevitably got caught, or just fell down. Later, when I was older, I just stuffed it in a hood. It was easier that way, instead of spending the morning brushing and braiding." She smiled at the memory. "Our servant used to nag me constantly about it."

A glint appeared in Iain's eye and he laughed. "I can imagine it."

She gestured to it. "It's easier to manage this length, especially now that we're travelling."

"Mmmph," said Iain and the glint disappeared. He offered his arm. "I suppose we should make our way now."

Abby nodded and took his arm, regretting the last words that had pulled them back to the immediate issues at hand. It had been enjoyable talking for those few moments of matters that had no problems or tensions associated with them. She only hoped the upcoming evening held some time for relief and enjoyment. She could see by the small lines of strain around Iain's eyes that he needed a respite. So did she, for that matter.

The great hall at Edinburgh Castle was hung with tapestries and paintings on the wood panelled walls and lit with sputtering candles placed in holders on long trestle tables. Pewter and silver plate filled the cloth covered tables. A stone carved fireplace stood at one end with a fire brightly burning. Courtiers ambled towards their places at the tables, while a small band of musicians, dressed in the royal livery of red and yellow, played in one corner. Abby noted there were several rebecs, a lute, a harp and a recorder. Behind them was a trumpeter who sat sour faced, his trumpet in his lap. She turned to remark on it to Iain when Janet came up to them and slipped her hand through Iain's other arm.

"Och, there you are," she said. "And you are looking very fine as ever with your bonnet, Iain. I'm so glad you've finally come to your senses about wearing your plaid all the time. It was so silly since everyone knows you're a cultured and educated man and not some backwards Highlander, as you would sometimes have people believe."

Abby curtsyed and murmured a word of greeting while she suppressed an inward sigh.

Iain bowed low and raised a brow. "Lady Janet. Och, I am glad it pleases ye," he said. "It's good tae ken that my efforts havena gone unnoticed."

He'd spoken in an even tone, but, though it might have been Abby's imagination, she thought his accent had become slightly thicker.

Janet gave him a flirtatious smile and laughed. "So I insist you must sit by me, because I must know what you intend here and if I can assist in any way. These meals can be dull affairs if you are placed next to someone with no conversation at all."

"As ye mentioned, I am cultured and educated, and so I ken ye are too exalted tae be seated next tae us," said Iain.

Janet waved her hand. "We'll dispense with that tonight, and if anyone questions it, I will protect you," she said in a teasing manner.

Iain gave her a wry look and nodded. She took his arm and led him towards a table near to the head table, Abby following in their wake.

The steward, dressed in black with a red bonnet, approached Abby, bowed and laid a hand on her arm. "Mistress MacGregor, Her Grace wishes you and your husband to be her guest at the high table tonight."

"Husband?" said Lady Janet murmured. "But they are only handfasted, in that quaint Highland manner. It means nothing. Isn't that so, Iain?"

Iain smiled faintly. "It is a Highland custom, and among us Highlanders it has a most formal meaning." He bowed again to Lady Janet. "I thank ye for your kind attention."

"Och, well, you must attend the Dowager Queen for now. But we will dance later."

Her manner allowed no refusal. Iain nodded and bowed slightly.

"Until later," he said. He turned and weaved Abby's hand

through his arm and followed the steward to the Dowager Queen's table.

They were seated at the end, some distance from the Dowager Queen and for this Abby was thankful, on many counts. Not only did she not have to worry that she might have to elaborate on the exact nature of her relationship to Iain and reveal that she wasn't his wife, strictly speaking, but that she might also have to say more about her father, who was really not a relation of the Earl of Huntly. And she admitted to herself that she also was glad she wasn't seated near Lady Janet, who was fast becoming unbearable. She wouldn't think about what might come after the meal.

The trumpeter rose, lifted his instrument to his mouth and blew the sounds that announced the Dowager Queen's arrival. Everyone stood. The Dowager Queen entered the hall with her small retinue of lords and ladies behind her. The richly dressed man just beside her, Abby presumed, was James Hamilton, the Duke of Châtelherault, the old king's illegitimate son. In comparison, the Dowager Queen was soberly dressed in her dark velvets and ermine sleeves with ropes of pearls hanging from her neck. Other lords were just as plainly dressed, if not plainer, as if to make the point that they were men of thought, newly awakened in the Calvinist faith. The Dowager Queen seemed to be walking a fine line between the lords who thought culture included extravagant living and the Calvinists who espoused discipline and restraint in all matters.

From her time at Kilchurn, Abby knew that the two factions of the Scottish nobles often played off against one another, and such infighting had sometimes left them open to manipulations by the English as well as the French. She only hoped that the Campbells wouldn't use this strategy to victimise the MacGregors. That approach be all too difficult to combat.

Once the Dowager Queen, her retinue and the remaining courtiers were seated, the servants entered with the first course.

The food wasn't quite the marvel of innovation that Abby had observed and occasionally sampled at the French court, but it was the best fare she'd had since her arrival in Scotland. Her plate was silver and the juices and colourful sauces shimmered in its reflection. The strong aroma of spices filled her nose and battled with the odour of her companion on her right side, a large framed baron from some estate near the border, also visiting court to petition the Dowager Queen on some matter. He nodded at her and took a bite of his meat and gagged slightly.

"These spices burn your thrapple as ye swallow," he said with a full mouth.

He rolled his "r's" so strongly Abby had difficulty understanding him. "It's the cinnamon and nutmeg together," she said, trying to refrain from laughing.

He reached for his goblet and took a heavy swallow. "Aye, as ye say."

Next to her Iain gave a soft laugh. "I think ye might save your breath, lass. There's some ye willna convince that a slab of venison and a good swig of whisky isna the best meal a man can have," he said quietly.

She smiled at him and saw the twinkle in his eyes. Beside him was an empty chair, and for a moment she wondered who it might be for. Some lady, no doubt, caught up on an errand for the Dowager Queen. Would she know Iain from before?

She returned to her meal and listened to the musicians, enjoying their playing. She realised how much she'd missed music on such a regular basis, either playing it herself, or hearing her father and the other court musicians. The tune was a familiar one, only in her mind, the rebecs were playing too stridently. And one, she thought might be out of tune. She remembered the tone deaf harper, Andrew, at Kilchurn Castle. She looked at Iain, wondering if he'd noticed.

He caught her glance and gave a wry grin. "One of them has

something of Andrew's way of playing about him."

She stifled a laugh and felt the pleasure of the evening spread through her. "Perhaps his strings are faulty," she said.

Iain grunted. "Verra faulty."

Just as the first course was taken away there was a rustle by the door and a man entered and made his way to the front of the Dowager Queen's table. He swept his bonnet from his head and bent on one knee.

"Your Grace, I offer ye my most humble apologies for my lateness. The roads and dust were such that I couldna allow myself tae appear before ye until I had donned suitable attire."

Abby didn't need to see his face to know who it was. The red hair and the voice were enough. Her breath caught in her throat. Beside her, she could feel Iain tensing. Glenorchy. At the Dowager Queen's bidding, Glenorchy rose.

"You are forgiven and most welcome, Lord Glenorchy. Come take your seat and enjoy the rest of the meal. We have a place saved for you." She gestured to her left, in the direction of Abby and Iain.

Abby tensed. Though she knew now that Glenorchy had no real authority here or in Glen Strae, she was still wary. Had the Dowager Queen deliberately placed them together in some foolish attempt at reconciliation?

Glenorchy bowed again and made his way to the table. His eyes scanned the people arrayed there and halted when they came to Iain. He gave a curt nod and Iain returned it no less curtly. He didn't notice Abby until he was upon her.

"Our little runaway lute player…Gabriel was it?" he said. "Or should I call ye something else, since I see ye have taken on a different disguise now."

"Ye have nae reason tae address her, Glenorchy. But if ye must do so, ye can call her Mistress MacGregor."

Glenorchy looked at her, his eyes slowly roaming her body,

undressing her in the process. "A mistress now, is it? Aye, well I ken that." He ran the tip of his tongue briefly over his lips.

Iain started forward for a few moments and then drew back. "I would gladly answer that insult, if I kenned it was nothing more than a ploy tae get me tae strike ye in front of the Dowager Queen and the other lords," he said. "Added tae the fact that I still ken ye're married tae my cousin and are therefore related tae me."

Glenorchy laughed without any trace of humour. "And so many say ye're just a gowked stupid Heelander," he said in a thick Highland accent. He muttered a few words in Gaelic that only Iain and Abby could hear. Iain gave an equally unintelligible reply.

Glenorchy gave a "hrrmph," bowed slightly and worked his way past Iain to the seat next to him.

The second course arrived, but all the pleasure Abby had felt during the first course had vanished. Her food had little taste to her, though by her companion on her left side, it seemed more to his style. Stewed duck of some sort just sat on her plate congealing in its sauce while the tension on her right rose and filled the silence. It was at the conclusion of the next course that a time for dancing was declared and Abby actually welcomed the sight of Lady Janet signalling Iain to come join her on the floor.

Iain leaned over, murmured a few words of excuse to Abby and rose. He gave another curt nod to Glenorchy and bowed to Abby before making his way to Lady Janet. Once there, he led her through the figures of a galliard, executing the steps in an elegant fashion. Lady Janet matched his rhythm perfectly and with a familiarity that dimmed her appreciation of a beautifully executed dance.

"May I have the pleasure?" said a voice.

Abby looked up to see Glenorchy staring down at her, his

hand held out. "As a musician I would imagine ye're passing good at dancing."

Abby looked over at Iain, but he was busy with Lady Janet. She glanced at the Dowager Queen, who smiled at her and nodded approval. With a sigh, she slipped her hand in Glenorchy's and rose. He led her out to the crowded floor. She could only hope that Iain wouldn't notice. If he did, she reassured herself he would understand that it was none of her doing and would ignore it as a provocation on Glenorchy's part.

They took up the steps together without missing a beat. Abby remembered he had been a skilled dancer and so it was no surprise he matched her step for step. He lifted her high and with great dexterity when the dance called for it and small murmurs of appreciation were uttered from those nearby. Abby tried to scan the dancers for sight of Iain, but the intricate movements and twirls allowed her little time. She would just hope for the best.

The dance finished and she breathed a sigh of relief. She gave Glenorchy a curtsy to meet his deep bow and turned to find her way back to the table. A hand restrained her. She looked up to see Iain standing beside her.

"I think it's time I had the pleasure of dancing with my wife."

"Wife, is it now?" said Glenorchy. "Aye, ye did call her Mistress MacGregor. I suppose ye could do nae better than tying yourself tae a mere musician."

"Aye, the music is important and my wife has no lack of talent there, but she has many fine qualities that ye wouldna be able to ken in a lifetime."

Glenorchy eyed Abby, his eyes gleaming. "I think I had a little taste of those qualities when she was at Kilchurn. I ken, for example, her breasts are the colour of fresh cream and her rose-red nipples are as pert as a bud."

Iain flushed hard. "I'm surprised that ye find time tae note anyone else's appearance other than your own, even if ye have tae dip into your imagination. Except perhaps Elspeth. How is she? Are she and Lady Arbella still away from Glenorchy? Is that why ye have come tae court? Tae find your pleasures here, since ye canna at home?"

Glenorchy gave a slow smile. "I think we both ken why I'm here. And why ye're here."

Iain gave him a hard look. "Aye."

"Dinna imagine ye have an advantage just because ye put your case before mine."

"I dinna imagine anything," said Iain.

Glenorchy sniffed. "Give it up, MacGregor. Our clan is stronger than yours. It's only a matter of time before ye're made tae submit. Why not do it now and get it over with?"

"I ken ye canna imagine that a clan with such ancient royal blood as the Gregorach wouldna dream of submitting tae anyone except their sovereign king since ye are from an upstart clan, so I'll forgive that remark."

Glenorchy reached to his side where his ballock dagger would usually be and let it drop a moment later. He smiled slowly. "Ye're all words. But words willna get ye the pardon ye seek."

He gave a quick bow to Abby and then Iain and walked away. Abby let out a breath she hadn't realised she was holding. Around them, the next dance had begun.

"Did you still want that dance?"

Iain looked over at her and with an effort cleared his face of all expression. "Yes, I think I have something to prove."

"You do?" said Abby.

"Aye. That ye, who is without doubt the best dancer here, dance best with me."

He held out his hand and she took it. It was a pavane, in some hands a sedate and undemanding dance, but with Iain she found it the most sensual dancing she'd ever experienced. His arms brushed hers, the tilt of his head and the closeness when they passed each other; which evoked her own response in the sway of her hips and the movement of her arms. When the dance ended, he looked deeply into her eyes and she felt that the dangerous tension of earlier had been replaced by something else that crackled between them.

CHAPTER 15

They were silent on the way to their chamber and her body was thick with the desire that filled her. It seemed to her that Iain felt it too, if only from the manner in which he'd stroked her fingers and thumbs underneath the table after they'd resumed their seat when the dancing ended. Glenorchy had disappeared after making some excuse to the Dowager Queen, eliminating a dangerous distraction. Lady Janet had not claimed Iain's attention since the first dance, her own company in much demand from other attentive men.

Iain had offered their excuses shortly after the sixth and final course and the Dowager Queen had accepted. Abby was only too glad to follow him away from the throng of courtiers and noise, though her anticipation was mixed with a large amount of nervousness. She might be mistaking what was happening, after all.

Iain stopped outside the door to their chamber and turned to her. He put his hand under her chin. His eyes were now a deep blue, his expression unfathomable. He searched her face and gave a small sigh. He leaned over and kissed her. The kiss was warm and tender and she opened her mouth to it, surrendering to all that she was feeling at the moment. For a moment the kiss deepened and then Iain pulled away. He stroked her cheek.

"Ye're a bonny lass, quean. *Tha hu bóideach.*"

She leaned in to kiss him, but he pulled away further.

"It wouldna be right, quean. I'm sorry. As much as I want tae be with ye, it wouldna be right. We must mind the terms of the handfast."

Abby stiffened. "Would anyone know?"

He laughed. "Ye ken better than that, coming from the French court."

Her pride wouldn't let her argue any further. She knew he was right and was annoyed with herself that she was hurt by his words.

"Where will you go?"

"I'll go tae Lady Janet. She'll ensure that nae one doubts where I have spent the night."

"You're going to sleep with Lady Janet tonight?" she fought to keep the shrill note out of her voice.

"Och, *Francach,* I'll be in her chamber, that's certain enough, but I dinna think there will be much sleeping."

"Oh, I ken that alright," said Abby imitating that manner of speech.

"Nay, I'll be playing cards with her and others who like tae gamble. It's the best place tae find out information."

"Oh," said Abby, her tone contrite. She blinked. "Of course. You must do what you can to find out what the Dowager Queen might decide and influence it, if possible."

He pecked her on the head. "Aye. Sleep well, lass. I'll collect ye in the morning."

She nodded and watched him as he made his way back down the corridor. She had the urge to go after him and ask if she could join him in Lady Janet's apartments, but knew it was out of the question. He would fare much better without her at his arm.

She wasn't blind to the attraction he held for Lady Janet and without her as a reminder of his supposed "wife" he was more likely to have her favour and perhaps her help. She just hoped that was all she gave him.

A KNOCK SOUNDED at the door. Abby, already awake, rose quickly from the bed and pulled a plaid around her, making for the door.

"Who is it?" she asked wearily. It was probably only Iain, unwillingly to simply intrude on her without notice. She'd spent most of the night lying awake in the bed, her mind unable to settle. Now, in the early hours the morning, she was only glad for Iain's return, her irritation with him that she'd felt earlier now vanished in the rational light of day.

"It's Angus," came the voice in the corridor.

"Angus?"

Abby opened the door and saw the large bearded Highlander standing before her. At the sight of her dressed only in her linen nightdress and plaid he blushed and looked down at his feet.

"Iain asked me tae fetch ye."

"Now? Where is he?"

"In the stables."

"The stables?" she felt like a goose, repeating Angus's words but she couldn't help herself.

"Aye. I'll wait out here while ye dress and then come in tae fetch your kist."

"We're leaving? But why?"

Angus nodded. "I'll leave Iain tae explain that to ye. But ye best be making it quick. He wants tae be on the road soon."

Abby frowned and gave her assent. She closed the door and as quickly as she could manage she drew on the gown she'd travelled in and stuffed her hair into an old French hood. It was a tangled mess and bore little resemblance to the beautifully coiffed hair of the night before. When she'd retired she'd only bothered to remove the rope of pearls and made little effort to loosen the small braids that had held it in place, and hours' worth of tossing on an uncomfortable bed hadn't improved it one bit.

She hastily shoved the gowns back into the kist and fastened it shut. She opened the door to let Angus know she was ready and he removed the kist and carried it down the corridor while she followed him.

They found Iain waiting outside the stables, the early light shining weakly on him. Stubble shadowed his face and gave it a gaunt look, which was mirrored in his tired eyes. A long night, she guessed. When she got closer she was aware of the reek of perfume and sweat that clung to him. Perhaps he had played more than cards.

"Why are we leaving now?" she asked, a little more aggressively than she meant to. "And where are we going?"

"And a good morning tae yourself," Iain said evenly. He muttered a few words to Angus who disappeared inside the stables.

He reached up and put a hand on her shoulder. She gave him a quizzical look.

"I'm sorry tae have tae tell ye that I've just had word that ye're father isna at court."

"He isn't?" she said. She sniffed. "He's probably just gone to one the estate of one of his paramours for a short visit. He's done it before. It's of no account." She didn't know if she'd said that to reassure herself, as much as to reassure Iain.

"Nay, lass," he said softly. "He's been missing for some time. Even the Queen has remarked on the absence of her favourite musician."

"Some time?" she whispered. All the fears that she'd pushed aside these weeks came flooded back.

"Aye. Since about the time ye left. Many just assumed that he'd gone wi' ye tae Scotland, so it wasna until recently that it was remarked upon by a friend who knew he'd not done so."

"A friend?" she said, with a slight bitter note. "One of his women no doubt."

"It was a woman. One of the Queen's ladies. She'd left court around that time tae go tae her family and only returned a few weeks ago."

Abby stared at him as the full implication of his words hit. "And no one knows where he's gone?"

Iain shook his head. "I'm sorry lass. Perhaps there's a reasonable and quite innocent explanation. The sooner we get there and find out, the better."

"We're going to France?"

"Aye, *Francach*, where did ye think we were going?"

"I-I don't know. Back to Glen Strae, maybe. Angus said there was a need for haste and so I thought you'd heard something had happened at home."

Iain shook his head. "We're off now at such a pace in the hopes we can make the tide tonight at Leith. It's a hard ride, but I dinna doubt ye can manage it."

She gave him a weak smile. "But what of you? You should be here to receive the Dowager Queen's decision. And she won't be happy if we quit court without her permission."

Iain frowned. "Ye've tarried long enough on my account, *Francach*, it's the least I can do tae make sure ye get tae France safely and find out what's happened to your father." He shrugged. "And besides, one day more at court will make little difference tae my case. She'll either favour me, or she won't."

"But you can't just up and leave without her permission."

"I've written a letter and Lady Janet will see that she gets it and understands the situation."

Abby could only imagine what sort of explanation Lady Janet

might give for their departure. She only hoped that she felt well enough disposed enough to Iain after a night in his company, however the time might have been spent. She suppressed a brief picture of the two of them together and straightened. She owed Iain more than an irritated jibe.

"Thank you," she said and meant it. "Though you might deny it, I know this action may cost you greatly. I am more than happy to take my chances with only Angus for an escort."

"As much as I might trust that over large Highlander," said Iain, "I prefer tae go wi' ye myself. There's nae more tae be said, so that's an end tae it."

Angus emerged from the stables leading their horses. "What's this about an over large Highlander?"

"It's your horse, he's been complaining that he needs more oats wi' all the weight he's carrying," said Iain.

"Och, my horse has nothing on the shifty odours your horse will have tae endure. Ye reek, mannie."

Abby stifled a snort and took the reins of her own horse from Angus with a grin. Iain put his arms around her waist and lifted her up on her mount. She realised how glad she was Angus would be coming with them. His company would surely help distract her from the mixture of emotions she was feeling. Though she was comforted by the fact that Iain was going to help her discover her father's whereabouts, she was all too aware of the tension that still rose inside her whenever he touched her.

ABBY CLUTCHED the pewter bowl tightly. Her hair hung in large sweaty clumps around her face. She knew she had spittle at the side of her mouth, but she didn't care. Iain sat beside her on the small bed and stroked her back in a soothing manner. She had no thought for anything but stopping the waves of nausea that seized her with every motion of the ship. She'd been retching for what seemed hours. Surely there was nothing left inside her.

Iain reached over to take the bowl. "Here, let me empty that. I'm sure it doesna help tae keep down what's still inside when ye're staring at what was inside."

She held onto the bowl and shook her head. "No, I dare not."

He looked around. A moment later he came back with a small tankard. For a moment Abby thought he wanted her to drink some ale.

She groaned and shook her head again. "I couldn't drink anything. It will only come up."

"Nay, *Francach*, there's nothing in it. It's only for ye tae use while I'm away emptying the bowl. I willna be long."

She took the tankard and gave him a grateful look. She managed three deep breaths and found no urges to retch answered and felt a bit more confident. The door to their small cabin closed. Angus, she knew, was above deck somewhere. She supposed he knew what she'd be like and had disappeared before he could be roped into back rubbing and bowl holding. She gave a grim smile, remembering her sea journey with him at her side. To be fair, he had been kindness itself. And so, now, was Iain.

The door opened again and Iain returned. He cocked his head. "Ye have a bit more colour in your face, *Francach*, I'm glad tae say. For a while there ye resembled a corpse more than a living person."

"I felt like I could happily join the dead," said Abby. She smiled weakly. "Thank you."

"For what?"

"For your kindness."

He waved his hand. "Dinna fash yourself, *Francach*. I would do it for anyone. I ken what it is tae suffer so."

"You suffer from sea sickness? But why aren't you sick now?"

"Nay, I only meant I ken what it is tae have a stomach that

wants tae turn itself inside out."

She nodded. She could imagine how he would come to be in that kind of situation.

"Well, it isn't everyone who would be so sympathetic and kind."

Iain shrugged. "Ye'd feel better if ye went up above. They may prefer ye stay below, but if ye went up just for a wee while, I think ye might find your sea legs."

Abby tested the thought and eventually decided it was safe. Gingerly, she rose from the bed. Iain took her arm and escorted up the small ladder to the deck above. She could see the stars in the night sky radiant above her. A salt breeze stirred her hair as she stepped out on the deck and tickled the back of her neck. She could taste the salt on her lips and found that her stomach didn't object. She inhaled deeply, filling her lungs. Her head cleared. She took a few tentative steps forward and Iain put a steadying hand on her arm.

"Careful, now. Ye dinna want tae walk too much. Though the waters are calm, there are still waves enough tae unsettle your feet."

Iain led her to the rail of the ship and put his hands on the rails, his arms on either side of her body, enclosing her.

"Have you been on ships often?" she asked, for wont of anything better to say. Her stomach, much to her relief had settled a little, allowing her senses more liberty.

"Aye, some," said Iain.

"Anywhere in particular. Anywhere of interest?"

"Nowhere particular, or of interest," said Iain.

She could feel his breath on her face and the timbre of his voice vibrated in her ear. He pulled away slightly, creating a small space between them.

"How is it you know about my father's disappearance?" she asked suddenly. It had bothered her during the ride, but she hadn't had the opportunity or the mind to press him on it, until now. "Was it something that was mentioned when you were playing cards?"

She felt rather than saw his frown. "Nay, it was Angus who found out. I'd made some inquiries and Angus went into the town tae see if anything had come of them."

She twisted around to face him. "You made inquiries?"

"Aye. I could see that ye were sore worried."

"When did you do that?"

"Back at Glen Strae."

"Before the ceremony?"

He looked at her quizzically. "Aye. Does it matter when?"

It mattered to her, but she couldn't say why. She chose to say nothing. "Did you learn anything of importance at Lady Janet's chamber?"

He shrugged. "This and that. Nothing that I hadn't already thought of myself."

"Specifically?"

He grinned. "She praised your hairstyle. She said it had an 'antique' look about it."

"That's not praise, that's a badly veiled insult," said Abby.

"Och, it means she was impressed, *Francach*. She was jealous of your style."

"My style?" Her tone was sceptical.

"Aye. Ye have your own style, lass. Ye ken that ye do."

She laughed. "Is that what it is? I think my father might differ with you on that point. He was always telling me that my courtly manners were badly wanting."

The mention of her father brought her teasing tone to a halt. Silence hung between them for a few brief moments.

"Teach me some Gaelic," she said on impulse. Anything to distract her from her father's situation.

Iain seemed to sense her need. "It isna the easiest language tae learn, though it may be the most poetic." He paused. "Well ye ken some words, already, from the ballad."

"Not really. I know the general meaning, but not the exact words. Tell me what you would say to greet a person."

"*Ciamar a tha thu,*" he said.

She repeated the words the best she could. Iain nodded approval.

"How do the words translate?"

"God and Mary be with you," he told her.

She murmured the phrase again. "I like that. What was it you said a while ago… *mo bhilis?* What does that mean again?"

He looked down at her and in the darkness she couldn't read his eyes. "'My sweet' is the exact translation," he said.

She looked up at him, casting her mind back to the time when he'd said those words. Her breath caught and she opened her mouth to speak.

"Ye've had enough language instruction for now," he said. He glanced around. "The wind is getting up, so I think it's better that I get ye below."

Without further word Iain helped Abby back down the stairs and into the small cabin. He deposited her safely on the bed and placed the bowl on the bed beside her.

"Just in case," he said. "Though I think ye might fare a little better, now."

"You're not staying?"

"Nay. I'll go back on deck. I need tae speak with Angus."

She nodded, not trusting herself to speak further.

"Dinna fash yourself, *Francach*. We'll be in dry land before long."

Abby watched him disappear out of the cabin. She looked around the small space. The low ceiling seemed to close in on her for a moment. She breathed deeply. How much faith could she place in Iain's words, the words that counted?

CHAPTER 16

She entered the apartments and nearly stopped short at the sight of the familiar furniture and hangings. In some ways it was as though she had never left. The small room, cluttered with its scarred furniture, piled with sheet music and books, and the narrow window overlooking a turret and a limited view of the distant fields, was still the same.

Behind her, Iain put a hand on her shoulder. "Is anything amiss?"

It had been an easy matter gaining entrance to the apartments. Even if the household staff didn't recognise her, they knew her father and one mention of his name was all it took in the stables and entering the palace. Obtaining the key had been even easier, the steward remembered her, instructing his servant to escort her and her companions as far as the corridor. She hadn't even thought to be anxious or nervous until she stood here considering Iain's question.

She was tempted to say nothing was amiss in the rooms in the hope it would make it so, but she knew that was foolish. Instead, she moved forward to the table and began to shuffle through the books and sheets of music. As far as she could tell, everything was here but greatly disordered. She had no idea if that was because her father wasn't the most organised of men, or that someone had looked through them.

"I don't think anything is out of place here," she said.

Iain frowned. He glanced at Angus and gave him a nod. Angus moved towards her door and opened it carefully. He scanned the room, glanced back at Iain and gave a shrug. He moved over to her father's room and repeated the process, only this time when he looked inside he turned to Iain and raised his brows, muttering something in Gaelic.

"What is it?" said Abby. "What did Angus say?"

"He said that it's possible it might have been disturbed or it might be that your father isna the neatest person."

Abby gave a wan smile and moved to the room. Inside, she was greeted with clothes, shoes, boots and books strewn across the floor and spilling out from chests. The bedclothes were pulled off the bed and the feather tic was askew. She took a deep breath and studied the mess. True, her father wasn't neat, but this seemed more than his usual clutter and disregard for tidying. And wouldn't the servant have come in to tidy?

She moved over to the clothes and began picking them up, folding them carefully and piling them on the bed. Iain and Angus watched her in silence.

"Someone has been here searching," she said finally. "This is more than my father's sloppy behaviour."

"Ye're certain?"

She nodded. "And there are clothes missing, too. More than just what he is presumably wearing."

"Can ye say what kind of clothes? Court clothes or travelling clothes."

She cocked her head. "Travelling. His best riding boots, a good cloak, his leather gloves and a dark doublet and breeches and several linen shirts. Good ones."

Angus murmured something to Iain in Gaelic.

"Aye," said Iain.

Abby looked at Angus in frustration. "Could you please speak in English?"

"Sorry, mistress," said Angus. "I was just mentioned that it sounds as though your father went of his own will."

Abby nodded. "I apologise for my shortness. Yes, that's a good point. But why would he go without letting anyone know his destination?"

"This is out of character?" asked Iain.

"Yes," said Abby. She would be honest, now. No quips about paramours. "Completely."

She walked out of the bed chamber into the small sitting area and went over to the pile of papers. She could see nothing there that might look like a letter or note addressed to her. Just scratchings and notations of music. She went through to her own bedchamber and entered it. The room was tidy; the bed made, her own small collection of books piled on top of the chest that held her clothes. She rifled through the books, hoping he might have tucked something inside. There was no sign of a letter or note anywhere. But then her father had thought she was in Scotland. Why would he leave her a note?

She ran her mind over her father's friends and acquaintances, hoping they might provide a clue when questioned closely. His fellow musicians would be a start. She sighed. She knew, before she did anything else, she must let the Queen know she had returned. And perhaps the Queen would have heard some news about her father.

"Is all in order in your room?" asked Iain coming to the doorway.

She nodded. "It's more or less how I left it. And no sign of a letter or note here, either." She could no longer resist asking the question that had been bothering her since she knew her father was missing. "Do you think it has anything to do with the conversation I overheard?"

He looked at her long and hard. "Perhaps," he said finally. "But I dinna think so. Ye told me yourself that issue had been closed."

She nodded, letting the matter go. She was grateful to him, for he seemed to be giving his honest opinion. "I'll just write a note to the Queen, a moment. Let her know I've returned," said Abby.

It was good to be able to take some action and she cast around for a quill and some blank paper eagerly. Action took her mind off what she didn't want to speculate about. In the end she found a scrap of paper that only had a few musical notations on it, sat down and using the reverse side, wrote her note on it. When she was finished she rose from the chair.

"I'll just take this out to a servant to deliver."

"Nay, Angus will find a servant," Iain said. He looked at Angus. "When ye've done wi' that see what news ye can find out at the stables, and anywhere else your nose might lead ye."

"Aye," Angus said. He gave a quick bow and left.

"I'm sure will find there's a simple explanation to your father's whereabouts," said Iain.

She looked at him, but knew he was only trying to comfort her. He stood there, the light from the small window casting his face in shadow and she tried to read his eyes. She saw his mouth smile, but could see nothing else of comfort.

It wasn't long after Angus's departure that a servant came with a message that the Queen asked them to join her in her apartments as soon they were able. Abby looked at Iain when the servant had delivered his message. He was still dressed in his travelling clothes and boots which were stained with mud and dirt from the road. She knew she looked little better.

"We must change first," she said. "You and my father are of a size, so you may borrow some of his clothes, if you wish."

Iain glanced down at his doublet and gave her a rueful look. "Aye, I suppose it's for the best."

She made her way to her father's chamber and opened up one of the chests. She rifled quickly through the clothes she had packed away just a short while before, wondering what to give Iain to wear. Eventually, she settled on a deep blue and silver brocade doublet and matching breeches with light coloured hose. The shoes were fine calfskin and appeared to be sufficiently big enough for Iain. She handed the bundle over to him. He murmured his thanks and Abby left him there, shutting the door. She breathed a sigh. She mustn't think any more about the need for him to wear the clothes, or that her father wasn't here to object or give permission.

She went along to her own chamber and closed the door softly, wondering what she might wear herself. She opened her large chest and fingered the various dresses lying folded in a pile inside. The scent of lavender and other herbs wafted up from the sprigs laid in there to keep her gowns fresh. She found her way down to the bottom where she had buried her wedding gown. It seemed another lifetime ago that she'd worn the white and silver brocade gown when she'd wed Henri. How innocent she'd been then, and Henri too. She pulled out the gown and its kirtle and laid them on the bed.

Both the gown and the kirtle were richly made, so much more than the plainer gowns she'd customarily worn. The sleeves were one piece, with small slashes to reveal a sheer linen underdress. As the daughter of the Queen's lute player she was more at home wearing the plainer gowns, if she was being truthful. She'd preferred to go about court unremarked, for she found the etiquette and all the other aspects of the flirting and intrigue tiresome and unsuited to her temperament. But the occasion of her wedding her father had deemed an important event and one that needed to reflect her status as a member of the household and as the future member of Henri's family. Looking at it now, she was glad he'd insisted, for she knew she looked well in it and now, in front of the Queen and the rest of the courtiers, it was important that she appear her best. If not for her sake, but the for the sake of Iain and the MacGregors. This wasn't an opportunity to be missed. She would ask the Queen for her help in their cause, if she had the chance.

After removing her old gown and wiping the dirt from her face and hands with a wet cloth, she struggled into the farthingale that hung underneath and then slipped the brocade kirtle on, followed by the embroidered silver and white gown and the sleeves. She tugged them all into place, lacing at the side and fastening the ornate buttons that formed in the front.

It seemed tighter than before and she was surprised to notice that where no bust had been before, soft mounds appeared at the top. It was lower cut than she remembered. She searched for the pearls Iain had given her and put them around her neck. Her pier glass was small, but she could still see that her tangled hair was out of place with the elegant gown. Before, at her wedding, she'd worn her hair loose, hanging down to her waist. That was impossible now. There was no possibility that she could arrange it herself in the manner the French servant at the Dowager Queen's court had done, as much as she might wish it.

She frowned, running her fingers through the tangles to give them some semblance of order. She searched the small box of trinkets on her table and found a pair of hair combs decorated with pearls. They'd been her mother's, left behind with only a few other items when she'd gone. She'd never worn them, for reasons that had something to do with her father's sensitivities, though she'd never consciously gave thought to them. Now, it seemed the right thing and the only thing she could wear. No headpiece she owned would do.

She combed her hair through, and with a few pins and some twisting and turning, she slid the combs into place. She looked at the results in the mirror and gave a satisfied smile. Toilet complete, she turned and slipped out of her room into the small sitting room. Iain was lounging in one of the chairs. When she entered he stood and smiled. The light from the window caught the silver in his brocade and lit up his face, where his blue eyes seemed brighter than she remembered.

The doublet stretched tightly across his shoulders, but other than that, the clothes were a good fit. In fact they were more than a good fit, Abby allowed, and as handsome as she remembered her father had been wearing that very same outfit, Abby had to admit Iain outshone him, but only by a fraction. Her heart missed a beat. Though Iain seemed different to his father, there was similarity in their manner and temperament that only just struck her now.

"If it wasna for the evening at the Scottish court I'd hardly recognise ye, *Francach.*"

"I'll take that as a compliment," said Abby.

"It was meant as one. You are striking in that gown."

"Thank you," she said, allowing the pleasure of his words to warm her.

Iain tugged at his sleeve. "Och, this is tight enough and too fine to be afraid that I might inadvertently do it damage. There'll no be any sword swinging for me today."

Abby gave a laugh, though she noted that his ballock dagger was still belted at his side. "You would do best to leave that here. I doubt it will be allowed in the Queen's apartments, Scots or no."

He looked down at the ballock dagger in its sheath and reluctantly unbelted it. "Aye, though I canna help but feel naked wi'out it."

"But you had no dagger at Kilchurn, surely?"

He gave her a wicked grin. "Didn't I?"

She shook her head, but the smile was still on her face. "I might have guessed. But I suggest you leave that behind. They won't be as remiss here in light of the past history. Potential threats to the Queen's life are at the forefront of the guards minds here."

"Let's hope the court sees my potential in other directions," said Iain. "With ye beside me, I dinna see how they cannot."

He ended his words by tweaking a loose curl by her ear and offering his arm. She took it. In her mind there was no doubt that the court would see his potential in one particular direction. At least the ladies would. She only hoped the potential would stay just that. Potential.

CHAPTER 17

The Queen's apartments were large and spacious rooms panelled in wood and hung with paintings and finely wrought tapestries. Sun streamed in from the windows, shedding heat and light on the courtiers who sat and stood in clusters talking, sewing or playing a discreet game of cards. The air was heavy with the odours of sweat and perfumes that mingled in the heat of a summer's midday and the noise of chatter made Abby and Iain's arrival go largely unnoticed.

Abby threaded her way through the groups, nodding to one or two courtiers she recognised, Iain following in her wake. At first she was unaware of the stir she caused and it wasn't until the room turned virtually silent that she looked around and saw the mixture of admiring glances and curious stares.

The Queen, noticing the pair finally, beckoned them forward, her old governess, Madame Parois, sitting beside her, sour-faced and watchful of Abby. The Queen had grown taller in Abby's absence, and was now just about her size. Few other women matched that height, and for a brief moment Abby wondered how the Dauphin fared in growth in comparison to his bride-to-be. She was a striking beauty already with her fair colouring and

164

auburn hair, made even fairer by the jewels that dressed her neck and her fingers. Her green silk gown shot with gold thread enhanced the richness of her colouring and marked her as the centre of attention, even if she hadn't been the Queen.

Abby curtsyed low and Iain gave a sweeping bow on one knee before her and when bid, they both rose. The Queen greeted Abby warmly, which surprised her since she couldn't recall the Queen paying her much attention before.

"We welcome you back to court, Madame de Villiers," said the Queen in French. We are delighted to see you."

"I thank you, Your Grace," said Abby.

"And your father, have you news of him? We do miss him greatly."

"No, Your Grace. I have nothing to tell you on that score. I have only just returned from Scotland. I was hoping there might be news of him here."

"*Bien sûr*, I remember now. You went to Scotland to stay with a family friend and learn more about our great nation, *ne c'est pas?*"

"*Oui*, Your Grace."

"And did you learn about our fair Scotland?" The Queen looked at Iain and smiled. "I see you have brought back a keepsake, and a bonny one he is."

Abby smiled at the quaint way the Queen pronounced the word "bonny" and looked at Iain. He bowed to the Queen, his expression neutral.

"May I present, Iain MacGregor, son and heir of the MacGregor, Chief of the clan, who is my….." She searched a moment for the right term that sum up the relationship and could find none the Queen would understand. "My husband-to-be," she settled on eventually.

The Queen gave her a puzzled look. "Do you not mean 'betrothed?'"

"Not exactly, Your Grace. We are what the Highlanders term 'handfasted'. It's an ancient custom there in which the vows we exchange become final and binding only if we lie together." It was the best explanation she could give, but out of the corner of her eye she caught Iain's amused expression.

"And have you?"

"What, Your Grace?" asked Abby.

"Lain together."

Abby looked down, knowing her face betrayed her embarrassment. For the French court, the nature of her sexual relationship with Iain was of passing curiosity, not just for the Queen, but for all. It was what they fed on. Anyone would have asked and expected an answer. Knowing this didn't make Abby any happier about discussing it. Beside her, Iain shifted.

"No," she murmured "Not yet. We await my father's formal consent. We couldn't reach him from Scotland, hence my arrival."

The young queen clapped her hands. "A romance," she said with excitement. "How lovely. And such a handsome pair, too. Lord Iain, you are *trés beau* and most welcome. We will find the father of Mistress Gordon…or is it Mistress MacGregor now? I am a little confused about the proper term."

"As you will, Your Grace," said Iain, before Abby could reply. "And I must beg your pardon, Your Grace, but I am not a lord."

"But is your father not one of my earls?" asked the Queen.

Iain gave a wry smile. "No, Your Grace. My father is a chief of one of the most ancient and royal clans in Scotland, descended from MacAlpin himself."

"Ah, *bien sûr*," said the Queen. She laughed. "It is difficult to keep it all straight, there is so much complication in the history."

"There is that, Your Grace," said Iain.

"You must instruct us sometime on the particular history of your clan. We do so want to learn as much about our people as possible."

"With pleasure," said Iain.

"If I may, Your Grace," said Abby. "I would like to mention one particular bit of history about the clan now."

"Of course," said the Queen. Beside her, Madame Parois coughed discreetly and frowned at Abby, but the Queen ignored her. "Afterwards, we insist that you play the lute for us. We have missed your father's excellent playing so much."

Abby bowed her assent and then began a brief explanation of the situation that had brought Iain in danger of being arrested and the clan outlawed.

When Abby had finished the Queen spoke. "Oh that is terrible. We would hate to see someone as handsome as this fine young man be arrested and hung for such a thing. I will of course write to my *maman* at once."

"Oh, I thank you, Your Grace," said Abby. "With all my heart."

Iain bowed and offered his own thanks.

"But of course. What else would we do?" said the Queen. "We cannot have two young lovers separated so cruelly."

A commotion at the back of the room caught the Queen's attention. "What is amiss?" she asked.

"It's Lady Elizabeth," said Mary Beaton, one of the Queen's ladies and a close friend. "She seems to be unwell."

"Lady Margaret," said the Queen. "Will you assist her to her room?"

"Of course," said a dark-haired, large woman.

"I'm fine, really," came a small voice from the centre of a cluster of people gathered at the end of the room.

"Are you certain, Lady Elizabeth?" said the Queen.

A small figure moved forward. The deep red dress she wore set off her jet black hair and large dark eyes, and despite her full figure, she moved as though she was a feather, or more accurately, a delicate morsel.

Iain stirred beside Abby. She looked at him and for a brief

moment saw bewilderment and concern there, before he resumed his usual neutral expression. Abby's stomach tightened.

"You do look pale, though," said the Queen. "Sit while someone brings you some wine to restore you." She turned to Abby and gestured to the lute that lay on a chair nearby. "Perhaps some music, too, would help."

Abby nodded, welcoming the opportunity to occupy her mind and keep her fingers busy. She made her way over to the chair, took up the lute and sat. Settling it on her lap she tested the tuning. Once satisfied, she began to pluck out a tune she knew was a favourite of the Queen's. As she played she felt soothed by the notes and for a moment closed her eyes, determined to lose herself in the music. Eventually, she opened her eyes and her gaze drifted around the room. Some sat attentively listening, conscious that the Queen did so also. The Queen loved music, and was proud of her own accomplishments on the lute, some of which were due to the instruction of Abby's father.

With the piece finished, a smattering of clapping broke out. The Queen asked for more and Abby resumed her playing with an air her father had composed. It was then she noticed Iain talking earnestly to Lady Elizabeth at the back of the room. She watched them closely, unable to resist the compulsion to try to interpret their exchange. Lady Elizabeth's colour had flooded back, emphasising the fullness of her lips. She looked up at Iain from under long thick lashes that seemed to be working their magic on him. He had her hands in his and was rubbing the back of them as he spoke.

Abby pulled her gaze away and admonished herself to pay more attention to her music, which was all that mattered in that moment. If Iain chose to play the fool to some simpering girl, it was his affair. His behaviour galled her more than she cared to admit, not only because it was in his interest to play the besotted lover with her, rather than Lady Elizabeth, but because she'd never seen him act in this manner with any other woman before.

She finished the piece and the Queen called for a song. Abby obliged. She looked straight ahead, away from Iain and Lady Elizabeth and focused on words she sang. When she'd finished, the Queen released her. She placed the lute back on the chair and made her way back through the clusters of people, determined to speak with someone other than Iain. She found Jacques de Longueville, her father's friend hovering at her elbow and turned to him with a winning smile pinned to her face.

"Seigneur de Longueville," said Abby giving a small curtsy. "What a pleasure to see you here. I thought the ladies of Queen Catherine were more to your style."

"But how could you say such a thing?" said de Longueville, bowing low over her hand. He wasn't as tall as Abby, though his boots had heels. "Not with such a beautiful lady as yourself gracing the Queen's apartments. He smiled at her words and stroked his oiled, carefully trimmed beard. "Is it really Calum's *petite fille* that stands before me? May I say you look ravishing. The gown is a triumph. And your hair, *que c'est beau*. You have transformed since I last saw you. Is it perhaps the Scottish air? And please, as your father's dearest friend, you must call me de Longueville."

Abby kept the smile on her face. "Of course," she said. "de Longueville."

She wasn't certain how comfortable she was using that kind of familiarity with a man she hardly knew. He was usually found in her father's company when he was drinking or gambling. But she realised that fostering a closer acquaintance between them might be useful. He might have information about her father, or at the very least be willing to try to discover information.

She gave a trill of laughter that even sounded false in her ears. "You are too kind, Seigneur. *Non,* I assure you I am little different than when I left here." She patted her hair. "Though the hair is shorter, I grant you."

"You are modest, *ma chérie*. Take the compliment as truth. The sign of grace and elegance is to receive all the tributes as your right. It is only a pity the father cannot be here to reflect in the glory of his child."

Abby's face clouded. "Yes, I would wish my father was here, on many counts. But it seems he was called away."

"But I heard it was some kind of family concerns that called him away," said de Longueville. "I assumed it was you he meant." He smiled slowly. "I can see there's nothing to concern him regarding you."

Abby looked at him. Some instinct inside her made her decide it was better not to call attention to her father's absence to anyone in the court, not even one of her father's circle. Since overhearing the conversation threatening the Queen's life, she felt it necessary to be cautious.

"It wasn't on my account," said Abby and she smiled. "It was some other matter."

"Of course," said de Longueville, seeing her glance around the room. He gave her an inquiring look. "You're right. Things are rather dull here. Shall we go elsewhere for some more lively company? I know where some of your father's friends are entertaining this evening."

Abby looked at him, considering the possibilities. Would she be able to discover more information about her father? She nodded. "That sounds lovely."

He bowed slightly and offered his arm. She took it and he led her away, through the groups of people. Out of the corner of her eye Abby caught sight of Iain. He was still engrossed in conversation with Lady Elizabeth. She turned away and moved closer to de Longueville.

CHAPTER 18

The rooms were spacious and well appointed, denoting their owner was someone of rank. This evidence was reaffirmed by the luxurious manner of dress, though some clothes were draped on chairs or lying on the floor. Some men lounged with their linen shirts hanging loose, their doublets long discarded. Women had alarmingly low cut gowns and hair uncovered, with soft curls dangling suggestively. Drink spills were pooled on tables and floors that were laden with food and flagons of wine.

On closer inspection Abby could see that some of the women wore cosmetics that lightened their skin or reddened their lips and cheeks. One daring specimen had her eyes outlined in kohl, like some Mohammedan woman, something Abby had seen only once before when she was very young.

Men and women lounged around in groups dicing or playing cards, while in the background someone played a lute. In darkened corners couples entertained themselves in other ways. Abby's first instinct was to offer to play the lute herself. It was a comfortable role with which she was well acquainted.

"Should we play cards or dice?" asked de Longueville.

"Dice," said Abby on impulse. She had little skill in card play-ing, having only tried once or twice with her father. She'd preferred playing music to anything involving cards, which she found boring in comparison.

De Longueville led her towards a group of men and women gathered around a table. Besides an English lord and a wealthy Spanish merchant, Abby recognised two of the women as members of Queen Catherine's household, part of the intimate circle of women she favoured. They were both dark-haired and smoky-eyed and the Italianate manner of their dress and hair suggested they might be Medici relatives.

De Longueville made the introductions and they greeted her with indifferent smiles.

Julietta, one of the Italian ladies, spoke. "But yes, I know you now. You are Calum's daughter."

"No," said the other Italian lady, Maria. "Calum cannot have a daughter of that age, surely?"

"But can you not see resemblance?" said de Longueville. "Is she not *très belle?*"

Maria studied Abby, who returned her gaze calmly, and after a moment realised she was the woman she had stumbled upon in her father's bed chamber on her final day at court, months before. Abby raised her brows, showing she recognised the woman. Maria gave a little shrug.

"Perhaps," said Maria.

A liveried servant brought de Longueville and Abby fine Italian glass goblets filled with wine. Abby drank deeply, feeling the need for something to sustain her through this evening. The wine was strong, but it filled her with a warmth she found reas-suring. She put on her most charming smile and asked if she might play dice with them.

"*Bien sûr,*" said the young lord, whose name she couldn't

remember. He made a place beside him and she slipped in. de Longueville came to other side and pressed tight against her.

"I shall guide you," he whispered in her ear.

"What will you wager?" said the young lord.

"I'll just watch for now," she said.

The two Italian women exchanged glances and smiled. Before the dice was rolled the various players declared their wagers. Some wagered gold coins, others a small item of jewellery. When it came to Maria, one of the Italian women, she gave a little pout. There were no gold coins in front of her and she was wearing no jewellery except the large pearl fastened to her bodice.

"I shall wager a kiss," she said.

"A kiss where?" said the English lord.

Her eyes sparkled with mischief. "A kiss anywhere."

"Madamoiselle, your enrich the play with such a wager," said the Spanish merchant.

With every wager placed, the English lord handed Maria the dice. She held them in her hands and kissed them before throwing them on the table. She gave a little moue of dismay, scooped them up and handed them to the next person. By the end, it was clear the Englishman had won.

"Shall I collect the wager from you now?" he asked.

She cocked her head. "Oh, whenever you like."

He grinned. "Now, if you please."

She beckoned him to her and he came over, his eyes alight. She held out her hand.

"You may kiss me there," she said coquettishly

"Ah, madamoiselle, I protest. Surely it would be a kiss of my own choosing."

She fluttered her lashes. "Well, Seigneur, because it is you, I will agree."

He took her hand and pulled him in close, his freed hand

brushing her breast. He leaned down and kissed her hard, on the lips. Eventually, he pulled away, his eyes filled with desire.

She sighed, swaying slightly, "Oh, Seigneur," she said. "I wonder now, who it is that gained from this wager."

A flash of triumph passed over his face. He bowed. "I can count as a winner without a doubt."

"Another toss," a young blond haired French nobleman cried. "I demand a chance to win back my losses."

"Oh Montchamp," said Julietta, "I don't think that lady fortune is present with you today."

He gave her a charming smile. "Ah, but no. It is only a matter of time before I persuade her to return."

Julietta slipped her hand through the Spanish's merchant's arm and smiled up at him. "I'm afraid that you will have much difficulty persuading lady fortune to leave Monsieur Ortega's side. She seems particularly attached to him, tonight."

Ortega took Julietta's hand and kissed it. "My lady, it is you who have brought luck to my side."

Montchamp looked over at Abby. "Perhaps Calum's ravishing daughter can win fortune to my side." He handed her the dice. "Please, I ask you to throw for me."

"But what will you wager?" asked Maria.

He cocked his head and looked at his meagre pile of coins. He scooped them up, withdrew a ring from his finger and tossed them all onto the table. "There," he said.

Abby looked down at the dice. "Please, don't risk your possessions on my skill at throwing dice. I'm not experienced at this and can guarantee nothing."

Maria gave a little clap. "Oh no! Such high play gives it spice."

Montchamp laughed. "You see," he said to Abby. "It is about the interest, the excitement, rather than the winnings. Your father understood that very well."

"Do you know my father? I don't recall meeting you before."

"Of course, your father and I are well acquainted, but we see each other in places I don't think you have frequented." He gave her a dazzling smile.

"But you haven't spoken to him, or seen him recently," said Abby. She couldn't think how to phrase the question in a manner that seemed less like an interrogation. She only hoped he didn't take offence.

A flash of humour crossed his face and not the indignation she imagined he would feel. "Ah, sadly no. I hear he has gone away to settle some family affairs. But do you know more? He will be back soon? Please, tell me, for I miss my good friend. "

Abby glanced at de Longueville, but he merely shrugged.

"No, I'm not certain when he will be back. He didn't say," she said in a bright tone.

The others made their wagers; Julietta an earring and Maria pledging a ribbon that served a critical role in the closure of her bodice. With the ribbon removed, her bodice opened, revealing soft breasts pressing against transparent fabric. The English lord's eyes kept drifting to the game of chance going on with the lady's chest, instead of the play of dice on the table.

Abby drank from her goblet deeply and stared at the dice in her other hand. She had little understanding of the game, but how much skill could it take to throw some little wooden pieces? On impulse she kissed them as Maria had done. She privately doubted it would make any difference but it seemed to be the custom of an expert so she decided to follow suit. She rolled them carefully on the table and they came to rest.

"*Bien*," said Maria. She took up the dice, rolled them and gave a little cry of dismay. "Oh, non, and I did so love the colour of that ribbon."

The English lord threw his dice, but this time luck was not on his side. He turned to Maria, took her hand and kissed it. "Fear not my lovely lady. I shall give you as many ribbons as you wish to replace that one."

Maria looked up at him and gave her coquettish smile once more, murmuring her gratitude. The others made their plays and when all had done Montchamp took up her hand and gave it a lingering kiss.

"See, I was certain you, of anyone, could persuade lady fortune to return to my side."

His eyes held hers, a light blue, fringed with golden lashes that suggested an innocence his expression didn't match. He rubbed his thumb along the back of her hand. She felt liquid, her senses heightened to the point that she could it seemed as if every bit of her hand alive with his touch. The scent of his body, the traces of sweat and the sweet odour of his perfume enveloped her. She was seized with an overwhelming desire to pick up that thumb and taste it, to taste him, all of him. With effort she pulled away and gave a shaky laugh.

"I'm certain it was nothing of my skill that brought your luck back," she said.

"But we will prove it. You must wager and throw the dice," Montchamp said.

"But I have nothing to wager," Abby said. There was no question about the pearls. She put a hand to her combs. It was too much. They weren't hers to wager. By rights they were still her mother's combs. She looked at de Longueville and he smiled. He pulled a pair of gloves from his belt and gave them to her.

"Please, I insist that you use this for your first wager."

"Oh, I cannot." She bit her lip and looked down at her fingers, bare except for Iain's ring.

De Longueville put a hand on hers. "No, no. You must not. Take the gloves. These mean nothing. There is no sentiment attached to them. I would be very desolate if you didn't accept my offer." He bowed and kissed her hand.

She gave what she hoped was a tinkle of laughter and took the gloves with a murmur of thanks. Montchamp collected the dice from the table and placed them in her right palm, closing her hand over them. He raised the closed hand to his lips and kissed it slowly, his eyes holding hers. The same tingling desire flashed through her. With effort she drew her eyes away, opened her palm and kissed the dice as before. The others placed their wagers. Julietta pulled off an embroidered slipper.

"I shall win and help you place it back on your foot," said Monsieur Ortega with a guttural laugh. He wore crumbs of pastry on his dark beard. Julietta gave him a pat on his fat be-ringed fingers, cocked her head and smiled wickedly.

"I look forward to it," she said.

Maria, after much consideration and consultation with the English lord, decided she would offer a silk stocking. The English lord watched entranced as she lifted her skirt and carefully removed the garter and then the stocking itself. She held it up to him.

"Please, Seigneur, do you think it is fine enough for a wager?" she asked. She draped it over his hand.

The English lord licked his lips and nodded. "Most certainly, mademoiselle," he said.

Maria sighed and murmured her thanks as she picked up the stocking and placed it on the table. Montchamp nodded to Abby and whispered encouragement to her. She nodded and threw the dice on the table. She looked at the results blankly, still unclear if it was a good throw or not.

"*Bien!*" said Montchamp.

Others threw the dice in turn and when all who desired had thrown, de Longueville turned to her and gave her arm a squeeze.

"Such skill. I can see that you are your father's daughter," he said.

She blinked at him. "Have I won?"

"You have," said Montchamp. He took up her hand and kissed the inside of the palm.

"Did I not say you have lady fortune with you?"

She gave Montchamp a weak smile, caught up once again by the look of desire in his eyes. She felt his lips once more on her palm. This time it was not just her skin, but her very bones that seemed to be liquid. She was dissolving into him.

"You must go again," he said. He rubbed her palm.

She stared at the winnings on the table. She picked up the gloves, handed them back to de Longueville and pushed the rest into the centre. The others placed their wagers. Another shoe and stocking were removed with great ceremony which absorbed the full attention of the English lord and Spanish merchant. More gold coins, and a brooch and ring were added to the pile.

She took up her goblet and found that Montchamp had filled it again. "Thank you for such consideration," she said softly.

He raised his own goblet and gestured to her. "*La plus belle femme*," he said.

She blushed and drank from her goblet. There was no denying the quality of the wine or its taste. She took another deep drink and placed it on the table before scooping up the dice again. Montchamp placed his hand on her back and caressed it. She kissed the dice once more, feeling wonderfully happy. She smiled at the assembled group. This was a most enjoyable evening. All her tension and worry seemed to have gone, and all she could feel was affection for these people who had been such good company.

She threw the dice and watched them fall into place. A sigh went through the group. She stared at the little wooden pieces, trying to determine the outcome. The pieces were blurred around the edges and the painted images on them shivered slightly. She blinked again, but it was no use. She looked over at Montchamp and he gave her a little squeeze.

"*Quelle domage*," he said a look of remorse on his face.

She smiled back at him, studying his face. It was a wonderful face, such a noble nose, the way it sloped and the nostrils flared. And the lips, they were a marvel of sensuality and humour. The others threw the dice while she marvelled at his face, his arm still around her. "You will try again," he whispered in her ear.

"I will," she said.

She leaned into him, suddenly needing the support, for it appeared that her legs were finding it difficult to remain upright. He rubbed her arm and she felt the warmth of his hand through the fabric of her gown.

"You must wager now," he murmured into her ear.

She smiled dreamily up at him. "What shall I wager?" she murmured. "A shoe?" she giggled at the thought.

"A comb, perhaps?" he said.

"Oh, no," she said. "These are my mother's, I couldn't do that. She might want them someday."

"Ah," he said. "Your mother is returning?"

She shrugged. "Possibly." She looked at him. "A shoe it is," she said. She leaned over and her head swam. The wine was stronger than she'd thought. She teetered but Montchamp righted her.

"Allow me," he said.

Before she could object, he knelt down at her feet and raised her gown. She placed her hand on his back for support. He took up her right foot and ran one hand softly along her calf. His hands were light and caressing and she shivered under his touch.

"If my wife needs tae undress, I think it's best that she do it in our apartments and wi' my assistance."

Abby looked up and saw Iain standing there, a sardonic expression on his face. His tone had been light, no trace of anger or menace in it. Montchamp rose and stood beside Abby, his brow raised.

"Oh, Iain," she said and smiled. "I want you to meet my friends. They're so entertaining. They're teaching me a new game."

Iain eyed her suspiciously. "Is that what they're teaching ye? A new game."

"Apparently I'm quite lucky. I've won a few times." She looked at the empty space in front of her and placed her hand over her mouth. "Oops, I lost the last round, though."

He grasped her wrist. "I think it's time tae bid your friends a good night."

She looked up at him. "Is it?" She turned and looked at the group that had made her so happy. She blew them each a kiss. When she came to Montchamp she leaned over and kissed his mouth. "You have such a lovely mouth, you know. But it's your nose that I find is your best feature."

Montchamp took up her hand and kissed it lightly. "It was a pleasure to have your company tonight, Madamoiselle Gabrielle. You are even better company than your father and I look forward to spending more time with you so you may feast on my nose and lips as much as you desire."

"Weel, I am sore pleased ye enjoyed her company sae much, but I dinna think she'll have any time in the future to find her way tae your side," said Iain. He bowed to Montchamp and the rest of the group and took Abby away.

ANGUS WAS on the floor asleep when they arrived back at the apartments and Abby nearly fell over him in the darkness. Iain helped her into her room and after quickly removing her farthingale, settled her safely on the bed. That done, he set about lighting candles. He placed one beside her and cupped her chin, examining her eyes. She smiled at him, marvelling at his eyes.

"Your eyes are a darker blue than Montchamp's," she said. "Especially when you're angry." She knit her brow. "Are you angry now? You shouldn't be. Your eyes and mouth are even lovelier than Mountchamp's. And you're more handsome," she added for extra measure.

"Aye, well, I can imagine anyone would look good after what ye've been given." he said. He sighed. "I suppose ye dinna think tae eat anything since ye left here."

She considered his question and eventually shook her head. "No, I was playing the lute at the Queen's apartments and before I could eat anything afterwards, de Longueville had a wonderful notion to go to the other apartments and kindly invited me. And there—" she waved her hand in the air—"there were too many other things distracting me. And besides, the Spanish merchant made a pig of himself with the pastry." She gave a moue of distaste.

Iain shook his head. "I should give ye a right beating for your foolishness, but I canna. Ye've been played deftly and it isna your fault."

Abby sat up and pouted. "What isn't my fault? I haven't done anything wrong. I was having a good time. If you hadn't been taken up with your helpless little damsel you could have come along and enjoyed the fun." She prodded his chest with her finger. "She's that girl, isn't she? The one Lady Arbella mentioned when she teased you about the song. *Your upright handsome appearance has left me lovesick.*" She sang the phrase from the verse in a wobbly tone.

Iain frowned. "Ye'll leave Lady Elizabeth out of this. She has nothing tae do with what's happened." He pushed her back on the bed. "Now I advise ye tae go tae sleep."

Angus appeared at the door, rubbing his eyes. "What's tae do?"

"Och," said Iain. "She's been lured tae a gaming circle and drugged." He muttered a few phrases at Angus.

Angus grunted. "Any harm done?"

Iain shook his head. "I canna be sure. There's nae sense from her now. I'll see if she remembers anything in the morning. For now, I want ye tae keep an eye on her. Make sure she doesna go anywhere."

Abby drew her brows together and folded her arms across her chest. "I remember everything clearly, you know. Longueville said they were my father's friends and I went to see if they knew anything. And I'll have you know I did find out something."

"Oh, aye. And what was that?" asked Iain.

She sniffed. "You can wait until tomorrow, since you're being this way." She turned her head away and closed her eyes.

CHAPTER 19

*A*bby opened her eyes and then shut them quickly. She raised her hand to her head and gave a soft moan. There was a strong pounding behind her eyes that seemed to reach out to every part of her head. Her tongue felt swollen and dry. With effort she opened her eyes again and slowly raised her head from the bed. Light from the window poured in and she turned away from its brightness. She moaned again and fell back against the pillow.

With effort she tried to recall the events of the night before that had brought her to this state. Except for her farthingale, which was tossed on the floor, she was still in the clothes she'd worn to the Queen's apartments. Those events came back to her clearly, including Iain's engaging conversation with Lady Elizabeth. It was after she'd left the Queen's apartments that things became a little fuzzy. She remembered de Longueville, her father's friend, taking her elsewhere after sensing her discomfort with Iain's actions.

She thought hard, trying to piece together the subsequent events. It all came back in a flood. She moaned again, hoping her disjointed memories were much worse than the actual occurrences. It was unthinkable otherwise. She couldn't possibly have allowed Montchamp to caress her legs, nor could she have told Iain that his mouth and eyes were lovelier than Montchamp's. She buried her face in the pillow, willing the memory away.

She listened for any stirrings on the other side of the door. A slight noise and a clearing of a throat. A moment later there was a tap on the door.

"Mistress?"

She gave a sigh of relief. It was Angus. With effort, she pulled herself out of the bed, went over to the door and opened it.

Angus made no comment on the state of her clothes, he only sniffed. "Just wondering if ye were awake yet. It's gone the noon hour."

She glanced past him but could see no sign of anyone else. "Where's Iain?"

"Not back yet," said Angus.

"Not back yet?" She frowned.

Angus shook his head. Abby stared at him. The effort to concentrate was almost too much. Where could Iain be at this hour? She thought of Lady Elizabeth and her accusations from the night before came back to her. She repressed the urge to groan again.

"Will ye be wanting anything tae eat?" asked Angus.

"What?" she looked at him and it suddenly dawned on her why he was tapping at her door. "You must be famished, yourself. Why haven't you gone to for something to eat?"

"Och, Iain said I was tae keep an eye on ye. So I thought, now ye're awake, ye could go in search of food wi' me."

Anger flashed through her and then dissolved. At this moment it required too much effort to be angry at Iain and besides, she reasoned, he was only looking after her. Or rather making Angus watch her. She glanced at Angus. He gave her an expectant look.

"Just step outside a moment and flag down a servant. There's bound to be one out there. Ask the servant to bring some food and drink and some water. I promise I won't go anywhere."

He gave her a dubious look, but the rumbling of his stomach won him over. He nodded. "I willna be long," he said.

She watched him leave and shut her own chamber door. She'd make use of his absence by changing out of her gown. It was one action she could take to eliminate the memory of the night before.

By the time she had removed her gown and replaced it with a plain one of brown cloth and simple linen foresleeves, Angus had returned and she'd confirmed her presence with a greeting. She entered the sitting room, feeling slightly more herself and took the empty seat by the window, her back to its glare.

"Do you know where Iain went?" she asked.

She picked up the flagon from the table and saw that it was empty. It was from the day before, she knew, but it had been nearly full of watered wine when she'd last seen it. She raised a brow at Angus. He shrugged.

"He said he had some people tae see," said Angus.

"What people?"

Angus shrugged again. "Iain doesna confide in me."

She gave him a close look, but his face revealed nothing. She sighed.

They sat there in silence for a short while until a knock sounded at the door. Angus rose quickly and let the servant in. It was a young lad, dressed in Queen Catherine's livery. On the tray he carried were a flagon of watered wine, a plate of meat, bread and cheese. He bowed, entered and placed the tray on the table beside Abby. After another bow he informed them he would return shortly with the water required.

The two ate in silence. Abby was too intent on the reaction of her stomach and head to be able to manage any conversation, so it wasn't until the servant returned that she looked up from her lap, where she'd been studying a slight pull in the fabric while she slowly chewed a piece of bread.

The servant entered and Abby indicated he should put the jug of water in her room. Angus would have to take care of any ablutions elsewhere. Her body needed all the help it could get to refresh itself. When the servant returned from the room he bowed and withdrew a note from his doublet.

"For you, mademoiselle," he said.

Abby took the note, thanked him and the servant left. She glanced down at the writing, puzzled. It was addressed to her, there was no doubt, but she didn't recognise the script and the seal told her nothing. She broke it and unfolded the paper. *I have found the information you seek about your father. I must tell you in confidence. Meet me in the maze in one hour. L.*

She stared at the note, trying to take in the words and signature. It must be Longueville. Who else would write her about her father and in such a fashion? She looked up and saw Angus regarding her quizzically.

"What is it?" he asked.

She paused for a moment and handed him the note.

He shook his head and gave it back to her. "I canna read it," he said.

"It's from de Longueville. He says he has information about my father, but he must tell me in confidence, so he's asked me to meet him in the maze in an hour."

He frowned. "Nay, it's too risky."

"What risk?"

He snorted. "It could be a trap. Why does he no meet ye in public and whisper the words?"

She gave an exasperated sigh. "You know little of court if you think that is possible."

"But why there?" He shook his head. "I dinna like it."

"Well I'm not asking you to accompany me. I'll go on my own and if there is any danger, I'll leave."

"Ye willna be going anywhere on your own."

"Then you'll just have to come with me, because I'm determined to do what I can to find my father, even if you and Iain don't seem to be much concerned."

Angus frowned and shook his head. "Ye've got it wrong if ye think Iain isna concerned."

"Well there's little evidence of his concern at the moment," she said acerbically. She took a deep breath and adopted a more reasonable tone. "If you accompany me, I assure you the moment anything appears suspicious we will both leave."

Angus crossed his arms, a scowl on his face. "Och, verra well. If that's the only way I can keep ye from doing anything rash. And ye will promise tae stay by my side at all times."

"I promise," she said.

THE SUN BEAT down on her, causing the dull throb in her head to increase. A few beads of sweat formed on her upper lip and across her brow. Beside her, Angus, in his wrapped plaid and leather jerkin, shifted uncomfortably. The two crossed the large expanse of grass and neared the maze. Laughter drifted towards them from the distant rose gardens at the opposite end.

They entered the maze, the tall hedges providing much-needed shade. Angus gave an appreciative sigh. The way was narrow, not really wide enough for two, so he trailed behind as she weaved her way through the various hedges, choosing the direction with confidence. As a child she'd learned the maze's secret and spent many hours playing in here and taking refuge from her tutor, or from any other task she might need to avoid.

Just before they reached the centre of the maze, Abby slowed down and signalled Angus to silence. She neared the edge of an opening, where a bench overlooked a small formal pond. Sitting on the bench was de Longueville. At a distance were two men in Guise livery. The sight of the men surprised her. But perhaps they had the information. She edged her way forward. Angus put a restraining hand on her arm.

"Nay," he said in a low whisper.

She shook off his hand and stepped forward. De Longueville looked up, an apologetic expression on his face. The two men moved toward her, one drawing a dagger from his belt. From the shadows emerged a figure. The Comte de Damville.

Abby needed no more prodding. She turned. "Follow me carefully," she said.

She picked up her skirts and ran for all she was worth, twisting and turning, going down one narrow path and then another, until she was at the far end of the maze. Behind her, she could hear Angus's laboured breathing and further back, the shouts and sounds of pursuit. She stopped and paused. The men were close behind them. Angus stopped and withdrew his ballock dagger from its hiding place in his jerkin and prepared to fight. The two men pulled up at the sight of Angus and slowly approached. They both carried swords. Abby searched fruitlessly for something to help him as he moved warily back and forth, the dagger in his hand. She had little idea of his skill and only hoped that, being Iain's companion, he would be experienced.

Angus feinted and parried, surprisingly nimble for all his bulk. The men were quick enough but the space was tight and Angus used it to his advantage, ensuring there was only room for one opponent at a time. For a moment Abby stood there, frozen, until Angus shouted at her to run. She hesitated and then took off, leaving the sounds of fighting behind her.

She found her way back out of the maze and ran across the expanse of grass and slipped back into the palace without encountering anyone. Once inside, she made her way back to the apartments, wildly trying to think how to find Iain. She entered the apartments closing the door loudly.

"That blasted man," she said angrily. It would take her too long to find out where the Lady Elizabeth's quarters were. And there was no guarantee that Iain would be there. Angus needed help immediately.

The door opened and Iain entered, his eyes dark with tiredness, a day's growth of beard on his face.

"What blasted man?" he said.

Abby turned to him in surprise. "You're back." She collected herself. "Quickly, you must come. Angus is in danger."

Iain was instantly alert. "What? Where?"

"I'll explain later. Just follow me. Have you a spare dagger or sword hidden? If so, bring it."

He disappeared into her father's chamber and returned a moment later, slipping a large dagger inside his jerkin. They left the apartments quickly and went down the corridor, down stairs, as swiftly as possible without drawing attention to themselves. Once outside Abby raced to the maze, Iain close behind. Just as they were about to enter, Angus emerged hurriedly, his clothes dishevelled, but his dagger safely tucked away. He nodded at Iain and a message passed between them, puzzling Abby.

"We'll talk back at the apartments," said Iain in a low voice. "They wouldn't dare touch us there."

Silently the two followed Iain back to the palace and it wasn't until the door closed behind them that he turned an angry gaze at them both. Abby glanced at Angus, who was staring at his feet.

"Well?" Iain said. "What were ye doing in the maze? Must I pull it out of ye?"

"I went to meet Longueville just now, only it was a trap. He was there with Damville."

"Damville?" said Iain. He looked at Angus and frowned.

"It wasna my idea. I told her it wasna wise tae go, that it was a trap."

"Yet she went."

"It wasn't Angus's fault. He insisted on going with me and I promised I would leave at the first sign of trouble. And I did."

"Why did ye go in the first place?" asked Iain. He went over to a vacant chair, sat down and poured himself a cup of wine. "Now, start at the beginning and tell me everything."

Abby took a seat opposite, but Angus chose to remain standing, his body straight with only the slightest hint of defiance. After a bite of bread and a sip of her cup Abby recounted the events.

"And you say the men wore the Guise livery?" asked Iain. He sat back in his chair. "The comte and the Guises. Well it's nay surprise there, I suppose. But what does he and the Guises want wi' ye?"

Abby reddened and recalled the great walloping she gave to Damville's nether regions before she'd escaped from him in Scotland. "I suppose the comte was none too happy with the manner of my leaving."

Iain raised a brow. Abby sighed and briefly recounted the incident. Iain grunted and Angus tried to hide a smile.

"Still, I dinna think the comte would go to such lengths just because a slip of a girl got the better of him."

"He did think I was a spy," said Abby.

Iain looked at her and snorted. "I dinna think that's a serious concern of his now," he said.

"Well you might not have a high opinion of my potential as a spy, but that doesn't mean he doesn't. I have gone to the Scottish court and now here I am at the French court. It is possible, you know."

"Aye," said Iain. "Anything's possible."

"It might be something concerning my father," said Abby.

"Perhaps he has my father and wants to use me to force him to cooperate."

Iain shook his head. "Nay, he doesna have your father."

"How do you know?" asked Abby.

"Because I ken where your father is," said Iain.

She blinked. "You do? Why didn't you say?"

"There seemed to be other, more pressing concerns."

She put her hand on his arm. "Where is my father? Is he unharmed?"

"I dinna ken if he is unharmed, but I ken that he is being held somewhere in the southeast, in Burgundy."

"Burgundy? But who's holding him there and why?"

"I dinna ken that either."

"How did you find out? Who told you?"

Iain shrugged. "I made inquiries."

She looked at him and waited, but he offered up no more information.

"I must go southeast, then. Find him."

"Nay," said Iain. "I'll go. Ye'll stay here, with Angus." He looked at Angus. "And this time he'll do a better job of keeping an eye on ye."

She shook her head. "I'm not staying here while my father could be in danger or hurt."

Iain pressed his lips together. "Ye'll stay here and promise to mind Angus."

"I'm not a child, Iain, to be ordered about. I'm coming with you."

"It isna a matter of whether or not ye're a child. It's tae protect ye, tae keep ye safe," he said, his tone matter-of-fact.

"But how safe is it for me to remain behind with Damville here? And surely it's best if you have Angus with you. I promise I won't slow you down."

Iain frowned. Eventually he nodded his assent. "But ye must do as I say at all times. No arguing. Will ye promise that?"

"But…" said Angus, and he shook his head, clearly displeased.

"I promise," she said and gave a wide smile.

Iain sighed. "Make ready for the journey, then. And be quick about it. We'll be travelling light."

SHE WROTE a brief note to the Queen, explaining that it was necessary to depart to meet with her first husband's family and handed it to Angus to deliver to the Queen's apartments. She rose from the table and on impulse went into her father's room where Iain was examining her father's things once more.

"Are you looking for anything in particular?" she asked.

"Nay, just hoping there might be some indication about what he might be doing in Burgundy." He turned to her. "Did he have any connection to Burgundy? Any family or friends there?"

Abby shook her head. "No, I don't think so."

"What about your mother? Where did ye say she was from?"

"Lorraine."

"What about her parents. Are they still alive?"

Abby shook her head again. "I don't know anything about my mother's family. My father refused to speak about her after she left."

"She left? I thought ye said she'd died."

Abby bit her lip. "I said that because that's how it felt."

"Ye mean tae say she isna dead?"

"No," she said softly. "She left when I was young. We've never seen her since."

"What is her name?"

"Marie de Brezé."

Iain considered the name. "A Lorraine family, ye say. And she was in the Guise household?"

"Yes," said Abby. "At least, she was in the household of Queen Marie when she went to Scotland as a bride. That's where my parents met."

Iain looked pensive. "I see."

"Do you think there's a connection?"

"I dinna ken," said Iain. "But for now I would prefer if we took our leave from here with little fuss."

Abby looked at the clothes scattered across the floor. The bedclothes had been straightened somewhat and the doublet Iain had worn the night before lay across the bed. Little else had changed since she'd put his clothes away the day before. She bent over and picked up her father's doublet.

"I know they are ill-fitting, but should I don my father's clothes to help our progress east? I could ride astride and it also might render us less memorable along the way."

Iain gave her a speculative look. "If ye wore something less conspicuous, perhaps," he said reluctantly. "But ye would need better fitting shoes and hose than the last time." He gave a wry smile.

Her face brightened. "I could ask one of the pages to loan me clothes. I could say that a young male servant has arrived from Scotland and only has his plaid, which I, of course, find completely unsuitable for the palace."

"Aye, well," said Iain, an amused look on his face. "I can do that. It's best ye remain here. Hopefully Damville doesna ken that I'm here and he's less likely to discover such a request coming from me."

"Of course," Abby said.

"Wait here. Dinna open the door to anyone but Angus or myself."

Abby nodded and Ian left. She looked at the doublet and

folded it back into the chest. That finished, she straightened the bedclothes and then the piles of papers on the table. She picked up the sheet of paper on top. It was a musical score. The words of the ballad were written underneath. It was a song she was familiar with, but when she looked at the music she discovered it was a different air. An air that was meant to be in Dorian mode, but on this sheet it had been set in Aeolian. Something wasn't right. She looked at it again and matched the words, but they wouldn't fit. The writing wasn't her father's, so her first thought was that it was a mistake.

She studied the piece again and then looked at the words. On impulse, she turned over a scrap of paper, took the quill and began to work out the letters in a different sequence, using D as an interchange for the letter A and so on, with each letter in the alphabet. She looked at the result and snorted. It was an indecipherable mess that had no meaning in French or English as far as she could see. Even her sketchy knowledge of Latin and Greek made her discard her idea.

The outer door opened and Iain entered, clothes draped over his arm, Angus behind him. He came into the room and placed the clothes on the bed.

"Is something amiss?" he asked.

"No, I was just playing with an idea, and it seems I was wrong."

"What idea?"

Abby explained what she'd been doing. Iain came over and looked at the paper where she'd scribbled her letters. He picked up the scrap and stared at it. After a moment he took the quill from her and began crossing out some of the letters. When he was done he laid the piece of paper in front of her. With the letters crossed out she could read the message there, clearly laid out in French: *Come. You are needed. Chateau of the Four Towers.*

"Does this mean anything to ye?" asked Iain.

She shook her head slowly. "It means nothing. I don't know of any Chateau of the Four Towers."

"And the handwriting?"

Abby studied the original piece of paper again, looking for any familiar signs. "No," she said softly. "I don't recognise it at all."

"Well, if this is his reason for his departure, it seems as if he went willingly and to someone he knew."

Abby nodded silently. All he said was true but it gave her no comfort at all.

CHAPTER 20

Abby shifted uncomfortably in her saddle and pulled the bonnet down lower on her head. The pace of their journey had been steady and they'd been riding for several hours now so she was feeling it in the ache of her thighs. The boots Iain had obtained for her pinched her feet, the bonnet was too large and the doublet was tight across her chest, but at least it was better than riding side-saddle in a gown. Iain had made her promise that she would act as his servant and say nothing to anyone, so she would attract little attention. She only hoped that, dressed in a mixture of the Queen's livery and the Dauphin's, she would remain unnoticed.

"Angus, see if there's a stream ahead where we can water the horses," said Iain.

Abby gave an inward thanks. She would welcome the break. With any luck she might be able to ease her feet in the stream and have a bite to eat at the same time. She'd packed a bag with bread and cheese and a wine skin that would last them through the next day, if they were careful. She hadn't asked about sleeping arrangements so she had no idea if they would be dining at an inn or priory or be stuck in a field. Iain hadn't been forthcoming on the subject. In fact they'd spoken little since their hurried departure from the palace.

After a brief foray further afield, Angus returned and told them there was a stream a short distance ahead. They rode a little while more and pulled off the road and headed down a short slope to a glade. Abby could hear the burble of the brook before she dismounted and led her horse in Iain's wake to the water's edge.

The three horses leaned down to take their fill, the reins loose about their necks. Iain removed the sack containing the food from his horse and laid it on the ground. At that signal Abby sat on the bank and tugged off her boots, flexing her toes through her hose. Without thinking she removed her hose and then, suddenly aware of Angus and Iain's looks, draped her cloak over her legs and put her feet in the water. The coolness was delicious and she leaned back and closed her eyes in pleasure.

"It would be best if ye kept your cloak on when ye're in company," said Iain. "Ye're curves are in all the wrong places for a laddie."

"Aye," said Angus. "No many would see ye other than what ye are."

Abby looked down at her doublet and breeches. The breeches weren't full and puffed like the English custom and nearly covered all her thigh. The doublet, on the other hand revealed all the curves of her bust. She'd strapped herself in the best she could, but her breasts had seemed larger than the last time, or her doublet was that much smaller. She sighed and sat up and wrapped her arms around her chest, hiding the tell-tale curves.

Iain opened the pack and withdrew one of the loaves of bread and chunks of cheese. He broke off pieces and shared it among the three of them. They ate in silence and Abby was glad of it, for she was too tired to concentrate on anything but the meal. A little while later Iain murmured something to Angus, who rose, took up the reins of his horse and strode off.

Abby gave Iain a questioning look.

"We seemed to have acquired some friends. Angus is bringing them in," he said softly.

"Friends? How many?" she whispered.

Iain shrugged. "Two, maybe three."

"How long have they been following us?"

"The last few hours."

Abby stared at him. If it was Damville's men following them, why didn't they just overtake? Who else but Damville would be following them? There had been two men by Damville's side at the maze. Perhaps it was those men with Damville. If it was, Abby felt sure he wouldn't hesitate to seize the three of them.

Abby chewed her remaining piece of bread and cheese and tried to appear calm. It would do no good for Iain to see how nervous she felt. What if something happened to Angus and the men decided to attack? She glanced over at Iain, who was busy digging out the wine skin. He took a swig and handed it to Abby, who lifted the wine skin to her mouth and gulped back the wine. It was watered so there was little potency, but it tasted good and eased her tension just a fraction.

Pounding hooves sounded behind her and she looked around, her body tense once more. Through the trees she caught a glimpse of mounted men. She saw Angus's plaid and searched quickly for a sign that he was well.

"I thought ye might like tae meet our friends," said Angus loudly.

"Aye, I would," said Iain, rising. "Bring them here so we can get acquainted."

Angus emerged by the bank leading his horse and two others with men on their back, each with their hands bound and their mouths gagged. They were the men from the maze. Iain rose and dragged them from their mounts one at a time. Angus took hold of one and Iain the other. Iain released the gag from one man's mouth. The man shook his head and moistened his lips.

"Now, suppose you tell me why you were following us," said Iain in French.

The man remained silent, his eyes defiant.

"Perhaps you didn't understand me. I'll give you another chance." Iain slid the dagger from the scabbard at his side and held it up to the man's chin. "Why were you following us?"

The man Angus held made muffled protests until Angus shook him hard. "Be still," Angus said in French.

Abby watched Angus, astonished. She didn't know why she should be surprised that Angus spoke French, but she was. Always on the journeys he had spoken only in English or Gaelic and she'd assumed he had no knowledge of French.

The man in Iain's struggled away from the dagger's point. Iain pressed it closer, drawing blood.

"Someone has you more afraid of them than the point of my dagger," said Iain. "But you're a fool if you think I'm bluffing. I ask again and this is the final time I'll do it nicely. Was it the Comte de Damville who set you on us?"

The man shut his eyes and shook his head.

Iain sighed. "I'm not in the mood for guessing." He took the dagger and pressed it at the man's groin. "Perhaps you have more value for your privates than you do for your neck?"

To emphasise his intent, Iain reached down and clutched the man's groin, hard. The man bent over and moaned in pain.

"Who was it?" asked Iain, his voice deadly cold.

The knife pressed harder. The man howled. Iain squeezed hard again.

"The Duke," he whispered.

"The Duke of Guise?" asked Iain.

The man nodded.

"And why would he want you to follow us?"

The man shook his head. "He said to take the lady and bring her to him."

Iain narrowed his eyes. "What does he want the lady, then?"

The man shrugged. "I don't know, monsieur."

Iain glanced at the other man who stood angrily under Angus's grip. He nodded at Angus. With a quick gesture the man's gag was removed.

"Do you have anything else to add?"

The man shook his head sullenly. "He told you all that I know. We just have the orders, as he said."

"Where is the Duke of Guise?"

The man frowned. "At court."

"Very good," said Iain. "You've both done well."

Iain turned to Abby. "Come, mount your horse," he said in English. "It's time tae go."

While Abby did as she was told, Iain muttered a few phrases in Gaelic to Angus. Angus nodded. Iain packed up the food, gathered up the reins to his own horse and mounted. He gestured to Abby to go ahead of him and they made their way back to the track road silently. Once on the track, Iain urged his horse into a swift trot and Abby followed suit. She glanced briefly behind her and saw there was no sign of Angus.

They carried on without any exchange for a while. Eventually, Iain slowed down the horses and they continued at a fast walk. Abby still felt shaken by the scene she'd witnessed. The suppressed violence in Iain, the deadly intent that was nothing to do with defending oneself. It was something she hadn't witnessed first-hand before.

"Is Angus coming?" she asked, finally unable to hold back any longer.

"Aye, he'll be along."

"And the men? What will did you tell him to do with them?"

"I told him tae take care of them."

She gaped at him, channelling her rage and fear into her response. "Take care of them? What do you mean by that? Surely you haven't told Angus to kill them."

Iain gave her an amused look. "Is that what ye take me for? A cold blooded murderer?"

"How am I supposed to think otherwise? You threaten the man's very life, you draw blood to show your intent."

"Och, dinna fash yourself, *Francach*. Angus will just teach them a lesson."

"Lesson? What kind of lesson?" she asked, her tone suspicious.

"Are ye no worried about these men's intentions?" he asked.

She gave him a furious look. "Of course, but there's no need to murder two men who were only doing the Duke of Guise's bidding." She fell silent a moment. "Why would the Duke of Guise want me? I don't even know him."

"I was hoping ye might be able to tell me."

"No. I've never met him. Or anyone else in his family, except the Dowager Queen, of course. And Queen Mary."

"But ye did say your mother was from Lorraine?"

She nodded. "But I've never been there myself. Dada wouldn't hear of it." She bit her lip at the slip of her pet name for her father.

But Iain made no remark on it and his face remained passive. "Well, there's bound tae be some connection there, I think. We'll carry on for now, heading east and hopefully we can find some answers."

Abby said nothing more, lost in contemplation of his words. She reviewed all she knew of her mother and realised how little it was. Her father's reticence and her own determination to wipe her mother out of her life had made her less than curious about this woman who had chosen to leave her and her father without a word.

It was some while later that Angus caught up with them. He spoke to Iain in Gaelic and Iain nodded.

"Would you be so kind as to repeat that in English," Abby said. "I would like to know what happened to the men."

Angus shot up his brows and looked at Iain. Iain gave a quick nod.

"There's nae need tae worry about them, mistress," said Angus. "It will be some while before they find their way anywhere to make trouble."

"What did you do with them?" she asked.

Angus shrugged. "I let them off tae make their way back to their master on foot."

"But the horses? Where are they?"

"Och, I took them off to the west and set them loose. I dinna think the men will find them with any ease."

"But they belong to the Duke. Someone might steal them before they arrive back."

Angus and Iain looked at her, amused. "Dinna concern your-self wi' that. The horses wear the Duke's colours. Seeing them, some might think it as a chance to win the Duke's favour and hand them back."

Abby gave them a dubious look. She didn't know why she was so concerned about the Duke's horses, except that she felt she didn't want to bring his wrath down upon her for anything more. But was it wrath that the Duke felt towards her? She'd just assumed it was when she saw Damville standing with the two men. Damville who appeared to be working for the Duke of Guise.

It was only when the evening came that Iain saw fit to stop. But since there was no inn or priory to give them a meal and a bed for the night, he felt it best to find somewhere less public and sent Angus ahead to search out a suitable place. On his return, Angus led them to an old dilapidated stable. At this point Abby was grateful to have the chance to lay her head down anywhere, if it meant she could pull off her boots.

The summer evening was still warm and the sun shone on the back of her neck as she dismounted in front of the small stone barn. Angus took the reins from her and led her horse and the others to a stream nearby after Iain had removed the bags. Iain entered the barn and Abby followed. Old straw, some of it damp, was scattered across the dirt floor. The fading evening light shone through a hole in the roof and through some chinks of one of walls of the gable ends. A few stalls were half in place at the dry end.

Iain threw the sacks on the ground in one of the stalls.

Abby gave him a bright smile. "It's dry," she said. She eyed the sacks and the cloak she wore, thinking between them and the bits of straw she might make something of a bed. Iain took off his own light cloak and laid it down, gesturing for her to sit.

"We'll eat first."

She nodded and sat down on the cloak gratefully. Carefully, she unloaded the remains of the bread and cheese. Iain took a seat beside her and reached over for the wine skin. He took a long draught and handed it over to her. Grateful, she followed suit, suddenly aware of his close proximity. When she was finished she sealed the wine skin and put it aside for Angus when he returned. Iain broke off a chunk of bread and handed it to her, their fingers brushing. Abby felt herself redden. She took the bread from him and placed it in her mouth, avoiding eye contact. He picked up the cheese, and using his dagger, broke off a piece and offered it to her. She expressed thanks and when she reached for it he held on to it.

"Are ye well, *Francach*? Ye're no thinking about the Duke, are ye?"

She looked at him and saw the compassion in his startling blue eyes. She took a deep breath and shook her head.

"Och, dinna fash yourself, lass. Ye'll be safe and no harm come to ye. Angus and I will see tae that."

"I know," she said in a strangled voice, looking away. "And I appreciate it. You've been more than kind in helping me with my father."

"There's nae need for thanks, lass," he said softly. "I would do it gladly for ye anyway."

Her breath caught. She lifted her eyes again and regarded him carefully. "Would you?"

He took her hand. "Aye, I would. Ye've done more than enough for me and my kin."

She loosed her hand from his and forced a smile. "I assure you, you're not beholden to me on that account."

He scanned her face, frowning. "Are ye certain ye're no upset?"

"I'm fine," she said more stiffly than she meant to. "Save that chunk of cheese for Angus, I'm not really hungry."

Iain gave her an odd look. She finished the last of her bread. Silently, she worked at removing her boots, until Iain laid a hand on her legs.

"Here, let me help ye."

"No, it's fine. I can manage."

"Dinna be daft, it's easier if someone else does it."

She nodded and leaned back while he slipped his hand under the heel of one of her boots and carefully tugged at it. Eventually the boot came off and she wriggled her toes in her hose, letting out a soft moan of relief. Iain clucked, knelt down and started rubbing her feet, massaging to help the circulation. His touch was sure and so sensuous even through the thickness of the hose, it was all she could do not to snatch her foot away. She closed her eyes, pressed her mouth shut and tried to focus on the ease his fingers gave her feet, rather than how they warmed her body. She remembered Duchamp caressing her there, and despite the rustic surroundings and the unintended sensuousness, Abby felt aflame.

Slowly, Iain took off the other boot and applied the same method to her other foot, then working up her calves, stroking and massaging. Abby licked her lips and stared at the dark head bent so intensely at his task. His fingers stopped and he looked up, as if he sensed her stare. His eyes locked on hers and she could see the heat in them. She parted her lips a fraction, her own breath held and waiting. Iain straightened, his eyes fixing hers. He leaned in closely. The sound of horses hooves and Angus whistling broke the moment. Iain blinked and moved away.

"That should help your feet return to some semblance of life, *Francach*," he said.

Abby only nodded and bent her knees, putting her arms around them. Angus entered and bedded the horses down at the other end of the barn before joining Iain and Abby. He took up his bread and cheese gratefully and washed it down with the remainder of the wine. Abby watched him, saying little, and Iain only gave some half-hearted remarks to Angus's comments.

The meal finished, Angus wrapped his plaid around him, and with a murmur of goodnight, bedded down in the sparse straw. Abby gathered up her cloak and followed suit. The quicker she fell asleep, the better it would be for her peace of mind. She closed her eyes, but couldn't help be aware of Iain creating his own bed next to her, the only available space. It was ages before she was able to fall asleep because she was all too aware of the closeness of Iain's warm body.

CHAPTER 21

Abby dismounted her horse and handed her reins to Angus. She turned to go towards the entrance of the small inn and bumped into Iain. She flushed and muttered an excuse and moved to the right, only to find he'd done the same thing. Iain stopped, gave a mocking bow and allowed her to pass.

The jostling was the latest in a number of emotional and physical dances she seemed to have performed with Iain in the past few days since the first night in the barn. The more care she took to avoid touching him, the more it seemed inevitable that she did. And it wasn't as if Iain was deliberately making an effort to touch her physically, it was more like nature was conspiring to bring them together. Worst of all, part of her appreciated what nature was doing. Her mind however, tried to reason with the rest of her, citing Iain's indifference and determination that their relationship and handfasting was based purely on the needs of his family and his own precarious situation.

These thoughts had crowded her mind as they made their journey, riding with her on the horse and actively seeking attention at night when they'd stayed at various outbuildings in questionable states of repair. Angus and Iain took turns acquiring food and drink for them. Iain felt it best that they minimise any attention along the way, in case someone did manage to follow them, though Abby thought privately that Angus with his hulking form and Scots plaid would attract attention in any part of France. Iain merited attention on other scores, but those less noticeable than being Scots. In this part of France, anyone with little local dialect would be seen as a foreigner, so it mattered not that Iain's accent held hints of his origins.

But now he had decided to stay at this rustic inn, just outside a town. He gave no reason, but Abby was glad for the opportunity to have some privacy in which she could hopefully wash, remove the bindings around her chest and also minister to her sore, abused feet.

A plainly dressed man came out to them and removed his cap. He was small and wiry, with a day's growth of beard. His wife, a stocky woman with a frizz of curls poking from her cap, came behind him, wiping her hands on her apron. Iain greeted them in French.

"You are welcome to our humble inn, mesieurs," said the man.

"We thank you," said Iain. "Would you be able to provide a room for myself and my servants tonight, as well as some food and drink?"

"Bien *sûr*, monsieur," said the man. "We're not very grand here, but the rooms are clean and the plain food is hot and well cooked. My wife makes certain of that."

"That will suit me fine," said Iain.

Iain muttered to Angus to look after the horses and gave the bags to Abby to carry. She took them without a word. The man led Angus off to show him where to stable the horses while the woman led Iain and Abby into the inn.

"If you would like to wait in here by the fire, I'll just see to your room," said the woman.

She ushered them into a small front room where two men sat

by the fire drinking ale from tankards. It was cramped and dark, the only light the feeble fire in the fireplace which smoked badly. The fug from the two men was almost more than Abby could bear. She took a small stool at the opposite end of the room. Iain gave her an amused look and pulled up another stool and sat down beside her, facing the men.

"I hope it doesna take long for her to ready the room," said Iain softly. "I dinna fancy carrying you up the stairs in a dead faint."

She suppressed a laugh and just nodded. She felt giddy with the odour that wafted from the men, combined with Iain's presence, so close and so intimate. They weren't alone, but despite the odour, it felt as though they were. She was aware of the soft intake of his breath, the rise and fall of his chest and every other small movement his body made.

She tried to quash such deep awareness, to shift her mind to something else. Iain patted her hand and she nearly jumped.

"Is it that bad, *Francach*? We can go back outside for some air if ye feel it would do ye good."

"No," she said hoarsely. "I'll be fine."

She sat on the stool and counted her own breaths, taking each one through the mouth and tried hard to listen to the conversation the two men were having. It was difficult to understand, the French too local to catch more than a word or two. She judged by their dress they were farmers of some sort, perhaps come to town for the market.

The door opened and the woman appeared. "All is ready now, monsieur, if you'd like to follow me."

Iain thanked the woman and Abby jumped up, eager to be away. They made their way up the narrow stairs to the small landing. The woman opened one of the doors and went in, Iain and Abby following after her.

"This is our best room, monsieur," she said and gave a small curtsy. "The bed is large enough for the three of you, if you wish, but there's a truckle bed that pulls out."

Abby blinked. She realised how foolish she'd been to think that she might have had a room to herself. She was only a servant. And a servant stayed either in the stable or with his employer.

"I thank you," said Iain.

"Will you be eating?" she asked.

"Yes." He glanced at Abby. "If you don't mind I'll eat up here. And could I have some water for washing, too?"

"Very good, monsieur." She curtsyed again and left.

Abby stared around the room. The beams of the ceiling were so low that Iain had to duck to avoid them, and the small window was crusted with dirt. Two of the tiny panes were cracked. The bed was covered with a worn blanket and she could see the pallet atop it was filled with feathers and most likely lice, but though the sheets were grey with much washing and use, they looked clean.

She went over to the bed and leaned over to pull out the truckle bed that she'd no doubt was her place for the night. She gave the side of it a tug and brought it out from under the bed. It was about half her size.

Abby stared at it in dismay. "Does she think I'm a child?"

"Och, she thinks only that ye're a servant and will make do."

She sighed and lifted the thin blanket that rested on top. Underneath was a bare pallet, no sheet in sight. It was filled with straw that hadn't seen the field from which it was cut in several years.

Angus entered, scanned the room and gave a nod. "Food?" he asked.

"Requested," said Iain. "We'll eat here. The surroundings here are a wee more...salubrious."

"Salubrious is it?" Angus raised his brows. "Well ye might miss a chance tae ask about your wee four towers."

Abby looked at Iain. "Four towers? You mean we're near the area?"

"Aye," said Iain. "There are two farmers downstairs at the moment," he said to Angus. "And even if ye can get close enough tae ask them, I'd be surprised ye unearth anything from them. But still, ye have made a good point. I'll ask the owners and it might be well if ye did some drinking in the town tonight."

"Aye," said Angus. "I'll see what I can find out."

"Shall we all go?" asked Abby. "My French would be better."

Angus and Iain looked her, both amused. "No," they said in unison.

"Why?" she asked.

"Because, lass, ye may bear scrutiny from a distance, wi' your bonnet pulled down and no speaking, but ye'll no pass muster at any close exchange."

"I managed well enough at Glenorchy."

Iain snorted. "Aye wi' those wrapped up in their own affairs." He looked her up and down. "And ye're wearing clothes that do more tae reveal your womanly curves than hide it."

She glanced down again at her body and frowned. Was she so curved?

"If I kept my cloak on?"

"No," said Iain. "We'll take nae chances and that's that. Angus can go on his own. He'll be less noticeable."

"Not wearing that plaid, he won't," said Abby.

Iain eyed Angus. "Weel, maybe it would be best if ye wore my clothes."

"No!" said Angus holding fast to his plaid. "I willna wear the hose. I'd sooner go naked."

"That would certainly not go unnoticed," muttered Abby.

"Angus, man, just put on the doublet and breeches."

Angus looked at Abby meaningfully.

"I'll go outside a moment," she said.

She waited there until the door was opened and was just about to step back inside when the innkeeper's wife came up the steps with the jug of water and a wooden bowl. She handed them to Abby.

"I'll be up with the food shortly," she said.

Abby nodded. She entered the room and set the jug and bowl on the small table. She looked at Angus, awkwardly clad in Iain's other doublet and breeches. The doublet barely closed over his stomach and the ties of his breeches were only just fastened into a knot.

"You look very nice, Angus," said Abby.

Angus glowered at her. "Aye, well it'll do for the night."

True to her promise, the innkeeper's wife arrived a moment later with the food and set it down on the floor beside the bed, the only available space. The fare was unpromising. A hunk of cheese and three bread trenchers filled with an uncertain liquid content were on the tray. A flagon of watered wine was also there, along with three small tankards.

Angus took his trencher first and ate a big mouthful while the other two eyed him dubiously. After the second mouthful he looked up and shrugged.

"It's filling," he said.

Abby sat on the bed and took one of the other trenchers while Iain took the remaining one and stood beside Angus. He had been overzealous in his praise. The soup was thin enough, but at least it was hot. The three of them ate in silence. When Angus was finished, he wiped his mouth with his sleeve and glanced in the flagon.

"If ye dinna mind, I think I'll do my drinking in the town."

Iain smiled and nodded. "Aye. Ye're so kind tae leave us your share."

Angus disappeared out of the door and Abby turned back to her food. There was only her small portion of cheese left and she decided to save that for later. Iain poured some of the watered wine into her tankard and gave the rest to himself. Abby took a mouthful. The amount of water it contained couldn't disguise the sour taste. She made a face.

"Not the finest vintage, is it?" said Iain.

"Best given to the horses."

"They have likely fared better."

She gave a slight smile and put down the tankard. "I think I'll leave it for now."

Iain gathered up the tankards and the flagon and put them onto the tray. "I'll just take these down and talk to the innkeeper. See what I can find out."

After he left Abby sat on the bed for a moment and sighed. She looked down at her boots and on impulse decided to remove them and give her feet some ease. She stood up and took off her doublet first, to improve her movement while she tugged. The boots came off eventually and she groaned at the relief of releasing her toes from their captive agony. There was a little blood on the hose at her heels and at her toes. Carefully she removed the hose from one leg and examined the foot. Two of her toes had blood crusted on them and the heel was red raw. When she removed the hose on her other leg, she found the other foot in no better condition.

She reached for the jug, poured some water into the bowl and used one of her hose to clean the crusted blood away, cooling the heat in her feet at the same time. When she was finished she lifted her feet on the bed and examined them. The bathing had improved them somewhat, but they still looked angry at the heels and the toes were tender with newly formed scabs. The door opened. Iain entered the room and halted abruptly when he saw her on the bed her legs up.

"Och, your poor feet," he said.

Abby swung her legs off the bed. "Sorry, I was just tending them." She reached for the hose, but they were wet.

Iain knelt down beside her on the floor and raised one foot to examine it. He gave a tsk, put it down and examined the other one. Abby stared down at his dark tousled hair, marvelling at the manner in which it curled. She resisted the urge to run her fingers through them. She could feel his hands, warm and tender in their touch.

"They're in a right state," Iain said.

He looked up at her and his eyes darkened. She leaned down towards him, drawn by his eyes. His hand reached around her head and pulled her towards him. Their lips met. The kiss deepened and he rose, lifting her up with him so that they stood together. She slid her arms around his neck, embracing him. She felt his arms enfold her, sweeping her against his body. She moaned softly, the taste of him filling her mouth and setting her on fire.

He pulled away and shook his head. "Nay," he said. "We canna do this. We canna break the terms."

"No one will know," she murmured.

She kissed him again and he groaned. She felt him give, drawing her in closer. She pulled away and removed her shirt, keeping her eyes locked with his. Slowly, she unbound the cloth that around her chest, unwinding the fabric in a sensuous movement. She took his hand and placed it on one of her breasts, her body responding to his touch. He groaned softly and leaned down to kiss each breast, at the same time unfastening the ties that held her breeches. The breeches dropped to the floor. She lifted up his head and kissed him on the mouth, fumbling with his doublet. He pulled away, removed his boots and clothes quickly, and drew her onto the bed with him.

He ran his hand along her skin, kissing her mouth, her neck

and breasts. He caressed her thighs slowly, eventually inserting his fingers inside her. She arched slightly and pressed her body closer to his, wanting more. She could feel him hard against her and she parted her legs, knowing that this was what she wanted above all things. Reading her body, he complied and with a sharp pain she found him inside her. She stilled a moment, registering the pain, but then responded, matching his rhythm, her skin and bones melting into his.

When they were both spent, he lay for a moment on top of her, looking at her, his eyes still clouded with desire. She ran her hand through his curls, as she'd wanted to do earlier and pulled him in to kiss her, parting her lips. He kissed her back for a moment, then pulled away.

"Och, quean, ye'd have me go again if ye're no careful."

She laughed and kissed his nose. "Would that be a bad thing?"

He gave her a sheepish grin. "I dinna ken if my body can withstand many seizes of that nature so soon."

He rolled off her body and propped his head on one arm, scanning her body. He felt her thighs, frowned and looked up at her.

"I thought ye were a widow."

"I am."

"But--. This was your first time? How can that be?"

She reddened. "My husband couldn't bed me. He was too ill."

Iain rolled on his back and put his hand over his eyes. "My god, what have I done?"

Abby rested a hand. "Why are you so upset? You assumed I wasn't a virgin and so does everyone else."

"Ye mean your father doesna know?"

"No," she said sharply.

He looked at her carefully. "Ye kept that all tae yourself, why?"

She sighed and looked away. "To spite his family, I suppose. And because I didn't want to have people saying I wasn't even attractive enough to get my husband to bed me. They certainly inferred it often enough before we were married."

Iain shook his head. He ran his hand along her neck and down along her shoulder.

"Ye're beautiful, quean. Do ye no ken that, *mo bhilis?*" He stared at her, his blue eyes filled with desire.

Abby blinked back the tears that came and he leaned down and kissed her again. She wrapped her arms around him and pulled him down on top of her, wanting him to make love to her again, have him fill her up again with his desire and she would fill him up with her love.

IN THE DARK, Abby lay in her truckle bed and smiled. Underneath her paltry blanket she was wearing her breeches and shirt once again, with the cloth binding her breasts. In the other bed next to her was Iain. He was still awake, judging by his breathing. Angus hadn't returned but the two of them waited for him, like soldiers awaiting battle. It wasn't as if she feared that Angus might discover what they'd done. No, for her it was that this special time would end and they would behave as if nothing had happened.

Such a deception would be difficult for her. How could she ever act as though she didn't desire him with every bit of her, every moment? But he had said nothing more about providing opportunities for them to make love again and she hadn't brought it up. She took a deep breath.

"Iain?" she said softly.

"Hmm?"

"We could get my father's agreement to the handfast. I'm sure he would have no objection."

She heard him stir. "Abby, dinna do this. Ye're father willna agree."

"You don't know that," she said with a hint of pleading.

"I do. I'm an outlaw, all but. And my family's standing is uncertain. No father would want that for his daughter."

"No, you're wrong. If I asked him, he would. And besides, the problem with your family will all come right. The Dowager Queen will see to it."

"It's no a certainty," his voice hard and firm. "I've nothing tae offer ye but hardship and I willna do that."

"I see," she said quietly. She wouldn't press it. It was clear the matter was closed. He didn't want to marry her and that was that.

CHAPTER 22

*A*ngus glanced at Abby and Iain, his face puzzled. "That wine seemed tae have soured your temper as well as your stomachs. The pair of ye look as miserable as death."

He had returned reeking of drink and other odours Abby didn't want to name, soon after her conversation with Iain. He fell into bed and was snoring almost immediately. Now, in the light of day, they all looked worse for wear in one way or another.

"I'm fine," said Abby.

Iain muttered something indistinguishable, but Abby refused to look at him. She'd lain awake all night nearly and had decided she would say as little as possible to him and avoid him at all costs.

"Did ye find anything in the town besides a sore head and a possible dose of the pox?" asked Iain.

Angus gave him a rueful look. "I did try. But they had little to say, though they werena averse tae a drink or two. At my expense."

"Or even three," muttered Iain.

"Aye, well. The end of it is that there's nae Four Towers around here. At least none that I could discover."

Iain frowned. "There must be something. Perhaps they dinna call it Four Towers. Did ye ask if there were any holdings with four towers?"

Angus shrugged. "Aye, but that doesna mean there isna a place like that around here. Do ye want me tae go search?"

Iain shook his head and glanced sideways at Abby. "Nay, we'll go together."

ABBY RUBBED HER ACHING BACK, glad for the opportunity to rest a moment. They'd been riding for three days and still they'd found nothing. They'd asked a few carters they'd encountered on one of the roads and that had brought no further enlightenment, except that there were two estates further east where they might glean information.

Though she was tired, she'd made no objection to the gruelling ride since it gave her little opportunity to mull over the events of that night and it made speech to either Angus or Iain impossible. Her body ached physically, but it was the ache of her heart that caused her the most pain. Iain had kept his distance at night but she made an effort to brush off his behaviour and listen to the little voice in her head that persuaded her that all would be fine. Once her father's freedom was secured he would give them permission to marry. He would see how much she cared for Iain and wouldn't refuse her.

In front, Iain and Angus spoke in a low undertone in Gaelic. Angus nodded. He urged his horse forward and headed down a small track that led off in a wide curve from the road on which they travelled and disappeared into a woodland.

Abby sat in silence for a while, until she couldn't contain herself any longer. "Why did Angus go down there?"

"The track is wide enough for a carriage. I sent him down it tae see what lay at the end of it."

She nodded, cursing her own stupidity. Of course, with a track that wide it made sense that a large building of some note was at its end. The silence continued between them. Abby shifted in her saddle, took her left boot from one of the stirrups and stretched it out. Eventually, she heard horse's hooves and gave a sigh of gratitude.

When Angus appeared he halted his horse and gave a nod. Iain urged his horse forward. Quickly, Abby replaced her foot in the stirrup and followed. They drew up alongside of Angus.

"Four towers?" asked Iain.

"Ye could say that," said Angus, grinning. "And then again ye could say there are three and a half. One is falling down."

Iain snorted. "Aye, sounds promising. Did ye see anything?"

"I dinna get too close. I stayed at the edge of the wood and watched for a wee while, but didna see anyone. The shutters are open on one side, though."

Iain nodded. "We'll wait until dark and then see if we can find out."

"But what if he is in there? What will you do?" asked Abby.

He looked at her, his face impassive. "We'll find a way in and get him out."

"But how?"

He sighed. "Trust me, we'll find a way. In the meantime ye can bide here, where you'll be safe."

"But why not approach whomever is there directly? See what's going on inside and what manner of people they are?"

He gave her an amused look. "Aye, and I'll introduce myself and make inquiries after your father."

"No," she said coldly. "I meant something more subtle. I could approach them as a servant, offer to sell them some of my wares."

"Och and what wares would that be?" he said, an edge to his voice. "They would ken ye were a woman right away, *Francach*. I've told ye that."

"But what if I was dressed as a servant woman and one of you came with me?"

"Nay, and that's an end tae it."

Angus eyed Iain. "She has a point. It might work."

Iain frowned at Angus. Eventually he grunted. "We'd have tae get ye the right clothes."

"Surely we could buy some from a small farmholding around here."

Iain looked at Angus and nodded. "Aye, I suppose. See if ye can scare some up. We'll stay here and keep a watch up by the edge of the woodland."

ABBY BLINKED her eyes and tried to sharpen their focus. A soft rain had begun. She'd been staring at the house for what seemed like days and still had observed nothing. It was large, sprawling three-storey stone building forming a square, towers at each corner. The tower that faced them was half in ruins. But for the open shutters on one window, the place appeared deserted.

Abby fidgeted again. She had a cramp in her legs from sitting with them bent close to her chest. Beside her, Iain remained motionless. They'd exchanged only a few words since they installed themselves at the edge of the wood and began their vigil. They'd left the horses tied to a tree in the woods.

She eased her back and moved her head a few times to either side. When she turned her head back she saw a slight flicker at the unshuttered window. She nudged Iain and pointed. He nodded. At least now they knew there was definitely someone in there.

A faint rustling came from behind and Angus crouched beside them. He thrust a bundle of clothes at Abby.

"Any signs?" he said softly.

"Aye, something in thon window, bottom left, first one."

"Thanks for the clothes," Abby said to Angus. "Shall I go and change then?"

Iain looked over at her, glanced at the bundle and his eyes hardened. He nodded.

She rose and made her back towards the horses. Upon unwrapping the bundle, she saw with dismay that Angus had neglected to get shoes. She sighed and quickly donned the skirt and jacket he'd brought and frowned at the result. Her hair hung in damp locks, but there was nothing to be done about that. The jacket, however, was low cut and tight enough that she could barely breathe. She made some adjustments. Her breasts, released from their bindings, were all too visible. She tugged at her shirt, pulling it up. The ties hung loosely outside of the jacket, and after a moment's hesitation she decided to let them be. Perhaps it wasn't so bad that she was revealing some of her attributes. Wouldn't that be the best way to distract them?

She stuffed her remaining clothes into the bag, tied it to her horse and made her way back to Iain and Angus. The two were deep in conversation in Gaelic. She crouched down beside them.

"Is all well? Has something happened in the house?"

Iain looked at her and started to open his mouth and shut it.

"Nay," said Angus.

"I want ye tae promise ye'll no take any risks and do as I tell ye."

She nodded. "Of course."

"There's nae 'of course' about it. I want ye tae promise."

"I promise," she said solemnly.

Satisfied, he turned to Angus. "Ye'll stay close tae the house, by the door. I'll let ye in when I can."

"Aye," said Angus.

Iain shoved a small basket into Abby's arms. "Here, Angus brought this as well. Ye're tae make like ye want tae sell them to the owner."

She looked down and lifted the worn cloth that covered the basket. Four barely ripe apples and a jug rested inside.

"Apples?" she said. "You think that will tempt them to let us in?"

"Nay, I dinna think the apples are tempting at all," he said, his tone sardonic.

She looked up at him and flushed. "Oh. Of course."

"But ye're no tae leave my side, do ye hear?" he said.

She nodded. "As you say."

Iain unfastened the belt that held his dagger case and hid the dagger inside his doublet. With a nod to Angus, he rose and held a hand out to Abby.

"We'll walk back a ways. Until we're out of sight of the house and make our way tae the track, walking from there."

He led her back through the woods and then across to the track. They emerged in the half light of the dusk that was falling and walked towards the house. Abby could feel the tension build inside her. Part of her hoped there was no one inside, except perhaps a decrepit old steward, or that the flicker they'd glimpsed had been a trick of the light.

Carrying her basket, Abby followed Iain to the side of the house and through a small archway that opened up to the court-yard beyond. Pieces of cut stone and loose cobbles were scattered at the far end where the ruined tower lay. Iain gestured to the small door to the left. Abby gripped the basket tightly, went up to the door and knocked hard. She could feel Iain looming behind her, making his presence known.

There was no sound behind the door. Abby knocked again, harder, her knuckles stinging smartly with the force. She waited and was about to turn away when she heard a faint noise. A few moments later the door opened and a stocky, swarthy skinned man with dark hair stared at her, his expression surly.

"*Oui?*" he asked.

Abby gave him a bright smile and pushed the wet hair from her face. "*Bonjour*, monsieur. I'm so sorry to disturb you, but I wonder if I might show you these goods I have in my basket. I see you have no orchard on your estate. My father is only a small farmer but he produces only the best quality apples and cider. If you like them, indeed he will be glad to supply you."

Abby pulled back the cloth that covered the basket and held it up beside her chest. The man glanced at the basket and then the soft swell of her breasts just visible in the opening of her shirt. He smiled and grunted, making way for her. She mounted the small step and went through the door. The man put up his arm, barring Iain.

"Not you. You can wait outside," the man said in thickly accented French.

"Oh, please don't make him wait in the rain," said Abby, cocking her head. "He is a halfwit and my brother. You'll get no trouble from him."

Iain gave the man a daft smile and nodded. He held out his hand. "Friend?"

The man frowned but in the end let Iain pass, then stopped him just inside the door. "Stay here and behave."

Iain nodded brightly. The man pushed Abby through the corridor to another room beyond. Inside she could see it was a kitchen. There was no fire lit, but a soft glow from a single candle on the table gave a little light. Another man was seated at a worn table. He was younger, fairer and slightly built, but his clothes were better quality. He spoke to the other man in rapid Italian.

The man shook his head and muttered something. He took Abby's basket from her and set it down on the floor.

"Come closer," said the younger man.

Abby edged forward. She reached down for her basket and plucked out an apple. "Would you like to taste the apple? My father has an orchard and makes the finest drink with it."

He reached out and instead of taking the apple he grabbed her wrist and pulled her towards him.

She pouted at him and moved away slightly. "You don't like apples, monsieur?"

"Never mind the apples," he said. "I have my eye on other treats." He grabbed her around the waist and pulled her onto his lap. She pulled away and tapped him on his arm in a playful manner.

"Oh, monsieur, I can understand you want some entertainment, but can I have your assurance that it will be worth my while?"

The man reached for the pouch at his side and threw some coins on the table. He grabbed her again. She pulled away.

"Surely we can go somewhere private?" she glanced at the other man who stood staring at her.

The younger man hesitated a moment and then nodded. Abby scooped up the money on the table. The younger man took her by the arm and led her through another door to a hall beyond. He stopped at the first door and opened it. It was dark and Abby could barely make out the sparse furniture arranged in the large room. The man drew her inside and shut the door behind them.

"Is this private enough?" he said.

He pulled her in against him and locked his arm around her waist, then planted his mouth on the swell of her breast and sucked, one hand hoisting up her skirts. She put her hands against his chest and tried to push him away.

"There's no need to rush. Let's have time so we both can enjoy this."

"I paid for my enjoyment, not yours," said the man.

Abby glanced at the door, praying for it to open, but it remained firmly shut. She glanced around the room, looking for something with which to hit him. He backed her up against the wall hard and pressed his mouth down against hers while he fumbled with the ties of his codpiece. She attempted to raise her knee to his groin but he caught her leg and forced it aside, spreading her legs wide.

"Playing it that way are you?"

He grinned and shoved his hand at her groin, searching, while he pinned her arms behind her with his other hand. She leaned over and bit his ear hard. He yowled in pain dropped his hand. She shoved hard and he staggered back, but recovered immediately. He grabbed at her, threw her to the floor and came down on top of her. Holding her hands together above her head, he hoisted up her skirts and forced her legs apart, positioning himself to enter her. Abby closed her eyes. A moment later she felt the full weight of his body on hers. She opened her eyes and saw Iain looming over her, the jug in his hand.

"Took you long enough," she said, making an effort to keep the tremble from her voice. "But then I could expect nothing more from a halfwit."

"My apologies, *Francach*," he said. "By the time ye'd disappeared and I let Angus in another man decided tae join us. He took a bit of persuading tae allow me tae come here."

He rolled the man off of her and she sat up, straightening her clothes. It was an effort to keep her hands from shaking. "Any sign of my father?"

"I've been a wee busy yet, tae find out. Angus is looking for him now."

Abby rose and shook out her damp hair. She could still smell of the man's sweat on her. She sniffed. "Is he dead?"

Iain shook his head. "Nay. He'll be out for a while, but we'll want tae question him."

She nodded and looked at Iain. "They spoke Italian."

"Yes."

She gave him a searching look. "Did you understand what they said?"

"Aye. It was nothing of importance."

He held out his hand to her. "Come, let's find Angus and hopefully your father."

She allowed him to lead her out into the corridor, half of her mind still on the floor with that man and what might have been. They made their way silently down the corridor, checking each room, through to the next wing, until they met Angus standing by a door, listening. Angus held his finger to his lips and pointed to the handle, shaking his head. Locked. Iain gestured with his head and Angus disappeared back down the hall. Abby waited tensely beside Iain, listening for all she was worth. A stirring came from within.

"Who's there?" came a whisper in French.

"A friend," said Iain softly.

He spoke a few words in Gaelic.

"Iain?" came the voice, louder.

"Father?"

"Abby!"

"Yes, Father. We've come to get you out of here. We're just getting the key."

"What are you doing here?"

"Shhh. I'll explain later," she said.

A short while later Angus returned, holding up a key. He put it in the lock and turned it. The door swung open and Calum stood there, bearded and unkempt. Abby rushed into his arms.

"Father, oh thank God, you're safe!" She kissed him on the cheek and hugged him tightly.

Calum stroked her head and made some comforting noises.

She drew away and looked at him. "What happened, how is it you're here?"

"Never mind, we'll talk about that later." He looked at Iain, a question in his eyes.

"Two men are bound and gagged in the kitchen and the other one… is incapacitated in another room."

"Horses?" asked Calum.

Iain nodded. "Three, tied in the woodland."

Calum nodded. "We must be quick, though. There are more and they could be back at any time. Angus, bring the horses to the courtyard. Iain, take Abby outside tae wait. I'll just have a word with the captives."

Angus disappeared down the corridor. Iain put his hand on Abby's shoulder and steered her back along the way they'd come, Calum following closely. Even as they moved Abby could hear the sound of horses in the distance.

"Quickly," said Calum. They ran down the corridor and back through to the small side door where Abby and Iain had entered less than an hour before. Darkness had descended completely now, and only a few stars lit the sky. Abby grabbed her skirts with one hand, trying not trip in her effort to keep up with Iain. Her father grabbed her other hand and the two dashed through the archway in Iain's wake. They made for the woodland, running hard now, as the horses came into sight. Abby prayed that they wouldn't notice the three of them in the noise and confusion of their arrival. There were four or five men, all armed with swords and wearing a livery she didn't recognise.

Her father jerked her forward to close the distance that remained to the cover of the trees and she collapsed on the ground, breathing hard. He picked her up with a quick kiss on her cheek and led her on again. Iain glanced back briefly and began weaving his way through the woods. They crossed the track to the other side, out of sight of the house, making their way back to where the horses were tied. Angus waited there and gave a relieved smile when he saw them.

"I heard the horses," he said. "Thought it best tae wait here and see before doing anything more."

"Good man," said Calum.

Angus handed Calum Abby's horse. He mounted and then hoisted Abby up behind him, astride, her skirts spread. She threaded her arms around her father's waist and rested her head on his back. Iain and Angus mounted and they urged their horses onward.

CHAPTER 23

She dismounted with relief, not realising how often she'd held her breath during their mad dash across the countryside. Fortunately, the stars had provided them with enough light to prevent any mishap with the horses' footing. Still, the ride had left her exhausted. Any moment she'd expected to hear horses thundering closer towards them, giving chase.

It was only when the night was half gone that Calum allowed them to stop at this old ruined cottage, with its roof half caved in. She sighed now, yearning for a place to collapse and permit the joy at her father's safe return to fill her. Iain entered the cottage, propping open the door and making way for Calum and Abby to enter.

"I'll just help Angus with the horses," said Iain, flatly.

"Nay, come in. There are things we need tae speak about."

Abby looked at her father in the dim light and tried to read his mood. The tension was evident, but there was something underneath it. She put her hand on his arm and he gave her a considering look.

"Aye, both of ye."

Calum ushered Abby through the door, his arm on her back,

as if to ensure she wouldn't slip away. Iain came in behind them and shut the door. He leaned against it, his body braced.

"Well?" said Calum.

"We had word ye were missing. We came tae find ye," said Iain, his face expressionless.

Calum looked at Abby. "And how do ye explain my daughter?"

"I made him take me with him," she said. "If you're going to blame anyone for my appearance, blame me."

Calum looked at Iain. "Made ye, did she? And just how did that happen?"

Iain looked at him silently for a moment. "As she said, it wasna my choice, but I was persuaded that it was best she come with us. It wasna safe for her tae remain at court."

Calum's eyes narrowed. "Court? What court? I thought she was safe at Glenorchy, companion to Lady Arbella."

"Aye, well, she had tae leave Glenorchy," said Iain.

"And why is that? Did ye have anything tae do with that?"

"Nay, I'd already left."

"You'd left?" He glanced at Abby. "Aye, well, we'll save that for later."

"I left of my own accord, Father," said Abby. "It had nothing to do with Iain."

"And how is it the two of ye are here together now?"

Abby took a deep breath. "It's a long story."

"I'm listening."

She rested her hand on his arm and gave a brief account of the events that prompted her to leave Glenorchy and go to Glen Strae. She squeezed his arm. "It's fine, Dada," she said softly. "Iain has been more than kind. He's a good man."

"Aye, I ken Iain well enough." He glared at Iain. "He is a man tae have at your side when the fighting is fierce, but not when ye want your daughter's virtue cared for."

"You're wrong. Iain is good and honourable." She squeezed

his arm. "Please Father. We were handfasted in front of his father who gladly gave his permission. I ask now that you give it."

"Handfasted!" Calum shook her off and moved towards Iain, his face filled with anger. Abby reached out and pulled her father back.

"Dada, please. What are you doing?"

Calum turned to her. "Ye canna marry Iain. It's impossible."

"But why? I don't understand. The MacGregors are an ancient family. We would do well to be linked with them."

"It's nought tae do with the family," said Calum with a growl.

"Then what is it about Iain that makes him unacceptable?"

She looked at Iain. He stared at her father intently.

"What is it between you two?" She narrowed her eyes. "Just how is it you know each other? I never met Iain before Glenorchy. As far as I know, he was never at the French court the whole time I was there. And no mention was made of him, either."

Iain looked at Calum and raised a brow.

Abby glanced at the two men. "What is going on? Your manner towards each other back at the chateau, it was like people who knew each other well and are used to taking orders from you, Father." She planted herself in front of Calum. "Tell me. I have a right to know," she said firmly.

Calum frowned at her. "Iain is commissioned to do things that often involve great danger. It takes a reckless man tae do these kind of things. And reckless men make poor husbands, and they often make dead husbands. I dinna want that for my daughter."

"You mean he's a spy?" She gave Iain a disbelieving look. His eyes were fixed on her father, his face expressionless. "And who gives him these commissions?"

"Supporters of the Queen," said Iain softly. "I work tae protect her. There are many who would have her dead or remain in France under French control."

Abby turned to her father. "And who does he report to, Father?" she asked softly.

Her father looked down at her and patted her arm. "Enough of this. I'll hear nae more about marriage tae Iain." He glanced at Iain. "I expect Angus and yourself tae be gone at first light. I'll see tae my daughter."

"Where are you taking me, then?" she said, her heart sinking.

"Ye'll go home, tae Scotland, where ye'll be safe."

"Home?" she said. "What home?"

"Strathbogie."

She looked at him, puzzled. "Where's that?"

"In the Highlands. It's the seat of the Gordons."

She went to open her mouth, but he put his finger against her lips and kissed her cheek. "Nay, they'll be nae more talk for now. It's time for rest. There's a long journey ahead of us."

She looked over at Iain, but he'd turned away, his face in shadow. She allowed her father to lead her to a corner of the room and settle her on the floor, her mind awash with emotion. It was almost too much to take in and her body was protesting with all she'd put it through for too long. Her father sat down beside her and pulled her in close against him. She shut her eyes and with that, tried to shut out the misery that was beginning to weigh her down.

ABBY WATCHED Iain swing his bag up on the horse and tie it there. She'd heard him and Angus stir in the early morning and quietly prepare to leave. Silently, she'd waited for him to signal her, or approach her so that they could say goodbye, away from where her father slept fitfully. When he and Angus had made their way outside, she'd crept quietly after them, watching from just inside the doorway.

Iain turned and caught sight of her. He glanced over at Angus, who nodded and led his horse onward, towards the track that would take them to the coast. Iain took her by the arm and led her to a small cluster of trees.

"So, you would have left without saying goodbye?" she asked, fighting for control.

Iain raised a hand to her face, but she shook it off. "Nay, lass. I would say goodbye tae ye. And that's what it must be, goodbye."

"Why didn't you tell me?" she said querulously.

"Tell ye?"

"Tell me that you were a spy?"

He gave her a weary look. "Ye ken why."

"How long? Were you spying at Glenorchy?" she asked. She thought about all the little incidents that at the time had her convinced of all manner of things, except that he was a spy. "So, it seems that it wasn't me who was the spy at Glenorchy."

"I was there to observe Glenorchy's interaction with the French and also to see if he had any contact with the English."

"At whose orders? My father's?"

He blinked at her, his expression unreadable. "I canna say, ye ken that."

"And the reason you left Glenorchy? Was it because of the man who died? The one you said you knew?"

"Partly."

"And what part would that be?"

He took her hand and held it, his thumb caressing hers. "Dinna fash yourself, lass. All I spoke tae ye was true, ye must believe that. I dinna care tae see ye in any more danger than ye were in. And I dearly regret that I had tae leave ye."

She struggled against his grip. "All of this...ruse between us, was that part of a greater plan to unearth information, to spy?"

He frowned at her. "Ye mustna believe that, quean," he said quietly. "It's because I do care for ye, care for ye too much that I tried to part with ye, keep ye at a distance as much as I could. I had nae illusions what your father would think about me as your betrothed, or connected tae ye in any way."

"So you care for my father's opinion so much do you?"

He gave a frustrated growl. "This is no a game, *Francach*. There's real danger involved and it's many's the time I've barely escaped wi' my life." He touched the mostly healed wound at his side. "Your father's right. I'm no the person for ye."

"He's wrong," she said. "But if you don't want to marry me, then that's fine. We'll dissolve the handfast." She started to slip the ring off her finger, but he closed her hand and held it.

"Nay," he said. "I would have ye keep the ring, quean." He lifted her hand and kissed it tenderly. "Remember me as a feckless Scots who loved ye madly, but also poorly."

He released her hand and turned and Abby watched him walk away, speechless. She blinked back the tears.

SHE STOOD at the ship's rail and felt the breeze blow against her face. It reminded her of the journey across to France with Iain. He'd been so careful of her and helped her through her sea sickness. Now, though her stomach churned, she knew she was much better here, above deck than down below, retching the whole time, fighting her feelings of despair. Her father stood silently beside her, his thoughts elsewhere. He'd refused to answer any of her questions, brushing her off with his own words of concern.

They'd arrived at Calais after a week's hard riding. It was there he'd arranged for better clothes and a woman to attend her. The woman stood on her other side, dark haired, stocky and middle aged. A solid woman, widowed with no children. Her father had beamed at the sight of her.

Abby glanced at her now, wondering what a French servant, used to town life, would make of the Scottish Highlands. Probably a lot less than she had. Still, she'd never been to Strathbogie.

"Are we staying at Strathbogie for good?" she asked her father.

"Ye will stay as long as it's necessary," he said. His face softened. "Dinna fash yourself. Ye'll be fine."

"But what about you?" she asked, studying his face. In these past few days she'd found herself looking at her father carefully, trying to reconcile this strange person with the womaniser, the lovable drunkard, gambler and musician that she'd known her father to be. This new father, this person who courted danger and carried an air of danger himself, would take some getting used to. Yet still, there was some deep current underneath that was still her father. The man who loved her, had ensured she knew of that love, even when her mother had left and it was just the two of them.

"Och, I canna stay. I've matters tae tend."

"Where are you going then?" she asked sharply. "You're not going back to court, are you? What about those men? They may try to find you there and take you again."

"Nay, I'll not be going tae court. Not for a good while."

She cocked her head. "You know who it was that drew you to that place, don't you? Who was it?"

"I canna tell ye. I'm no sure myself."

She narrowed her eyes. "You know."

"Hush, child."

"I'm not a child, Father," she said firmly.

She stared down at her finger which still carried Iain's ring. "You will see that Iain and his clan are pardoned, won't you?"

He stared at her hard. "I will. On one condition."

"What condition?"

"That ye agree to never see Iain again. The handfast will be revoked."

She took a deep breath, fingering the ring. "I agree," she said quietly.

They stood in silence for a while. Abby stared out to the sea. The waves rocked against the ship. She could feel the tug of the sails pulling them forward.

"The Gordons," she said, eventually. "So we are related to the Gordons at Strathbogie. The earl's clan."

"Aye, in a manner of speaking."

"What manner of speaking?"

"A manner that amounts tae little at this time," he said, his face set. "But I will have ye safe."

She sighed, realising she would get little else from him. Ahead, she could make out the shapes of a landform. Scotland. The place that held her next home and the place that held Iain. Would she ever see him again? In her heart she was certain she would, no matter what her father said. She would see to it. She couldn't imagine anything else.

TRY the next novel in the series that concludes Abby's story. Read the excerpt from The **Braes of Huntly** *at the end of the book.*

As mentioned in the previous novel, *The Hostage of Glenorchy*, during the time of this novel, Scotland was in tumult. King James V had died when Mary was days old and, as his only living child, Mary became Queen. Her uncle, the Earl of Arran, was appointed Regent, much to the dismay of Mary's mother, Mary of Guise. The Earl of Arran was weak and a poor enough soldier. The Scottish lords and chiefs, used to years of exercising their authority, argued among themselves, vied for greater power and manipulated Arran while Scotland's borders were constantly overrun by soldiers of King Henry VIII. Mary of Guise decided the best course of action to counter this issue was for Scotland to form an alliance through a marriage of her daughter to the heir to the French throne. Many Scots were against such an alliance, fearing that the French would annex Scotland. When Mary was five, a treaty agreeing to the marriage was signed and Mary went to live in France, at the French court. The lords, the Earl of Arran, the French and Mary of Guise continued to plot, quarrel and vie for power in the following years.

This novel takes place when Queen Mary is fourteen. A few years before, at the end of 1551, an archer of the guard, Robert

Stuart, was arrested and accused of attempting to poison Mary. He confessed and implied that he was an English spy, though it was never entirely clear who instigated the plot. Stuart was executed as a traitor in France, before it was ever clear who had planned it.

The rivalry between the MacGregors and the Campbells is based on fact. Originally the MacGregor holdings stretched from Glenorchy in Argyll to Perthshire. They claimed descent from Grogar, a son of Alpin and they had the motto, 'Royal is my name.' But their lands bordered the Campbells who in the late 15th century used every possible legal and illegal means and various representations to the king to encroach on larger and larger tracts.

The Guise family were based in the French province of Lorraine and were very powerful. Mary/Marie of Guise married King James IV of Scotland. Her father was the Duke of Guise and her uncle the Duke of Lorraine. Marie's daughter, Mary, became Queen as a newborn, after her father's death on the battlefield. At this time Marie of Guise's father had died and her brother assumed the title of Duke of Guise and together with her other brother, the Cardinal of Lorraine were highly influential at the French court. On the death of her husband Marie of Guise became the Dowager Queen and her powerful family negotiated for Marie's daughter Mary to be raised in the French court with a view to Mary becoming the bride of the heir to the French throne.

The Queen of France and mother to the heir to the throne was Catherine de Medici. Her father was the powerful Lorenzo de Medici, banker to half of Europe's royalty. As Catherine's power and influence grew at court, so did her rivalry with the Guise faction, causing tension and drama among the courtiers and nobles who jockeyed for power. It is against all this setting that The Highland Ballad Series is told.

AUTHOR'S NOTE

Originally from Philadelphia, Kristin Gleeson lives in Ireland, in the West Cork Gaeltacht, where she teaches art classes, plays harp, sings in a choir and runs two book clubs for the village library. She holds a Masters in Library Science and a Ph.D. in history and for a time was an administrator of a large archives, library and museum in America. She also served as a public librarian in America and now in Ireland.

Kristin Gleeson has also published *The Celtic Knot Series* and *The Renaissance Sojourner Series*, as well as *In Praise of the Bees*, a novel of 6th century Ireland. A free novelette prequel, *A Trick of Fate* is available free on e retailers. In addition to her novels, a biography on a First Nations Canadian woman, *Anahareo, A Wilderness Spirit*, is also available.

If you have enjoyed this book please post a review. It helps so much towards getting the book noticed.

If you go to the author website and join the mailing list to receive news of forthcoming releases, special offers and events you'll receive *Along the Far Shores*, and *A Treasure Beyond Worth* a **FREE prequel e-novelette** and the **ebook** *Along the Far Shores*.

www.kristingleeson.com

Music is a big part of Kristin's life and many of the books have music connected to them. Listen to the music while you read- go to www.kristingleeson/music and download the files. Keep checking back as more pieces will be added to the library in the course of time.

THE BRAES OF HUNTLY
BOOK THREE OF THE HIGHLAND BALLAD SERIES

KRISTIN GLEESON

AN TIG BEAG PRESS

EXCERPT

The arrow whizzed by Abby's ear and lifted a curl that had dried tightly after the morning's rain. Before she could open her mouth to shout a warning, her father, Calum, had dismounted and pulled her from her horse, his sword drawn and his eyes scanning the landscape around him.

"I thought this was your family's land," said Abby in a soft whisper.

"It is," he said darkly.

He frowned at Jeannette, the sturdy French woman who might have been excellent at scything grass, scrubbing floors and passable as Abby's maid, but was not a horsewoman. She'd promptly fallen from her little highland pony in fright and now lay moaning on the track, complaining of an injured leg.

Abby made a move to go to Jeannette, but her father stopped her, his eyes narrowed. He drew a dagger and handed it to her. Surprised, she took it. It was the first time he'd acknowledged that she might have some idea how to use it since she and Iain had rescued him over a month ago. She shoved the thought of Iain from her mind. It was too painful right now. A month and more gone by and no word. Nothing.

Calum scanned the area again. The track bordered a wood-land. It was from there the arrow had come. At least she thought so, and judging from her father's careful scrutiny, he did as well. He had the horses and pony in between them and the woodland. A moment later, several horsemen emerged from the wood and headed in their direction.

Calum studied the figures, tightened his jaw and pressed his lips into a smile. She gave him a quizzical look and turned to look at the men. Some were dressed in unfamiliar livery and carried a variety of weapons including bows, spears, daggers and swords. The two not wearing a livery were richly dressed, and as they drew closer, Abby noted they were also young and extremely handsome.

"Do you know them?" she asked. She went over to Jeannette and knelt beside her. Other than a bruised dignity and possibly a bruised thigh, Jeannette seemed unharmed.

"Nay, but I can hazard a guess as to their identity." Calum walked from behind his horse and slowly sheathed his sword.

"Who do you think they are?" she asked, losing patience.

"The two richly dressed boys are my nephews. Or my great nephews, to be precise."

She stared at the two young men, surprised. She knew she shouldn't be, but after years of thinking she had no family at all other than her father, here she was, confronted with two—what were they? Cousins.

She stood up slowly, helping Jeannette who clung to her arm, a dead weight. Abby glanced down at Jeannette and realised she still had the dagger in her hand. With Jeannette safely on two feet, she handed the dagger back to her father and he replaced it at his side.

She took a moment then to smooth her travel stained riding gown and check that her hair wasn't too wild after the hasty dismount. Except for the usual stray curls that always seemed to escape, the bulk of her hair was safely tucked in the dark velvet hood she wore.

She studied the approaching men. Her cousins. It seemed strange to think of them in that way, if indeed they were her cousins. But as they approached she could find no cause to doubt it. She could see the hair on both, glinting red gold in the sun. Her hair. The shape of the face and something in their bearing reminded Abby of her father.

They drew up in front of her and her father. The taller and broader of the two swept off his hat and bowed slightly from his horse.

"Greetings," he said in English. "May I offer you welcome to the Gordon lands." He spoke in clipped tones, with only a little trace of any accent.

Calum swept off his bonnet and bowed. "I thought the 'welcome' had already been given. My daughter's ear nearly found itself reshaped," he said.

The young man turned to eye Abby with interest, his expression only faintly curious. Beside him, his slimmer and presumably younger, brother stared at her with remarkable large blue eyes, unlike his companion's striking hazel eyes. His hand rested on his sword, poised and ready.

"Forbye, there's little need for alarm," said Calum said to the younger of the two. "Your cousin wilna harm ye. Unless ye give her cause."

The younger of the young men stiffened, his eyes taking on a deadlier look. "Cousin? What is this? We know naught of such a cousin."

"John, leave this to me," said the older one. He gave a slow smile and turned it full force on Abby. "Forgive my younger brother. He can be overly eager at times. And I cannot think for the life of me why he would object to any claim of relationship to one as lovely as you." He gave another bow, slight this time and directed at Abby. "I am George Gordon, the eldest son of the Earl."

"Well, nephew," said Calum. "I'm glad tae see ye're mending your manners. I am Calum Gordon and this is my daughter, Abby, and her servant. Though by rights ye should be escorting us tae a proper welcome and leave the questions for later."

George gave him an amused look that didn't reach his eyes. "Of course…uncle? My apologies again. And for the unfortunate incident with the arrow. We were out hunting and arrows were loosed. One was sent mistakenly in your direction."

"Oh aye," said Calum. "I would omit that fella from your hunt in future since he obviously suffers from poor eyesight. Either that, or he doesna ken the difference between a horse and a boar. I presume that's what ye were hunting in the woods?"

"Yes," said John, his voice stiff. "One of the men was over eager. There was no harm intended, I assure you."

"Yes, well. Maybe we'll save that for another day. For now, I would trouble ye for an escort tae the castle and a word with your mother, or your father if he is at home."

"Father is at court, of course," said George.

"Of course," said Calum.

"But we will happily escort you to the castle and offer you hospitality. Any hope for the charming company of your daughter is enough inducement to accompany you anywhere."

"Indeed?" said Abby. "You speak very prettily, my lord."

Abby had viewed the whole exchange with growing puzzlement and alarm, too stunned to say much. Her father had called George "nephew" and he, in turn, had referred to him as "uncle", albeit with a great amount of scepticism. But George had mentioned his father was an earl. Did that mean her father was also related to an earl? There were so many unanswered questions.

George studied her anew. "You inspire such speech, cousin.

And your own speech, do I hear trace of an accent? Have you been abroad?"

"You have a good ear," she said, resisting his probing. She tried for a different subject. "Are you a musician?"

He tilted his head. "I am, but nothing compared to John here. I only dabble in it. My time is taken up so much with my duties that I find l can only enjoy others playing on occasion."

"Perhaps I will hear you play." Abby tried to maintain a casual manner, but her words came out stiff amid the underlying tension in the air.

"We'll no be playing much if we dinna bestir ourselves," said Calum, with studied good humour. "Darkness is falling and there's every chance that that boar ye were hunting will show his face and gore us all tae death."

George and John gave a polite laugh, but the point was made. Their story about the boar was not believed.

They rode on mostly in silence, except for George dispatching one of the men ahead to alert the castle to their arrival. Abby considered her new relatives. Where did her father figure in all this? She tried to remember what she knew of titled members of the Gordon clan. Her knowledge wasn't large, but there were few candidates. She added to it the numerous times people had asked her if she was related to the Earl of Huntly since her arrival in Scotland and it didn't take long to confirm what she'd just heard.

She looked over at her father, studying his face and those of her newly met "cousins". There was no doubt, the resemblance was there. But with her recent knowledge that her father's light-hearted lothario attitude was merely a ruse to cover a deadly acuity that served him in his years spying for Queen Mary, anything was possible. Was her father exploiting a likeness and a distant connection to gain some end? Something beside his spoken desire to find her a home safe from the tentacles of those that wished to entangle her in the plots at the French court?

It was when they drew in sight of Huntly Castle that it became clear to Abby that the Earl of Huntly was every bit as powerful as she'd suspected. She knew he was close to Marie of Guise, the Dowager Queen and current regent along with some of the noblemen. Was he one of the noblemen? Looking at the impressive castle clearly built for comfort as well as defence, she had little doubt the Earl was one of those noblemen. What was her father's real reason for coming here? He'd never had an interest in his relatives in all the years she'd known him. Not even when her mother left them, when she was five. So why the sudden desire to see them now?

THERE WAS no shortage of servants. From the time they arrived through the gate into the courtyard amid servants unloading carts, dogs barking from the kennels, the ringing of the smith's hammer, scent of new baked bread from the bakery house and the clanging from the weaving shed, it was clear that the household was large.

Servants took their horses and George barked a few orders. There was no doubt that he was used to command and he carried it easily. John seemed the more gallant as he led her over to the mounting block and helped her down from her horse and then turned to do the same for Jeannette. By the time they were ushered through to the hall Abby was prepared to be impressed. There was no doubting the wealth of this household.

The hall was lined with highly polished linenfold panelling. Faces with severe expressions stared out of the cluster of portraits on one wall and several tapestries depicting hunting scenes hung on the remaining walls. A great table, chairs, kists and cupboards filled the room, all made with skill that would rival anything she'd seen in the homes she'd seen in France.

Standing in the front of the room was an elegantly dressed fair haired woman of no great height and past the first flush of youth. If Abby thought her size made her easy to handle, the steely grey eyes that turned to her and her father told a different story. Two women, less elegantly dressed, but no less fashionable, stood at either side of her.

George approached the woman, swept a bow and then kissed her briefly. "Mother," he said. "I thank you for welcoming our guests so handily." He turned to Calum and Abby. "May I present by mother, Elizabeth Keith Gordon, the Countess of Huntly." He looked at his mother. "This man, or so he informs me, is my uncle. And the young lady is his daughter…my cousin?"

The Countess raised her brows. "Uncle?"

Calum bowed deeply. "Your pardon, my lady. I am Calum Gordon, son of Alexander Gordon and Elizabeth Gray. And may I present my daughter, Gabrielle."

The Countess studied Calum carefully, barely giving Abby a glance. "Yes," she said finally in a careful voice. "I see. Elizabeth Gray's son. We haven't seen you…in some time. I understood the family connection had been…."

"Severed?" said Calum, his voice bland. "Aye."

"And yet here you are," said the Countess, matching his tone.

"I have a matter to discuss with your husband," said Calum.

"I'm afraid my husband isn't here. He's at court."

"Aye, so your son told me." Calum glanced over at George, who eyed him suspiciously. "Will he be detained there long?"

Elizabeth stiffened slightly. "My husband is a man of high rank. An adviser to the Dowager Queen. His presence at the court is required for as long as she needs his services."

"Of course," said Calum. "Perhaps I might discuss the matter with ye, then. Can I impose on your hospitality in the meantime?"

"The hospitality at Huntly Castle is unrivalled," said the

Countess. "You will of course be accommodated. The orders have been given already." She gestured to the table. "Please, join John and George and have a seat. Some refreshments should be here shortly for you to enjoy while your rooms are readied. I'm afraid I must leave you for now, but rest assured I will speak with you about this matter of yours, later."

The Countess swept from the room, her ladies in tow. Abby followed her father's lead and took a seat at the long, heavy carved table. The mullioned windows gave the room an airy feel and a newly lit fire blazed in the hearth opposite.

Moments later, a plate of meat, bread and a flagon of French wine were laid on the table by two male servants. George and John sat down with her and her father, obviously hungry after their ride. John glanced across at Abby and Calum while they all ate, clearly sizing up Abby and her father. He caught her eye and smiled a little. It was genuine.

The meat was deliciously seasoned and the wine expensive and smooth. It was evident that the tastes of this household had been shaped by the Earl's time at the Paris court. Abby noted this only briefly, her mind consumed with recent events. Her father had never mentioned his father's name, or his mother's – at least not in context to his relationship to the Earl of Huntly. She still found the relationship difficult to believe.

She glanced at her father quizzically. How much more had he kept from her all these years? And why? When anyone with the slightest connection to noble blood would flaunt it widely, why had her father kept this relationship secret? Illegitimacy? Though many wore such relationships lightly, perhaps there was something unsavoury about this one.

"You've not been in these parts for some years, I take it, uncle?" said George.

Calum gave a polite smile. "That is so. It was before ye were born. Your parents were young and newlywed, I believe."

John nodded. "Much has changed since then."

"Aye. It has," said Calum. "How many of ye are there now, besides ye and your brother?"

"Too many," said John with a laugh. "There are ten of us since Thomas died four years ago. But Elizabeth doesn't live here, now. She's married to the Earl of Atholl."

"And neither of ye are married yet?" asked Calum.

George shrugged. "I've been busy. I was appointed Sheriff of Inverness this year and I've been carrying letters for the Dowager Queen."

"Following in your father's footsteps," said Calum. "Commendable."

"Have you come far?" asked George.

"Aye," said Calum. "From France."

"France? Is that where you've been biding?"

"Aye," said Calum.

Abby cast him a glance. He was giving little away and she didn't wonder at it. She wasn't certain she trusted them either.

"Have you been to court there?" asked John. "Father was there, with the Dowager Queen."

"Aye, I've been," said Calum.

John turned to Abby. "And were you there too?"

Abby gave a small smile. "Yes."

"So you're familiar with the Queen," said John.

"Aye," said Calum.

"And were you in France a while?" asked John. "I've heard nothing of any uncle biding in France."

The unspoken additional question hung in the air. Why hadn't they heard about him from their parents? Abby was interested in the answer too.

Calum regarded John carefully. "Your father and I haven't met for some time, as ye might have gathered. And we were never on the best of terms."

"And you're here seeking to mend things?" asked George politely. "I'm certain my father would be happy to receive you if he was here."

Calum gave a wry smile. "Many thanks. Your mother has been most kind."

"Father may be here in a fortnight's time. Or perhaps sooner. He has some business to attend to here," said George. "You'll stay until then?"

A liveried servant entered and bowed. "The rooms are ready for the guests, my lord," he said in a thick lowland Scots.

Calum rose and gestured to Abby to rise. "If I may beg your pardon, my daughter and I will refresh ourselves a moment in our rooms. I'm the sure the servants will have our chests there now. Would ye be so kind and tell your lady mother that if she has a moment to spare later I would be pleased tae speak with her?"

George and John rose and gave a curt bow to both Abby and Calum. "Of course," said George.

Abby and Calum followed the servant along to the winding stairs and up to the floor above. They travelled the corridor to the end, until the servant stopped in front of a door. "Your room, my lord," he said. "And your room, my lady is next door. The kists have been placed inside and your servant should be unpacking them now." He bowed again and left them.

Abby nodded and looked at her father. "I'll join you in a moment."

"There's nae need," said Calum quietly. "I'll speak with Lady Elizabeth and come to ye later."

"No, there's every need. I intend to acquaint myself with Lady Elizabeth as soon as possible. I want to determine the sort of welcome to expect." She kept her voice firm, her eyes directed on her father. She wouldn't take no. "You owe me that much."

"I'm trying to protect ye, lass, that's all."

"You'll forgive me if I question your ideas of protection," she said. "What I do appreciate is that all you're doing is your level best to keep me from Iain. And the only reason I've complied is that you promised to ensure his name is cleared of treason."

Calum gave her a tired smile. "'Tis done, lass."

"What? When?"

"I wrote the letter before we left France," he said. "I keep my promises."

Her face softened. It was most likely true. She knew that he had secret messengers and it was possible that he'd arranged for a message to be sent without her noticing it.

"So he's pardoned? Is it certain?"

"I've no had confirmation yet, but I'm sure it will be soon if it hasn't happened yet."

She allowed herself to believe it and her temper cooled. It was only for her to honour her side of the bargain and keep away from Iain. "Thank you."

She walked on towards her room and turned just before she entered. "I won't be long."

A soft sigh was all she heard from her father. She entered the room and saw Jeanette there by a large four poster bed, Abby's gowns and other items strewn across it and her chests on the floor.

Jeannette gave her a tight smile when she entered. "Well, madame," she said in rapid French. "I can only say I was giving up hope that we might stay in surroundings that are some way close to civilisation in this godforsaken country." She fingered the rich brocade coverlet. "At least they understand some luxuries." She gave a nod to the small brazier filled with coals. "Though they still have strange notions about what it means to warm a room. It is like ice in here."

Abby laughed. "Ah, you just haven't acquired the hardiness for this climate."

Jeannette sniffed. "I hope that I will never have to remain here long enough to do so, madame. I shall pray every night to the holy mother that your father will see fit to send you back to the French court soon."

"But, Jeannette, I will have no need for you if he sends me back to court," said Abby. "There are plenty of servants there. So I'm afraid if you want to remain with me you must pray that I like it here well enough to stay."

If her first few hours were any indication, except for her promise to her father, she knew that she would have done all she could to get away. She gave a deep sigh. Could she keep away from Iain when all she wanted to do was get on a horse and ride all the way to Glen Strae? Was she a woman to keep her word? A word she'd given solemnly to her father? In her heart she knew the answer.

Abby entered the drawing room next to the great hall in her father's wake, steeling herself against Lady Elizabeth's manner. A large fire crackled brightly in the hearth and there was a lit brazier situated near the countess. Fresh herbs scented the air and a large array of candles gave the room a cheerful outlook. Outfitted with plenty of chairs and benches, all comfortably cushioned, the panelled room gave off an air of welcome and refinement that Abby couldn't help but appreciate.

The Countess was seated in the middle of the room with several women gathered near, chatting softly or intent on needlework. On the other side of the room some boys were gathered around a table containing a chess board, two of them seated and studying the board carefully. A young woman embroidered half-heartedly nearby in the light of a candle, while a girl, no more than eleven, read a small book intently.

Abby regarded the group with open curiosity. She could only guess that they were the large Gordon brood and the Countess's ladies assembled to greet the new guests. Or perhaps intimidate them. Abby placed a smile on her face, determined to remain unruffled by this encounter.

Calum bowed and gave Lady Elizabeth a brief greeting and Abby quickly followed suit, curtseying deeply. "My lady cousin, I thank you for this kind welcome."

Lady Elizabeth acknowledged both greetings with a nod of her head. Her jewelled hooded cap caught the light from the group of candles placed on the table near her. She had embroidery in a framed hoop on her lap. The light was softer, creating a warmer expression on her otherwise stern features. Her light hair and thin nose were reflected in the children that surrounded her.

She gestured briefly to each child, starting with the oldest to the youngest, and introduced them. "My married daughter, Elizabeth, is currently with her husband, Lord Atholl. These are my other girls, Margaret and Frances."

She pointed first to the fair haired young woman who was seated with her needlework near the chess players. She was somewhere in her mid-teens, with grey eyes and a full, sensual mouth. Presumably that was Margaret. Frances, then, must be the slim girl seated with her book. The eyes that held Abby's were a lively blue. Each Gordon girl rose and gave a quick curtsey when their names were mentioned. Abby noted the appraising looks the older daughter gave her. The younger daughter seemed happy enough to meet her new cousin and gave Abby a beaming smile. Abby returned it.

Lady Elizabeth indicated the boys gathered around the chessboard. "This is James, William and Adam, my middle boys, and here beside me are the youngest boys, Patrick and Robert."

James, William and Adam already had the family resemblance punctuated on their face along with the fair hair, though in varying shades. They studied Abby and Calum, the oldest boy, James, fingering his chess piece idly. Mischief lurked in the two youngest boys, and with only a half a head between them Abby was certain they were more allies in high jinks than enemies in this household. The middle boys held themselves with varying degrees of correctness that their years of training in the tiltyard and the care of their tutor most likely had much to do with. And of course a heavy dose from the parents, or at least Lady Elizabeth. Abby had no doubt that Lady Elizabeth was conscious of every bit of consequence she was entitled to.

Abby and her father made all the appropriate greetings and words of appreciation, though there was no discernible softening or increased warmth in Lady Elizabeth's manner. The children themselves spoke to Abby and her father with courtesy and marked interest, though no inappropriate word was said.

"George said you wished to have a word with me," said Lady Elizabeth eventually.

"Aye," said Calum. "If ye wouldna mind, I would prefer to have the conversation a bit more private." His tone was neutral, but Abby could see a trace of tension in his jaw.

Lady Elizabeth raised a brow. "Ah, indeed? And this cannot wait until tomorrow, when I would have a private moment for you in my own rooms? Now is the time I enjoy the company of my family."

"I beg your pardon for intruding on an hour that I'm certain ye hold of great importance, but it is a matter I would wish to have resolved soon. If ye will have it otherwise, I can only bow to your wishes."

"I understand there are matters about the family to resolve that you can only be anxious to deal with quickly. But you must remember...cousin," she said with an edge to her voice, "You're the supplicant here. And I am not at all certain my lord husband would even approve of your presence."

Abby glanced at her father. His expression was unreadable, but the tension in his jaw increased.

"I apologise, my lady. I will of course await your pleasure. Tomorrow it shall be." He bowed. "My daughter and I will take our leave of ye, then, so that ye may enjoy the company of your family and your companions."

Calum placed his hand along Abby's back and after a quick curtsey, she allowed him to usher her from the room. Lady Elizabeth had made no protest over their departure, but Abby was full of questions.

The questions barely waited until they were outside her father's chamber door. They'd been silent as they proceeded up the staircase and along the corridor. When her father opened his door she followed him in and closed the door behind him.

She looked at him expectantly. "Well?"

He gave her a surprised look. "I think it's time for ye to seek your rest."

"Rest can wait. Are you going to tell me what the countess meant about matters to resolve between you and the Gordon family? Why are you the supplicant?"

"Och it's too late for stories of that nature," said Calum in an amicable tone. "We'll save it for another time."

"No, you'll tell me now." Abby kept her tone forceful. "You've kept this from me for too long already. I'm tired of your evasions. What did you do that caused them to discount you?"

Calum gave a mild snort. "I'd say my biggest offence was being born. George and the others were nae too fond of my mother, or me. I was born just before my father died. So ye could say that I never knew him. The family bundled us off tae one of the remote houses and if my mother had been the lying down sort, there we would have lingered."

"So, it's true. The Earl is your brother?" asked Abby.

"Nay, lass. He's my nephew. His father, John was my brother, but he died long before I was born."

Abby blinked, trying to make sense of this. "But George, being the oldest son of John, the Earl at that time, inherited the title?"

"Aye, more or less."

"But he could have been no more than a young boy when he became Earl. How is it he had you and your mother banished?"

Calum gave a wry smile. "Well we werena banished, more like provided with alternative living quarters in the Highlands. It was comfortable and befitting my mother's station, but far enough away from court. But George's mother was a daughter of the King. From the wrong side of the blanket, but royal nonetheless. He and the rest of the family have great influence and power. I was too lowly for them."

"I gathered that," Abby said with an acerbic tone. "So, did you grow up in this remote place?"

"I was there for some years." He gave her a wry look. "Hence my speech. Eventually, though, my mother negotiated with her family tae arrange for another marriage that would be advantageous. And marry she did, tae a man that had no liking for me, nor I for him. My mother didna seem tae mind his disdain for me. She was safe and that was all that mattered." Calum shrugged. "I left as soon as I could."

"But you were at court, you said, when you met my mother. You were a musician."

"Aye, it was the music that drew me there. Cormag Kerr. I'd seen him the rare time I'd been tae court when I was young." He shook his head. "When I first heard his music I kent only that it was pure, without taint and it reached out tae me. It cared not who I was or wasn't."

Abby nodded. She knew the feeling and could appreciate what it must have been for her father, disregarded and for the most part unwanted. And she knew Cormag Kerr's undeniable talent from her own experience of him at Kilchurn Castle.

"But didn't they know you were related to the Earl? Surely he was there?"

"Aye, he was there. But he gave me nae countenance and I was happy tae keep it that way. There were a few rumours initially, but George quashed them."

"But there is enough of a resemblance…" Abby said.

Calum laughed. "Och we're all related among the nobles, one way or another. They just took me for someone's byblow. And my mother was dead by then so there was nae person willing tae deny it."

"But why now, then? Why are you choosing to renew the connection now? It's not just that you want me to stay somewhere safe is it? Surely we can find somewhere else among your connections, that network of spies you've been running for how many years?"

Suddenly Abby's frustration at the number of secrets he'd kept, the lies he'd told her welled up in her and gave heat to her words. All of her understanding of who he was and who she was formed over years had crumbled in just a matter of months, so that she was no longer sure of him, or of anything.

Her father put his hand on her shoulder and cupped her chin. "Abby, lass. Ye must believe I want only what is best for ye. Everything I've ever done, or said, has been tae protect ye. Always." He kissed her forehead. "Ye're my daughter. I'd never harm ye in any way."

Abby allowed him to take her into his arms in a comforting manner. But though his arms around her might give him some assurance, it did nothing to allay the turmoil and suspicion in her heart.

ABBY PAUSED QUIETLY OUTSIDE the door to the drawing room. The door was slightly ajar so she could hear her father's voice and Lady Elizabeth's answering murmur. She held her breath, suppressing the anger that arose. That he should discuss her with

Lady Elizabeth without her knowledge! Even though she'd suspected it was the case when she'd found his chamber empty a few moments ago, it still angered and disappointed her that her suspicions had been confirmed.

"I owe ye a great debt," said Calum.

"The understanding, of course, is that I'll undertake this only if my husband agrees," said Lady Elizabeth.

"Aye, of course. But ye say he will be here soon?"

"He will. Perhaps in a fortnight's time, maybe longer. He's meeting someone here."

"A fortnight?" Calum sucked in his breath. "I dinna think I can wait that long. Would ye be happy if the lass remained here for the time? If you husband doesna agree then I'll return as soon as I may. Ye can leave word with my man at Edinburgh."

"So you would leave your daughter here, regardless?"

"If ye permit. I must away today. Tomorrow at the latest."

"Very well," said Lady Elizabeth. "You'll explain this to your daughter before you leave." There was no question in the tone, it was an order. "I expect no problems with this, whatever the choice may be."

"I'll talk tae her," said Calum. "And there should be nae resistance if ye go with what I've outlined."

"Again, it will be as my husband sees fit, Calum. He will probably agree to your wishes, though. After all, if it is as you say, and overtures have already been made, I imagine he'll want to exert himself as little as possible."

"Good," said Calum. "I'll take my leave of ye, then."

Abby backed away from the door and looked around her. The corridor was empty but there was nowhere to hide. She quickly headed down the corridor and bore right, looking for a door other than that which led to the Hall. She located one, opened it and slipped inside. She paused on the threshold, listening for sounds of any presence and was relieved to find none. She moved forward quietly and realised it was a bedroom. The bed was draped in a rich deep velvet and brocade, the wood finely carved. Large kists and chairs were placed around the room, but there was no sign that anyone had been here recently. It was too tidy.

Suddenly, the door opened and she turned to see George, a serving girl in tow, giggling excitedly. George pulled the woman inside and kissed her roundly, not noticing Abby at first. He began to raise her skirts, biting her neck and shoulder lightly. The servant spotted Abby and her eyes widened. She pushed George off and he looked up at her, puzzled. It was then he noticed Abby. Annoyance crossed his face for a brief moment, but then his face relaxed into a grin.

"Cousin," he said easily, releasing the serving maid. "I must say I didn't think to find you in my father's bedchamber."

"Oh, I am sorry," Abby said feebly. "It's only that I seem to have lost my way."

"Easily done," said George. "It can be confusing which floor you're on, I'm sure. Your chamber you might recall, is on the floor above. You have stairs to climb, first."

Abby flushed. "Yes. I remember. I've come from there. I was looking for the kitchens. In search of breakfast." She eyed the servant. "It appears you have your own breakfast got," she couldn't help but add.

George laughed and patted the servant girl's bottom. "Thank you, Fenella That will be all."

Meg bobbed a curtsey and took her leave. When the door shut behind the servant, George moved close to Abby, took her hand and kissed it. "Perhaps we might breakfast together. It isn't often I have the pleasure of one as lovely as you to keep me company here at Huntly." His tone was playful and friendly.

Abby forced a smile and kept her own tone light. "I'm certain you could have any of the court ladies you chose."

"Ah, but this isn't the court, and the women are either too

young, or too old." He raised a hand to tweak a lock of hair that had escaped the French hood she'd hastily thrust on earlier. "And even at court you'd rival the ladies, I've no doubt."

"I thank you for the compliment...cousin."

"It more the truth than any courtly compliment," George said. He took her hand and drew her close. "Come. Will you not give your cousin a proper greeting and grant me pardon for its lack yesterday? I plead only that I was ignorant of our connection and now I would like to rectify that."

Before she could reply George leaned down and kissed her fully and deeply, his hand supporting the back of her head. Startled, she felt her mouth give way and then she pulled back, stunned and breathless.

"I-I had no idea kin greeted each other in that manner here," she said, confused. "I confess I have no great experience of family, other than my father."

George brushed her face with his hand. "I will happily acquaint you with all the ins and outs of it."

She gave a small smile. "That's very kind of you, I'm sure."

"It's my pleasure," said George. He took her hand. "I'll start by showing you where to get a bite to eat. We generally do that in the dining hall." He gave her a sly smile and raised a brow. "You know the place?"

Abby nodded and allowed him to take her out of the chamber and down along the corridor from whence she came not so long before, trying to fathom her cousin. She had little success except to note that she mustn't take him for a fool.